JASON GARMAN

Reflections in the Dark

A Horror-Noir

G A R M
Press

*For my wife, Lyndsey —
you've inspired me in ways I never thought possible.*

*For my boys: Greyson, Asher, Rhett, and Max —
the light and chaos of my life. You are the best part of me.*

We live inside a dream.

— PHILLIP JEFFRIES

Contents

1

CHAPTER ONE

Overture of Shadows

Dusk settled over the campus in a wash of thickened blue, the last light of day caught in the spires and old brick facades. Pathways glowed under the first flickers of lamplight as scattered students hurried past, their voices hushed against the quieting air.

Nestled inside a building that looked shut down for the night was a small classroom, filled with the pale hum of overhead lights. The room felt forgotten, its paint dulled, its chalkboard scarred, its windows rattling faintly in the evening wind.

At the front of the room stood a diminutive lecturer who passed for a student. She tried to hide this fact by donning an oversized sports jacket, reaching for professionalism. She wore glasses that she habitually pushed up on her nose. She wasn't lecturing; she was unraveling.

Her voice carried a nervous quiver, but she spoke with relentless urgency, each sentence stacking onto the next like a fevered mantra. The students weren't sure if they were attending a psychology lecture or witnessing a breakdown, but they scribbled, sighed, or stared, caught in her torrent of thought.

"Jacques Lacan," she began, eyes darting across the room without ever truly landing on a face. "His theory of the mirror stage: identity formed in infancy. The recognition of one's reflection. But what if it isn't just infants? What if the mirror stage lasts a lifetime? What if we wrestle with our image every day, shaping and reshaping who we think we are?"

She moved like a current, pacing, arms fluttering as she spoke faster and faster. "Each moment, each emotional experience rewrites us. It alters our trajectory. A single choice redirects perception. And from those changes: new possibilities, new realities."

The interruption came sharp, slicing into her rhythm. Students didn't bother raising their hands anymore in the middle of her "speeches." "What does that even mean?" a voice cut in. Another muttered from the back: "This is psychology, not philosophy." The room shifted, restless at last.

For the first time, the lecturer paused. Silence settled. She drew in a breath, and when she spoke again, her cadence slowed. Measured, deliberate, each word crystallized. The students leaned in despite themselves, knowing this sudden change meant weight.

"What if what mirrors reflect back… is not always who we are?" she asked quietly. Her eyes scanned the class, but her gaze seemed to pass through them, as though she were watching another world beyond their shoulders.

The lecturer blinked once, then turned, her voice sharpening. "Psychology is the study of the self. The mind. Consciousness. Metaphysics is the study of reality, existence. And what is consciousness if not existence itself? The two are bound. You can't untangle them."

Several students rolled their eyes, others smirked into their notebooks. Someone whispered just loud enough to carry: "Somebody got high before class."

She heard it. She did not flinch. Instead, she looked through the room, her voice softening into something like prayer as the windows rattled with autumn air.

"Immanuel Kant believed reality itself is unknowable. We do not experience things as they are. We experience them as filtered through consciousness. Which means reality is ambiguous. We live inside ambiguity's prison."

Her words landed heavier now, sinking into the uneasy quiet. "That means there is not one reality, but infinite realities. Infinite possible selves, infinite planes of existence waiting behind each mirror we dare to face."

A few students shifted in their seats. She continued.

"What if all we encounter is only the tip of the iceberg?" she whispered. "What if there is more waiting just beyond perception? What if the mirror isn't simply reflection at all … but a vault? A vault holding the answer to every question that we haven't figured out how to ask?"

She let the silence swallow her words. Outside, dusk bled into night, and the students sat in stillness, unsure whether they'd just attended a lecture… or witnessed something they weren't meant to hear.

2

CHAPTER TWO

The Sound of a Thought Turning Inside-Out

Reed Ashland's apartment looked like the lair of a madman fighting off the last threads of sanity. Stacks of dirty dishes, bottles of booze, and unopened mail battled for space on every surface.

The microwave clock glared: 3:33 a.m. The number had begun to feel like a signature.

In the living room, the television glowed permanently. He couldn't remember the last time he'd actually watched it. The muted box flickered with late-night reruns, but Reed heard a voice whispering from behind the screen. Not from the broadcast.

The bedroom? A landfill of fabric. Nothing worth salvaging.

Deeper inside was his true habitat: the office. Three cluttered tables and a single creaking chair that threatened collapse.

The walls were barren. The boards once covered with clippings and photos of every oddity imaginable had collapsed to the floor, swallowed by the mess. It was an apt analogy for Ashland himself. Once a respected professor, now a hermit buried in conspiracy theories and pseudo-science. Reed rubbed his face, eyes raw, temples throbbing from another sleepless stretch.

Sleep never came easy. He'd closed his eyes, sure, but the dreams had started to talk back. They weren't content to be symbols or half-memories anymore. They were prophecies waiting to be revealed and understood. But understanding was just out of reach. Dreams were cryptically condescending and confusing.

He didn't like that. He preferred being the smartest voice in the room, even if the room was mostly unpaid bills and half-empty gin bottles.

Reed stared out his window. He turned his head ever so slightly, but his reflection in the glass didn't move. Outside was a night sky polished to glass, every star a pinprick.

He looked down at one of his cluttered tables and peeking out at him was a framed picture of a young girl. Pretty and energetic, blond hair and green eyes. A replica of her mother. She had a smile that was frozen in time from another life. The image smacked Reed in the heart.

Somewhere in the distance, Reed thought he heard her laughter. The heavy weight on his chest reminded him of her head resting there.

"I miss you, Em," Ashland muttered with a lump in his throat. His eyes were red and watery. "Tell me I'm not crazy," he pleaded.

He could see his reflection slightly in the glass portion of the frame and what was staring back at him was not a pleasant sight. He looked older than forty-three, though proper care might have made him seem younger. Bookish good looks were covered by the disheveled nature of his thick brown hair, streaked with a little premature gray; the heavy bags under his deep, brown eyes and his perpetually smudged glasses.

A shadow shifted in the back of the room.

He sipped from a chipped coffee mug filled with warm gin. "Ex nihilo nihil," he muttered in Latin, raising his drink to no one. He drank. Out of the corner of his eye, he could swear his broken clock ticked irregularly.

His eyes drifted to the open journal on one of the tables. The Prison of the Human Mind, he'd written in red Sharpie on the cover. Inside, the last page held a phrase scrawled in his own hasty, impatient handwriting:

Reality is a story badly translated from another dimension.

Beneath it, something new. Someone else's handwriting in crayon: *REED, BETWEEN THE LINES.*

The muted television started making noise in the living room. A low hum, collapsing inward. A sound that he had never heard before yet gave him the feeling of familiarity.

Dr. Ashland looked up. He peeked out his office door into the living room. He slowly prepared himself for it but stopped. For some unknown reason, he turned and stared into the corner of his office. Looking at something that wasn't there.

No one was there. Reed stood and looked straight into the corner of this now very malleable room. He had the feeling that he was looking at something. "Why?" he asked the darkened corner.

The humming from the living room was washing over him now, overtaking him.

Then the room folded. Not metaphor, but fact. Origami in reverse. Colors bleeding from their edges as if reality itself was misprinted. Furniture bent without creasing. The room twitched. Something unseen was pressing to get through. And then: a pop, like a soap bubble dying in reverse.

Everything changed.

***

Reed now stood inside what resembled a library built by a lunatic geometry professor. Shelves curled and spiraled, intersecting in ways that defied architecture and possibly morality. Some looped back into themselves. Others whispered indecipherably when passed. Books floated lazily mid-air like koi in a pond made of suggestion.

When Reed tried to move, he moved in slow motion. Running internally, but going nowhere.

He blinked once. Then blinked sideways.

Reed then felt himself twitching, as if he was snapping in and out of existence. Finally, everything seemed to go back to normal speed, and he turned to look at what he thought had been the entrance to this den of the bizarre.

He moved toward this spot to try to leave, only to find the entrance had become a mirror. It didn't reflect him. It just watched.

His head throbbed. The gin, he thought. The gin was not helping.

From behind a stack of books, a voice like wind caught in a throat whispered, "Language is permitted but not required. Use carefully. It echoes."

Ashland couldn't hear the words per se. He felt them. Subtitles in his mind.

A tall figure emerged, draped in sheets of shimmering glass. Its body refracted with flickering images from Reed's own memories. Where a face should have been, there floated an antique rotary phone, turning slowly in the air. It rang once.

Ashland, ever the philosopher, did the only thing that felt rational in the moment: he answered it.

"Reed Ashland," said a calm, detached voice.

"Am I dead?" Ashland asked.

"Dead is not here," the dark cold voice replied.

Reed closed his eyes slowly and muttered, "I'm hallucinating."

"Hallucinations obey metaphor. Elsewhere does not. Remain calm as your soul adjusts to the curvature. Pay attention to the curtains."

His throat dried, his mouth shaping words meant for ghosts. "Curtains?"

The voice on the other end of the phone managed to yell yet still be completely devoid of emotion—"REED!... BETWEEN THE LINES!"

The phone melted in his hand.

The room tilted. Or maybe it was his balance. Reed gripped the edge of a shelf that pulsed gently beneath his fingers.

Then: a new sound. A door creaked open from above. Its tone warped and stretched like a cassette underwater. A staircase grew beneath it like a tongue rolling out of a mouth.

Down came a woman. Or close enough. She wore gloves the color of unfinished thoughts. Her coat may have once been a window. Her hair moved even when the air did not. Her voice was out of sync with her mouth. Her motions were unnatural and seemed to stop and start suddenly.

She gestured. The library collapsed in on itself, reforming into a room shaped like regret. A table. A single chair. A mirror that didn't reflect either of them.

From her coat, she retrieved a teacup filled with crackling static. She placed it in front of him.

He drank. The taste was like remembering something before it happened.

She handed him a pen. "Write."

"Write what?"

"What wants to be written."

A journal appeared in his hands. It bore a strange geometric symbol embossed in black. Its first page was already filling itself out:

You have been selected to observe the structural decay of the Real. Take notes. Do not interfere. Do not believe anything that cries.

The woman leaned close, her voice now identical to Reed's own.

"The story is folding in on itself, Reed. You can't stop it. But you can record it. And sometimes… that's enough."

He looked up. She was gone.

Only the mirror remained. It still refused to reflect him. Instead, it began to laugh. Not cruel laughter but not kind either. This mirror laughed the laugh of amusement. The amusement of someone who has all the answers to questions people don't know how to ask.

Ashland suddenly stepped forward toward the mirror and sank three inches into the floor. He shivered. The air thickened, humming with the low vibration of a storm about to break. Somewhere above him the sky blinked and the abyss expanded.

Behind him, a dozen strange, abstract beings whirled in slow circles, laughing and murmuring to each other in palindromes. The taste of winter and nostalgia filled his mouth.

"Unlearn the alphabet," they whispered.

The beings then drifted into the air, resembling ash floating above a fire, forming an oddly meaningful formation. They encircled him and hovered near him, asking questions:

"What lives in the spaces between the Where and the Elsewhere?"

"Why does déjà vu feel like homesickness?"

He didn't answer. Each syllable split his skull open wider. Reed clutched his temples—his migraines had finally decided to hire a choir.

Then silence and stillness.

A bird made of negations landed on his shoulder. "Welcome," it said, "to the place where meaning comes to be assembled… in the wrong order. Pay attention to the curtains."

In the distance and right in his ear at the same time, he could hear a distorted chuckle. Reed mumbled, "What fucking curtains?!" Then everything turned upside down. Literally.

The mirror only mocked him with silence.

3

CHAPTER THREE

Echoes in Glass

The house was quiet. Too quiet, Maria thought. Not just because it was empty, but because it felt cleansed. Someone had tried to erase the echo of violence. But echoes don't erase. They hang in the walls like smoke. It wasn't just that someone's life was gone. It was the happiness of the home itself. The memories and moments of a family: a baby's first steps, a child's first day of school, birthdays, and holidays—all wiped out by a senseless, brutal act. More than a life had been taken here. Much more.

Mary Johnson's home was modest. Two stories, pale blue siding. A small porch with wind chimes that barely stirred in the breeze. Maria stood in the doorway with blue nitrile gloves already on, breathing through her mouth. Not because of the smell, but because of the weight.

Detective Maria Voss had the aura of someone who'd seen too much and learned too early that justice doesn't always wear a badge. A Chicago homicide detective, she moved through crime scenes with a confidence born of experience. Quiet, efficient, unshaken. She was sharp as broken glass, fluent in sarcasm, and carried the weight of every case that went cold.

Her face told stories: too much coffee, too little sleep, and the kind of grief that doesn't go away. Her skin was warm olive, the tone of faded summers, and her eyes gave the impression they had seen the end of the

10

world and taken notes. Dark, wide, and tired. Those eyes held a persistent spark beneath the cynicism. A pilot light that refused to go out.

She wasn't the kind of attractive that made people look twice. Just once, and remember her for a long time. Maria had the build of someone who took care of herself, not for vanity but for survival. Lean, strong arms. Quick on her feet. Functional clothes. Always boots. She wore a silver ring on a chain under her shirt. Personal. Private. Untouchable.

When she entered a room, people noticed. Not because she wanted them to, but because the air changed.

Maria stepped into the bedroom. Neutral colors. Overstuffed dresser. Laundry basket half-full in the corner. A few stray children's toys on one side of the room. The bed looked almost made. Except for the dark stain at the center, a grotesque crimson flower blooming on the sheets.

"She lived here with her husband and three kids," Officer Darnell said from the hallway. "Husband's at his sister's with the kids. He found the body."

Maria moved slowly toward the bed where the victim was sprawled out. Her face was locked in a mask of terror. Mouth open. Her scream had been cut short mid-breath. The whites of her eyes bulged against the bruising around them, glassy and unblinking. Her fingers had clawed into the sheets so hard that half-moons of blood rimmed her nails. The body told the story: she had fought, she had begged, and in her last moment looked straight into madness.

Maria approached the corpse and gave it a visual scan, starting at the feet and moving very deliberately upward.

Darnell continued reading Detective Voss the facts from his file, which he held in front of him protectively, shielding himself from the reality of the scene. "Husband's Robert Johnson, forty-nine. Runs his own insurance agency. Alibi's being checked."

"Husband didn't do this," Maria quickly interrupted, now focused intently on the forehead of the victim. A cryptic marking carved grotesquely into the skin with precision. In this domestic space, it felt especially invasive. Like someone had brought madness into a place of order.

"You see the kids' drawings on the fridge?" Darnell asked from the hallway, clearly trying to change the subject.

"One of 'em real sweet. Stick figures. Mom, Dad, kids. Happy sun." He was trying to bring a little happiness into a horrific scene of violence and sorrow. It only made everything more tragic and desolate.

Just beside the bed, the carpet sank in a deep, perfect impression. Oddly geometric, heavy, too sharp-edged to be furniture. Maria crouched, running her gloved fingers along the outline. Not a chair. Not a nightstand. Too narrow for a footprint. The fibers were pressed flat, as though something had stood sentinel there for hours. Watching. Waiting.

"Has something been moved from the room, Darnell?" she asked, somewhat accusatory.

Darnell stared blankly at Detective Voss, caught off guard by the question and tone. "Uh, no. No, I don't think so. Why? What is it?"

Maria studied the young officer. She believed him, but skepticism was more than a defense mechanism for a seasoned investigator in this city. She looked back down at the imprint in the carpet, studying it in vain. The shape and placement made no sense. The perplexed detective answered by shaking her head and moving on.

"Signs of forced entry?" she asked.

"No."

"Anything stolen?" the investigator continued.

"Nope."

Maria sighed loudly and began talking aloud, but clearly not to Darnell. "Didn't break in. Didn't rob the place. No sign of a struggle outside of the bed, where she was clearly killed."

After a moment of silence, Darnell intruded on Detective Voss's self-interrogation. "That John Doe case? You think … it's the same guy? He had that same weird symbol on the head."

Maria stared at him briefly and then turned away. "Don't get ahead of yourself, deputy." She didn't want to overexcite the green officer, but she knew he was right. The symbol carved into the forehead was what concerned her.

Whoever this was, it wasn't just some random psycho. It was deliberate. Careful. John Doe and now Mary Johnson. The first body in an alley. This one in a bed. Opposites. Public and private. Seen and unseen. And both had been... watched. This killer had very specific reasons for what he had done and who he'd done it to. Those reasons were hopelessly obscure at the moment.

She stood up and walked to the bedroom mirror. Tall, narrow, mounted to the closet door. Something drew her to it. Something unexplainable. She stood in front of the mirror, not understanding why, but she studied her own reflection. The way the light fell wrong across her face seemed... unusual. The way the background felt delayed, off by a frame. Out of sync with life.

She could swear she heard some sort of faint humming in the distance.

Staring hypnotically into the looking glass, she slowly reached forward and touched the surface.

It was cold. Too cold.

Maria had a sudden feeling of not just being watched but that her mind was being invaded by some kind of force. The air around her felt... warped. She had the oddest feeling that if she looked up, she would see the roof of Mary Johnson's house spinning wildly. For a brief moment, she was in a daze, then noticed in the mirror that the bed was freshly made and clean. Mary Johnson's body was no longer lying dead in the middle of it.

Maria gasped. "What—?" She spun around with the reflex of prey sensing a predator.

In front of her, plain as day, was Mary Johnson. Dead. Cold. Just as she had been since Maria first arrived on the scene.

Maria quickly looked back in the mirror and saw the reflection of the reality in front of her own eyes. Mary Johnson was once again lying dead on her bed, the reflection bouncing almost mockingly back at her from the mirror.

"You alright, Detective?" Officer Darnell asked sympathetically.

Maria looked up with a feeling of self-doubt. A feeling she was unaccustomed to. She sighed long and deep. "Yeah." She paused. "Just need some black coffee and a lobotomy."

4

CHAPTER FOUR

The Silence That Wasn't There

Reed Ashland woke with grass in his mouth.

He lay face down in the middle of a wide, empty field. Cool earth beneath his cheek; the smell of soil and something faintly metallic drifting up into his senses.

It was night. Early morning.

Or maybe, somewhere in between.

The sky, once familiar, now seemed subtly altered. It was too deep, too black, like someone had switched off the stars and painted over the heavens. Pregnant with something unseen.

Conventional wisdom might say that Dr. Ashland was just a drunk, once again waking up in a strange place. The disorientation was not brought on by inebriation this time. The palpable strangeness hanging in the air made it much more obvious.

The hair on his neck didn't just rise. It bristled.

He rolled onto his back slowly, bones aching with memories that not even alcohol could erase. His clothes were damp with dew, and his glasses were missing. He fumbled until his hand found them near his shoulder, twisted at an odd angle. He fiddled with them clumsily for a few moments, contorting them back into something wearable. He slid them on and blinked. The

14

world swam, then snapped into something resembling focus.

No landmarks. No buildings. No roads. Just the rustle of grass and a low electric hum, coming from nowhere and everywhere at once. Reed was engulfed in it. Silent, yet deafening. It was less a noise than a symphonic message penetrating his soul.

He sat up. Wobbled. His head felt full of smoke and echoes.

Then, a light. Dim at first, then sharpening into clarity, emerged without a sound, without warning. It didn't blink or waver. It hovered. Steady and geometric, impossible to mistake for a star, plane, or satellite. The symphonic humming was overwhelming, diving deep down into the essence of Reed's existence, permeating the fabric of his reality.

Reed stared up at the sky with wide eyes. Amazement and veneration flowed from every fiber of his being.

Another light appeared suddenly. Either it came from a great distance at impossible speed, or it simply materialized. Hard to tell.

Then another light.

A perfect triangle. Massive and indifferent to gravity or logic. There was no roar, no wind, no propulsion. Just presence. A weight. A knowing.

Reed had the odd sensation of time stopping. Everything felt *paused* except for him and this massive floating enigma above him. He and this wondrous levitating paradox were suspended in time and space.

The lights hovered silently above the field, motionless, soundless, weightless. Reed's skin prickled and some old part of his brain was triggered—fear, awe, and confusion all tangled together. Something beyond his senses was being awakened. Something cellular. Like the rules of reality had loosened around him.

The triangle began to move. Slowly, smoothly, it glided across the sky, pivoting on an axis Reed couldn't locate. Its movements were deliberate, choreographed. A performance meant for him and him alone. Time bent in its wake: moments stretched thin, elastic, untrustworthy.

He couldn't look away.

His hands were shaking. He had studied sightings for years, compiled reports, examined patterns, dissected blurry videos with the obsession of a priest over scripture. But none of that had prepared him for this. Seeing is believing, they say, but this went beyond that. Staring into the face of God was even a poor analogy.

The craft made no sound.

And then—

It stopped.

Mid-air.

Directly above him.

And then, just as quietly as it came, it was gone. Vanished into the sky. Or into the thoughts of the universe. As if it had never even been there. But something lingered. Not just in the sky. Inside. A residue. A question. A silence that wasn't there before.

The air buzzed with static. Somewhere in the distance, a bell began to toll. But it was muffled, like his own funeral heard from underwater.

Reed's feet left the ground. Just an inch. Maybe two.

He was weightless. Briefly. Peacefully.

He wasn't folding. This was different. Something was scrutinizing him. A cryptic examination.

Then—

Reed collapsed back to the ground with a thud that shook through his bones. Face down in the grass again, he felt a bewildering mixture of exhaustion and astonishment.

In a way, his whole life had been leading to this experience. He had spent so much of his life researching these types of things. Imagining what this experience would be like. So rarely do experiences meet the weight of anticipation. This one exceeded it.

Silence. The cliché kind of silence. The deafening kind. Reed had an anticipatory feeling of excitement tinged with dread. The feeling you get when you reach the peak of a roller coaster and are about to drop. It wasn't the foreboding quiet that made him feel this way. He noticed his phone had fallen out of his pocket and onto the ground near where he lay. It was face up in the grass, and he noticed the time.

3:33 a.m.

"Of course," Reed muttered with a combination of knowing and sarcasm. He collected himself from the ground and stood slowly.

He was taking this moment in.

He had been disoriented before. Drunk. Depressed. Angry and alone. But he was different now. Whatever this was had cleared him. He was suddenly sober. Clear-headed in a way that he couldn't remember ever feeling.

What was all this?

Whatever it was, Reed had been imparted with the sense that this was unique and unlike anything he had ever felt or experienced before.

He closed his eyes and took a deep breath, tilting his head upward toward the heavens. After exhaling, he slowly opened his eyes and stared up into the early morning sky. He wanted to inhale it all, to burn it deep into memory.

This unfamiliar hilly meadow. A ghostly ocean that breathed with the cool dawn. The horizon glowed faintly, a thin line of silver light hinting at the sun's slow approach. He wanted to drink it all in.

This meant something. But the meaning was as elusive as a faded memory wrapped in a forgotten dream.

5

CHAPTER FIVE

Carved in Silence

The Cook County Medical Examiner's Office smelled faintly of antiseptic and old linoleum, the kind of place where silence hummed under fluorescent lights. Maria pushed through the double doors, her badge swinging against her hip. The air was colder here than outside, a chill that clung to her skin and bones.

In the examination room, two bodies lay beneath white sheets, anonymous and still. Hovering over them with her gloves snapped tight was Dr. Krista Rutkowski.

"Rose," Maria said, her voice cutting through the hum of the vents. Maria called her Rose, a nickname her kids had invented when they couldn't pronounce Rutkowski.

Krista looked up, eyes bright above her mask, and her grin came quick, like she'd been waiting all day. "Hoss," she shot back. The old nickname still had its sting of affection. A play on Voss. A nod to Maria's toughness.

They embraced briefly, not caring about the latex and the cold. They'd been through too much together: crime scenes, courtrooms, Christmas mornings with Maria's kids for formality's sake.

"How are my lil' buttcracks?" Krista asked, pulling off her gloves with a snap.

"Stealing my will to live one tantrum at a time," Maria said dryly. "Tommy's in a dinosaur phase. I swear if I hear one more word about velociraptors."

Krista laughed, that warm, sharp bark that Maria hadn't realized she needed tonight. "Good. Keeps you human."

"And me?" Krista said, not waiting for Maria to ask about her day.

"I've been through it today, three autopsies, a courtroom sideshow, and a rookie who nearly fainted. Same old song. I speak for the dead while the living drive me crazy."

Maria gave a tired smile. Normally, she hated small talk, but Krista was the exception. She was her one true friend in a lonely world.

Maria tilted her head, smirking. "And the dating life? How goes it?"

Krista rolled her eyes, tugging at the sleeve of her lab coat. "Rotating cast, no headliners. They either can't keep up or they want me to play house. I've got a career, a wardrobe, and a standing reservation at Avec. If a man wants in, he's on my terms. If not ..." She shrugged. "Plenty of fish."

Maria chuckled. "Still breaking hearts, huh?"

"Better theirs than mine, Hoss."

The levity lingered for a moment, then Krista's eyes flicked toward the bodies. Work. She stepped forward, tugging the sheet from the first.

Mary Johnson stared up at them: pale, bruised, lips cracked. Her body told a story in purple and red.

"Your victim: beaten. Badly," Krista said, her voice now clinical, steady. "Held down. Merciless, and no puncture wounds except the carving." She paused, letting her words hang.

Maria crossed her arms. "Weapon?"

Krista arched a brow. "If I had to guess? A surgical scalpel or a calligraphy knife. But that's just a couple guesses. Whatever blade it was, he only used it for the carving. Everything else was bare hands."

"And get this," she leaned down, gesturing toward the carved symbol on Mary's forehead. "It was done before she died."

Maria's eyes narrowed. "Before?"

"Yep." Krista's tone was matter-of-fact, but her gaze stayed on the corpse. "The bruising patterns, tissue response. She wasn't dead. And here's the kicker: she wasn't restrained. No ligature marks on the wrists or ankles, no defensive wounds. Nothing. She didn't even fight back when he carved this into her."

Maria's jaw tightened. She said nothing for a long moment. She noticed a mirror to the side of the room and glanced quickly at it with dread. She returned to the corpse.

Maria leaned closer to the carving. "She just… let this happen?" she asked, her voice low.

Krista slowly shrugged. "That's the story she's telling, Hoss."

Maria let her gaze linger on the victim's forehead, pondering. She stole another glance at the mirror in the room. Krista noticed this time but said nothing.

"Remember that John Doe?" Maria blurted out, suddenly breaking the silence.

Krista straightened, already moving toward the second table. She grabbed the sheet and pulled it back. "Already there, partner."

The homeless man from the alley, his head marred by the same grotesque carving.

"I did a deeper exam this time," Krista explained. "The first exam wasn't mine. Homeless guy in an alley. No one really gave a shit, you know?"

Maria nodded with sorrow and understanding.

Krista continued, "But I went through it like I did with Mary. Same result. Beaten. Symbol carved while alive. No resistance. And then strangulation. Same as your Mary Johnson over here."

"So both fought the beating. But then they let him carve them and strangle them?" Maria asked, hoping for an answer that would yield different possibilities.

"Well," Dr. Rutkowski began, "there was a struggle to begin with. From what I can tell, the victims put up a fight when your killer was beating them. In the case of the John Doe over here, a fierce struggle. But then, yeah, the victims don't seem to show any signs that they put up a fight when it comes to the carving and then the strangulation."

Maria stared at John Doe somberly. "Bizarre…" she said, just above a whisper.

Krista shrugged, palms out, "It is what it is." Maria hated how easy she made resignation look.

Maria studied both bodies, her mind grinding against the impossible. "Why would they fight and then let the killer do that?" she asked aloud, mostly talking to herself.

Krista didn't answer. She just watched Maria, her face a mixture of sympathy and unease.

Krista followed Maria's gaze to the mirror. "What are you looking for?"

Maria stared into the mirror. After a long silence: "I don't know. Truth?"

6

CHAPTER SIX

Night Drive

The night spread itself like ink across the windshield, smeared by the wipers' sluggish rhythm. A silver Lexus, spotless and humming low, cut a clean path through the wooded outskirts of the city, far from the buzz of streetlights and sirens. The city had vanished behind him in layers—first the neon, then the sodium haze, and finally the sense of consequence. Now there was only the road and the black swell of trees pressing close on either side. His car glided along effortlessly.

He checked the dashboard clock. 3:33 a.m. Time had lost its meaning a long time ago, but ritual demanded its record. He appreciated moments. A man without ritual was just an animal with a watch.

He focused on the dark road ahead. The silhouettes of the night rippled across his expressionless face like lunatics dancing to some deranged melody that only they could hear.

He drove with one hand on the wheel, the other resting loosely near his mouth, fingers curled as if he'd forgotten a cigarette there. He didn't smoke. But he enjoyed the affectation. It suited the profile he'd built: sharp, composed, a man of aesthetic and principle.

Habits, much like people, die in layers.

He wore black gloves. Always did. The kind you couldn't buy just anywhere. Italian leather, snug, with precise seams. He appreciated quality. Things that lasted. Most didn't. People especially.

"People," he said with a smug snicker in his voice.

"We're not people. Are we?" he continued, speaking to someone unseen.

In the rearview mirror, the vague shape of something lay beneath a heavy wool blanket, seatbelt strapped diagonally over it. He didn't look at it often. He didn't need to. Some things, once perfect, remained perfect without constant observation.

The rearview showed him sharper than he was. His smile stretched too wide, his eyes inked too dark, as if the reflection were rehearsing for a role he hadn't agreed to play.

"They don't see you," he said softly. "But I do. That first time. I was the only one who could. I understand you. Something connects us, you see. Something unspeakable, but true. The strange mysterious forces of attraction and coincidence cannot be ignored. We're both here for a reason."

Another glance up into the rearview mirror. His eyes blinked in the reflection and they were black. Blink again. Back to normal.

The car moved deeper into the woods, along a road that no longer had lines or shoulders, just gravel and overgrowth. A mile back, the last gas station had flickered out behind him like a dying planet. Awareness of his surroundings was of the utmost importance. He'd timed it all precisely. Timing was everything. The rhythm of movement, the weight of silence. Orchestration mattered. It's what made him as elusive and lethal as a demon's breath.

The highway was long behind him now. The road narrowed as tires hissed against the countless pebbles, shouldered by trees and shadows.

A single headlight flickered in the distance. An approaching truck, maybe, but he turned left before it could get close, slipping onto an isolated side road, unnoticed. With all the confidence and preparation he had put in, his presence was so discreet that he might as well have been invisible.

"I noticed you long before that party," he continued, speaking in that calm, instructive tone he used with people he didn't respect, which was most people. "They saw you laughing. I saw the silence underneath. That's where you lived. That stillness. That impossible stillness. I recognized your soul immediately. It was a mirror."

He smiled, a thin stretch of lips across clean teeth. He often found himself smiling when others would feel something else. As usual, he was smiling to himself, quiet and sharp, the way a man might smile at a hidden masterpiece hanging in his private study.

The gritty road snapped under the tires as the Lexus continued down a forgotten service road. Just wide enough for one vehicle. No lights. No signs. It wasn't on any maps. He'd made sure of that. He'd found it last winter while hiking with a woman whose name he couldn't recall. She'd been loud. Always narrating her own thoughts like someone expecting applause.

The Lexus climbed a narrow incline, tires crunching softly. The trees had thickened now. No moon tonight. Just stars, pale and diffident. He turned off the ignition. Darkness rushed in. Literally and figuratively.

For a long moment, he sat still, letting the quiet thicken. Minutes passed. He enjoyed this part. The weight of the pause. The airless space between the act and the echo. Savoring the success.

Heroin addicts got less enjoyment out of their fix.

"You deserve better than them," he said, still not turning around. "All of them, posing. Trying to be noticed. And then there was you." His voice seemed to reverberate even though the windows were up.

He paused for a few more moments and looked off into the black distance of the night, not really seeing anything. Just thinking. Lost in the thought of what this night had meant for him and for his existence.

He turned his head ever so slightly to the left, to look into the backseat, but never fully turned around. Just a little side-eye glance and he whispered very softly to himself, "Mirrors don't belong here. They belong Elsewhere. Just me, you know?"

Feelings of regret and determination washed over him. He was a man with a purpose, and he had achieved his objective. He let himself feel briefly and then he defiantly stepped out into the night. The door whispered shut behind him. The air smelled of moss and old rain.

Around the car, the trees stood with their thin limbs twisted upward. No moon. Just the cold. He embraced the cold. It empowered and inspired him.

He opened the rear door and folded the blanket back.

Her head tilted slightly, resting against the window. Her skin had taken on the calm, pale quality of something that no longer had to perform being alive. She was barefoot. He'd taken the shoes earlier, not out of necessity, but because they were wrong for her.

He touched her shoulder lightly.

"I told you I'd take care of it."

There was no struggle. Not anymore. There never really was. She had been delicate even in resistance, like paper refusing to burn. That was not typical of her kind. But she had joined the others in their collective fate all the same.

He lifted her from the seat—carefully, precisely, the way you might carry an expensive instrument, and turned toward the trees. The woman was beautiful in that hushed, final way. The delicate slant of her jaw, her dark lashes—ink drops on porcelain. The bruise beneath her eye was old now. The last punctuation in a sentence she never finished. Her dress was pale blue, torn near the hem. She weighed less than she had when he first noticed her. Strange, how death could feel like subtraction.

He disappeared into the trees. The woods accepted them both without protest. The branches swayed, though no wind stirred, bending toward him in the posture of parishioners bowing. Not in worship, but in mourning. The road would remember nothing.

The Lexus remained behind, still warm, its headlights dimmed but not off. The stereo blinked faintly, a cello's note held mid-breath, waiting. Even the music obeyed the hour.

The time was 3:33 a.m.

7

CHAPTER SEVEN

Messages in Flesh

Maria Voss stood with arms crossed, weight on one hip, staring up at the case board like it had insulted her.

The 18th carried the same worn weight as any precinct. Scuffed floors tracked with a hundred weary shoes, the stale reek of burnt coffee never quite gone, paper stacked in leaning towers that no one dared disturb. A constant murmur hung in the air. Phones ringing, keyboards clacking, and the scrape of chairs. All of it the background noise of people trying not to be here.

In front of Maria and her direct superior, Captain Solomon Bryans, were two photos, two bodies: a vagrant no one cared about and on the other side, a wife and mother who was beloved by all.

The overhead glow caught the photos at odd angles, giving the grainy prints a faint sheen, as if the dead themselves were half-emerging through the gloss. Each reflection bent the images into something else, something harder to look at.

Between the photos of the victims, tacked dead center, a grainy photo of a carved symbol—jagged, mystifying, impossible to decipher.

Captain Solomon Bryans was in his early fifties but you wouldn't know it from the way he moved: calm, economical, purposeful. His frame was

26

still strong, built from years serving in the army. The steel in his eyes hadn't dulled with age. If anything, it had sharpened. He wore command the way some men wore regret. Heavy but natural.

His voice had a low timbre—the kind that could de-escalate a tense room or silence a braggart without needing to raise it. He was a man who talked only when it mattered. And when he did, you listened.

His relationship with Detective Maria Voss was forged in the long shadows of unsolved cases and cold autopsy rooms. They didn't just respect each other; they got each other. He gave her hell, but only because he knew she could take it. And she gave it back just as quick. But God help the cop who thought they could talk down to her in his presence.

He had her back. Always had. She never had to ask.

Captain Bryans stood at the edge of the room, sipping burnt coffee from a chipped Cubs mug. "Two's a coincidence," he said. "Three's when we call the press." He said casually, trying not to let his favorite detective get ahead of herself. Even so, deep down he had the same sick feeling in the pit of his stomach as she did about these cases.

Maria didn't answer right away. She was staring at the photo of Mary Johnson, the second victim. Mother of three. Lived in a townhouse in Lincoln Park. Secretary at a law firm. Slightly overweight, dark hair pulled into a dated bun. Eyes wide in the crime scene photo like she'd seen something not of this world.

Mary Johnson's face made her ache in a different way. The kind of grief that came from knowing someone's children would carry the image of her last breath for the rest of their lives.

Maria never forgot details. But this time, she was forcing herself to. The image of Mary Johnson's absence in the mirror.

It was nothing, she told herself. But it hadn't felt like nothing. It had felt like something had looked back.

She was overworked and stressed. The wicked don't rest. So why should she? Seeing things in a mirror at a crime scene was just a mind pushed to its limits. That's all. Nothing more, nothing less.

Even if denial wasn't in her nature, she certainly was never going to bring up such a thing to the captain.

"You ever read Kierkegaard, Captain?" Maria asked, wanting to divert her thoughts.

"Every day. Isn't that the guy who does the comic right next to Marmaduke in the Tribune?" Bryans playfully asked.

"No." Maria closed her eyes. Annoyed, but not entirely.

Getting the conversation back on track, Maria continued, "Kierkegaard's a philosopher from Denmark. The 1800s. He's the one who said anxiety is the dizziness of freedom."

Bryans blinked. "Well, that clears it right up."

Maria half-smiled finally after the last crack by her boss broke her a little. A flicker of the woman she used to be. Before she traded music and metaphysics for crime scenes and cold cases. She'd walked into this job looking for answers. Somewhere along the way, she learned how to live with not having them. Cynicism is a welcome gift for homicide detectives. Especially the good ones.

Maria tilted her head wryly. "Don't strain yourself, Captain. Wouldn't want you accidentally stumbling while making an attempt at deep thought."

Bryans gave an abrupt exhale that masqueraded as a subtle laugh.

"Once you open your mind up to the possibilities, really open it, it makes you dizzy. But only then do you have a chance at finding the truth," Maria added, reflective now.

Bryans grunted, unimpressed on the surface, but the small flicker in his eyes betrayed the fact that her mind always impressed him.

"The symbol was identical," Maria finally said, getting back on topic. "Depth of the cut, shape, location. Forehead, dead center. That's not a coincidence. Both were most likely done by the same weapon. Some kind of modified surgical scalpel or calligraphy knife according to the ME. And, both victims allowed the carving to happen."

Bryans raised an eyebrow. "Allowed it to happen?"

"That's what Rose says. The symbol was put there before they died, and there's no evidence that they resisted this particular act." Maria explained.

Bryans sighed. "Still not a pattern. You got a John Doe and a soccer mom.

Nothing links them."

Maria watched him sip from that battered Cubs mug, jaw set too tight. He carried himself like the soldier he used to be. Disciplined, squared shoulders, always calm. But she knew the signs. The stillness wasn't composure. It was worry, locked down in parade rest.

Maria glanced at John Doe's photo. Male, white, late fifties. Unhoused, judging by the layers of torn clothing. Bludgeoned to death in a fierce struggle. Found in an alley near Halsted and 14th. No ID. Just another ghost in the city's long shadow.

Looking at him, she thought about how a man could vanish from the world so completely that only his absence was noticed.

If it hadn't been for the strange carving in the victim, the case would have been filed away as another insignificant death on the streets.

She rubbed her temple. "The killer wanted them found. Neither dump site was hidden. First was a dumpster behind a 24-hour deli. Second was Mary Johnson's own goddamn bed."

Bryans raised an eyebrow. "So, we've got a showboat?" he said, obviously beginning to drop the thin façade of disbelief.

"No," Maria said. "We've got someone making a statement. A symbol being carved into a victim is page one out of Sociopathic Manifestos for Dummies."

Bryans smirked to himself. She always amused him more than he would ever let on. It was his nature.

He grunted and walked over, folding his arms. "You're sure it's not just some sicko with a knife and a lucky streak?" he said. Challenging her because it was his job, not because he didn't believe her.

Maria gave him a look. Dry. Flat. A few years ago, she might've cracked a joke to defuse the tension. Now, she didn't bother. She hadn't had that black coffee she needed yet, after all. Or the lobotomy. The station's coffee was shit. Never tried their lobotomies though. Who knows?

She looked back at the board. "This symbol, whoever's carving it. They're not just killing. They're leaving a message." Voss knew her captain got the point but repeated herself for emphasis. Something she only did when she *knew* she was on the right path.

Bryans leaned over the table; eyes narrowed behind his glasses. A dozen printed photos were spread out all over.

Maria stood beside him, arms crossed, her jaw tight. Moving on to another point of interest in the investigation Bryans began, "Take a look at this one," tapping a close-up shot of the Johnson's living room.

"See it? The clock. Broken. Now the hallway. Another. And in the bedroom? A third." Bryans muttered, "Three broken clocks. You think that's a coincidence?"

"Don't believe in 'em," Maria said. Bryans concurred with a grunt.

Maria laid the three photos side by side, studying them. "Captain, look at the times on all three clocks." Bryans followed her finger, pointing to all three photos, directing his attention to the fact that all three clocks had been broken at the same time.

"Three clocks. All frozen at 3:33," she said, her voice quieter than before. "That's a message."

3:33. A time too exact to be random, too strange to be ignored.

She leaned in, noticing something. "Now look at the mirrors."

Two mirrors were visible: one above the fireplace, another in the bathroom. Both fractured. The bathroom mirror had a starburst impact, something had obviously been thrown. The one above the mantle was spiderwebbed, but still hanging.

"That's not random," she said. "Someone didn't just lose it in a rage."

"Clocks and mirrors," Bryans murmured. "Time and reflection."

Maria lingered on the photos of the broken mirrors, and the memory pressed in. The mirror in Mary Johnson's bedroom. How, in one glance, the corpse wasn't there at all, and in the next it was staring back at her. The moment had clung to her ever since. She was trying to bury it, but the fractured glass in these photos dragged it all back.

Maria exhaled slowly. Evidence bags weren't what she was thinking about anymore. "There's something else going on here." The memory of that mirror pressed at the edges of her thoughts until she forced it back with a nod.

"What is all this?" Maria wondered aloud.

"Well, whatever it is, let's hope it doesn't get answered with a third body," Bryans replied. He knew in his gut as she did that there would be.

Maria leaned closer to the blown-up photo of the second victim's forehead. The symbol was carved with meticulous care. Two angled shapes flanking a dashed vertical line, clean and geometric. It looked almost mechanical. Or religious. Or both.

Captain Bryans squinted at it from behind her. "Any luck figuring out what that's supposed to be?"

"None," Maria said. "Not in any cult databases. Not runic. Not any language I've ever seen."

Maria stared at the symbol. It felt like it was speaking a language she once knew but had forgotten. What did it mean?

"It's not a gang symbol. Not a family crest. It has no academic meaning." She continued rattling off an impromptu list of possibilities.

"It doesn't seem to have significance to either victim in their personal or professional life." Maria stated.

"John Doe had a résumé?" Bryans quipped.

Voss turned slowly and shot an annoyed half grin toward her captain. It was a mildly playful look but annoyed nonetheless.

Bryans snapped back to the seriousness of the conversation and grunted. "I'm seeing a pair of doors. Or a circuit diagram."

Maria's eyes narrowed. "Maybe," she squinted.

To her, it didn't look like doors or wires. It looked like a threshold. And thresholds were meant to be crossed.

"Or maybe it's not supposed to mean anything. Maybe it's just something he sees."

She didn't say what she was really thinking, that it was a message. Not to them. To the victims. Or worse, from them.

8

CHAPTER EIGHT

Discovery at Dusk

Dusk in the Midwest isn't quiet so much as it is holding its breath. The sun hadn't quite set, but the sky was bruising purple. The air pressed heavy, the kind of stillness that feels staged. Damp soil, sun-warmed bark, the faint musk of moss clinging to stone—all of it smelled alive and ancient. Mist clung low to the ground.

Majestic is one word, though it feels dishonest.

Deer tracks dented the mud near a rusted fence, half-swallowed by brambles that seemed to shift if you stared too long. Wildflowers, including Queen Anne's lace and goldenrod, were folding in for the night. Their petals curled inward as night took hold. Fireflies began to spark across the field, one by one.

Far off, a red barn leaned into the trees. Its tin roof caught the dying light in a way that made it glow from within, as though the building itself remembered something. The wind rattled loose metal on its siding, sharp and metallic. The treetops sighed long and mournful.

Serenity, or its imitation.

And imitations can be cruel.

Nevin Sauers—sixty-nine, ex-Marine, part-time land surveyor, full-time crank. He locked his back door with a grunt and stepped into the evening.

This was the part of the day he despised most: his nightly rounds. Checking the property lines. Watching for trespassers. Dragging off whatever scraps the coyotes left behind. The land demanded it, week after week, a ritual he'd never agreed to. His joints ached more each season, his body rusting in place, but the land never cared.

He used to love these woods when he was younger. Now they only looked back at him like strangers.

He stepped over a twisted root that resembled a hand reaching out. Cursed under his breath.

Nevin hated evenings almost as much as mornings. Hated the damp even more. If he wasn't complaining, he wasn't living.

The fence line had collapsed again. Damn deer. He wasn't about to let another neighbor's brat roll an ATV into his woods.

He squinted through the trees. His breath hitched. His boots were already soaked, but he hardly noticed. He moved carefully.

And then he saw it.

At first, fabric. Maybe a tarp, or laundry torn loose and snagged in the undergrowth. He took a step closer. Then froze.

A woman.

She lay on her side in a bed of leaves, her hair fanned out. A pale blue dress torn thin, clinging damply to her skin. Bare feet, gray with cold. Her arms were curled in tightly, trying to protect herself from something that hadn't quite finished. Her eyes were slightly open, catching the last shard of sunlight and holding it, glassy and unblinking.

Nevin didn't speak. Didn't dare. Years of hard living had taught him when not to interrupt the world.

It was only after the silence had deepened that he noticed the symbol.

Carved into her forehead.

Clean. Precise.

Meant.

The cicadas stopped all at once. The silence was so sharp it rang in his ears.

Nevin backed away, slowly, nervous that sudden movement might wake something. His hand made the sign of the cross almost without thinking. "God in heaven," he muttered. "What in the hell is this?"

The woods didn't answer. They only seemed to lean closer.

The air around her was wrong. Still but not silent. Like a choir holding its breath in the dark. And the mist moved, curling backward against the breeze, sliding the wrong way.

Nevin's hand trembled as he pulled out his phone. Dialed 911.

Behind him, high in the trees, something shifted. Long. Thin. Not quite shaped right.

And when he turned, the mist swallowed everything.

9

CHAPTER NINE

A Night at Home

The Voss house, a sturdy 1920s build in Villa Park, was chaos with corners.

Half-folded laundry slumped on the kitchen counter beside unopened packages and random items meant to be put away six months ago. Crumbs on the kitchen floor like settled dust. A half-built LEGO spaceship lived permanently on the coffee table, surrounded by out-of-place socks. Every chair leaned heavy with coats and jackets, long forgotten, thrown carelessly over the backs, ready to topple if bumped.

Maria Voss moved through it on autopilot, coat still half on, keys clutched in her hand. Burnout wasn't a state of mind. It was a way of life.

She dropped her keys into the chipped ceramic bowl by the door, the same way she did every night. The dull clink had become ritual. Proof she'd made it home, even if she wasn't fully here.

"Dinner in ten," she called out, not quite loud enough.

A short silence, then from the living room: "Is it real dinner or is it detective dinner again?" Eli, thirteen, dry, sharp, always watching.

Maria exhaled. "Define real."

"Something that doesn't come from a box or say 'Instructions: Pierce film before heating,'" he said, rounding the corner with a smug grin and a bowl of cereal in hand.

Maria threw her hands up in exaggerated annoyance and locked eyes with him. He knew what that look meant. "I was hungry," he admitted. "I still want actual dinner though."

She squinted at her oldest, whom she saw as more of an equal than she'd ever admit—because of his age, and because of that snarky attitude that could throw her off more than anyone else she'd ever met.

"Then no," she said. "It's detective dinner. Bonus points if you don't ask what the meat is."

He smiled like a kid who'd heard the same bedtime story too many years in a row. "It's fine. I'll pair it with a juice box and pretend it's a food truck."

Maria opened the freezer, fished out something vaguely rectangular, looked at it briefly without actually reading the label, then tossed it into the microwave. The hum filled the space.

Eli crossed his arms and, in his best mock-announcer voice, read from the box she'd ignored: "Instructions: Pierce film before heating. Stir halfway through. Let stand for two minutes."

Maria stared at him, too tired to laugh. "Thanks, you turd."

Just as she turned to rinse off a cutting board she didn't actually plan to use, a crash sounded from the hallway.

"Jesus, Tommy!" she shouted before she even looked.

She didn't need to. This crime required no investigation.

Her ten-year-old barreled in, Nerf gun raised imitating a SWAT commando. His shirt was on backward, his socks didn't match, his eyes were bright and slightly wild.

Tommy was her sunshine, and her high blood pressure rolled into one.

"It was an ambush!" he declared. "I was flanking Eli!"

"You broke the lamp," Maria said flatly.

"No, gravity broke the lamp. Gravity does all the breaking. *Ground gravity.*"

"Pun intended?" Eli asked snidely.

Tommy looked at him, confused and angry. Confused because he didn't know what a pun was. Angry because he knew his brother well enough to know he was making fun of him.

Eli leaned into the frame from the kitchen, spoon in mouth. "He's trying to redefine physics again."

"Because I read, Eli. You should try it sometime!" Tommy shouted, his perpetual pilot light about to flare into a full bonfire.

"Well, YOU should try not sucking so much," Eli retorted with his trademark sass.

"ELI!!" Tommy raised a clenched fist, ready to turn that spark into flame.

"Boys," Maria said, pinching the bridge of her nose. "Please. Can I just… can we not do this tonight? Just tonight?"

Both boys paused. Eli watched her, trying to read her thoughts. Tommy stared with a patented fire in his eyes.

Eli softened first. "Rough day?"

"Something like that," Maria muttered, touched and impressed at how socially intelligent her oldest was for being thirteen.

The microwave beeped. Maria opened it, pulled out the steaming tray, and tossed it onto the counter. She grabbed two forks. No plates. No ceremony.

"Split it," she said. "You get what you get and you don't throw a fit."

Tommy wrinkled his nose. "Is it meatloaf or lasagna?"

"Does it matter?"

"It matters morally."

Since she'd gotten home, Maria's words and movements had dragged, weighed down by cases and the need for sleep. But Tommy's absurd response jolted her; she spun and threw her hands up in an expression that said, *What the fuck?!* She bit back the actual words. Tommy would repeat it at school in a heartbeat.

Eli grabbed one fork and poked the mush. "It's either going to be amazing or medically inadvisable."

Maria turned away, toward the sink, trying to disappear into the running water and the scrape of utensils behind her. She wanted to sit. She wanted to talk to them. She wanted to be there. But her mind was still in a cold alley. Still in a warmly decorated bedroom destroyed by death. Still seeing an arcane symbol bleeding into her psyche.

She felt a flicker of guilt: how many nights had she come home too late, too tired, and fed them barely edible scraps instead of something she actually made? Too many. More than she wanted to count.

"Mom?"

She blinked back to Tommy frowning at her.

"You're doing that thing where you stare, but don't blink. It's weird."

Eli smirked. "It's her cop rebooting face."

Maria finally let out a short, bittersweet laugh. No one really understood her quite like her thirteen-year-old did.

If Tommy was her sunshine, Eli was her rock. Stabilizing and energizing her through this crazy life in this heartless world, her sons were her everything. Even if she couldn't always show it.

Maria exhaled and said, "Who wants to watch some episodes of *The Munsters* before bed?" She loved that the boys enjoyed classic television.

They answered together. Tommy shouting, "YEAH!!" while Eli muttered, "Okay."

Maria collapsed into the corner of the sectional and patted both sides. The boys hopped onto the sofa with the same enthusiasm, one loud, one reserved, both pressed close against her. The sectional smelled faintly of dried juice and stale fruit snacks.

Maria turned on the TV, settled into the glow, and let her thoughts begin to wash away.

The moment almost relaxed.

And then the phone rang.

Not her personal phone. The other one. The phone. The one that only rang for one reason.

Her eyes closed slowly. She hesitated, just for a heartbeat. For once she wanted to ignore it. For once she wanted to be mom, not cop. But she knew better. She sighed and picked it up on the first ring.

"Voss," she said, as she had a thousand times before.

Captain Bryans's voice, low and heavy. "Voss... I'm sorry. I know the time. Can you find a sitter?"

Maria didn't speak. The laugh track from the TV echoed behind her, tinny and hollow.

Bryans continued, "Northwoods area. Just south of North Avenue. The boonies."

Her eyes closed again. Eli stopped watching TV. Tommy didn't.

"What is it?" she asked.

"We got another one," Bryans said, reluctant. "You might want to start thinking about what you'll tell the press."

Maria nodded to no one. "I'll be there in twenty."

She hung up. Didn't move.

Eli nudged Tommy. Tommy ignored him. Eli nudged harder. Tommy scowled and mouthed, What?

Eli pointed at their mother.

Maria was frozen. Tommy spoke first. "Another dead person?"

Maria didn't look at him. "You know I can't talk about it."

Eli stood, quietly taking charge. "It's okay, Mom. Go ahead. We've got this."

She looked at them. Really looked. She wanted to memorize this. Mess and all. It was what kept her going.

"Be good. No more experiments in physics, please."

Tommy saluted. "No promises."

She swallowed, the words catching, but let them out anyway. "I love you both."

Eli's eyes softened; he gave her a knowing look. "Love you too, Mom."

Tommy grinned. "Bring back donuts. Sprinkles, please."

She smirked sadly, soaking in the moment for a few seconds, then slid back into the familiar motions of a tired cop and regret-filled parent.

Maria grabbed her coat, her keys, and walked out into the night.

10

CHAPTER TEN

The Knot

Reed Ashland's apartment was a cathedral of clutter. So was his mind. So was his life.

Half-drunk gin bottles. Photos curling at the corners. Books with more notes than pages. A stack of journals had collapsed against the wall, crooked and leaning. The odor of a hermit's despair hung in the air.

The television played static, but there was no sound. Not muted. Just absent. The flickering screen threw blue-white patches across the room, fractured light that looked like stained glass in a desecrated chapel.

Reed's world was not a place any reasonable person would want to inhabit. Not even he wanted to. Yet here he was: living it, breathing it. Waking up every morning, or early afternoon, with regrets stacked on worries.

A high-functioning drunk. Too damaged to stop the self-inflicted wounds. Too careful to ever hit rock bottom.

Some people need to hit bottom to change. Reed? He'd been digging through the sub-basement for years.

No growth. Not here. Not on this plane of existence.

He lay on the floor. Barefoot. Wearing a coat. A sock on one foot. A glove on one hand. Everything uneven. Everything wrong. But not wrong enough to fix.

Calling him "sad" was an understatement.

A Polaroid clung to his fingers. Emily, mid-laugh, her hair caught mid-motion, a golden ripple.

The gin still clung to his tongue, sour and metallic. His thoughts didn't move forward so much as stagger sideways. And yet, through the haze, her face was clear.

He remembered driving with her in the backseat, how he couldn't keep his eyes on the road because she was singing in her car seat. Off-key, feet kicking, arms dancing to a song only she understood. He remembered rocking her to sleep, her small head pressed against his chest, the weight of her body melting into him as her breathing slowed. It was the kind of moment he wished he could get stuck inside, a loop he'd gladly live in forever. He remembered the first time her little voice wrapped around the words, "I wuv you, Daddy."

Then came the memory he could never outrun. Emily pale in a hospital bed at ten, her skin cold with fever, machines ticking. The ache struck his body before it struck his mind: his throat tightening, chest caving in, stomach roiling.

Grief wasn't just sadness; it was theft. It had stolen not only her life, but every version of her he'd never get to see.

Reed stared at the photograph. Then flipped it over. His own handwriting on the back. Only it wasn't.

She remembers the real you.

Faint echoes rose from the distance. The joyful laughter of a family.

"Really?" Reed thought, expecting the picture to respond.

His eyes brimmed. Rivers trying to forget what they carried. He dropped the photo. It landed in a patch of moonlight and he began to sob.

He didn't notice the wall had begun to breathe. Slowly. Unevenly. Lungs learning to inhale. The plaster stretched and released, shallow at first, then deeper, almost panicked.

Reed tried to stand. Just the act made him wobble, grasping at air before falling backward. Almost comedic, if it weren't so familiar and tragic.

Drunk. Depressed. But the disorientation was something else.

Something was happening.

A shiver of intuition cut through the alcohol's fog. He felt as if the air itself were waiting. Thick with a cryptic importance he couldn't name, only sense. The world was leaning in close and whispering: pay attention.

Then, a knock.

Three taps. Soft. But sharp enough to pierce the haze in his skull.

Reed froze. His skin prickled; the hair on his arms stood straight. The sound hit him with the force of childhood fear; nights when he lay awake, imagining knocks on his bedroom door, certain the dark itself wanted in.

He didn't move. Maybe it was the wind. Maybe guilt had learned how to knock.

Knocks are usually mundane. Not these. These felt ritualistic, like something prescient had found his address. Reed's intuition, sharp even though dulled by gin, began to flare. His body thought it was midnight, and an intruder was already inside.

A second knock. Slower. Intentional.

Reed staggered toward the door. Past a stack of journals. Past a bottle clinging to its last drop.

He reached for the knob. Cracked the door. Slowly. Expecting someone to lunge.

He slipped his head through, a comically paranoid drunk.

Nothing.

Relief spread. He opened the door wider. Staggered into the hallway. Turned, slow. Not worried. Just confused.

He wobbled even while standing still. Looked left. Then right. Nothing. No one. No sound.

If anyone had been watching, they might have laughed.

Reed smirked, overconfident, drunk. He turned back toward his door.

And froze.

Sober in an instant.

Tied delicately around the knob was a fraying cord. Knotted intricately into a looping, tangled pattern. Almost a figure eight. Almost an infinity symbol breaking apart.

A wisdom knot.

Reed stared at it. His pulse slowed. Recognition rose, not in words but in sensation. Like the remembered smell of a house you once lived in.

He didn't think. He knew what to do somehow.

The streetlight flickered as he slipped behind the wheel of a black sedan.

He blinked. Startled. Not at the car, but at the missing stretch of reality between here and the knot on his door.

His car. Same dent in the rearview. Same stale coffee and cedarwood air freshener. But something was wrong.

The seat felt unfamiliar.

The radio whispered static.

The keys. He didn't remember picking them up.

The car was parked in a lot so wide it could have stretched to infinity. Black fog at the edges, hiding whatever lay beyond.

Reed sat still. Tried to gather himself. Center himself.

It didn't work.

Where am I?

How long had he been driving?

Did he start the engine?

What street was this?

A pressure built in the air. A dream leaning in, pausing before it chose how to enter. It felt both intimate and endless.

A shadow congealed in the passenger seat.

Reed turned. And there he was.

Not startled. He should have been. But wasn't.

A man sat beside him. Thin. Ageless. A face you couldn't quite focus on. Dressed in a gray three-piece suit from no decade that ever existed. His presence wasn't announced. He was just… there.

"Mr. Morrow," Reed said. The name arrived in his mouth before he realized he knew it.

The man smiled without teeth. "It's late, doctor. Or perhaps it's early. Time is a hallway with mirrors, not a line."

They stared at one another. Seconds stretched into minutes. It wasn't awkward. It was natural.

Reed's throat was dry. "What is this?"

"The knot was an invitation. And you accepted."

Reed blinked. "To what?"

"Recognition."

Mr. Morrow tilted his head. "There's a killer in your city, Reed. One who carves the memory of himself into others. Your soul has beheld this mark in its wondrous and macabre glory."

Reed's mind reeled. The test-you-never-studied-for dream. Only this was real.

He tried to think. Gin made that impossible.

He looked down. On the floor mat: a gingerbread man cookie. A single bite missing from its head. Reed hadn't eaten one since childhood. He didn't own floor mats. This was his car, though. Wasn't it?

"You mean the symbol?" His own voice sounded distant, half-knowing what he asked.

The image burned against the inside of his skull, but he couldn't place how it got there. For an instant, it felt less like memory and more like projection.

Morrow didn't answer. He leaned in slightly. "There are always two Marys. One to mourn. One to open the door."

"What does that mean?"

"You already know."

Reed felt the air tilt. He had the sensation that he was in a dream deciding whether to hold him or let him wake.

He knew Morrow was still there, and yet he also knew he was already gone; both sensations overlapped, indistinguishable, until Reed couldn't tell if he was watching a man vanish or remembering that he already had.

The seat was empty.

Reed gasped. Too late.

The desolate parking lot was gone. The car was parked at the edge of an industrial district he didn't recognize.

Rusted warehouses loomed, their windows blacked out, their walls sweating with condensation that shouldn't have been there in the cold.

A single streetlamp swayed above, its light stuttering in time with his pulse, each blink syncing his body to something outside himself.

The shift felt like shaking free from the weight of a dream. Only the dream was the part that had been real.

Waking wasn't clarity; it was dislocation.

He looked at the dashboard clock, 4:44 a.m.

The numbers hummed through his bones. Not sound. Not sight. Something more ancient. A secret whispered in a language he'd forgotten.

Reed exhaled and reached into his jacket for the knot.

It was gone.

11

CHAPTER ELEVEN

Between the Drop and the Dream

The lock clicked louder than usual. Reed stepped into the stillness of his apartment, the door closing behind him with a bang that woke everyone in his building who needed to go to work. The sun hadn't yet made up its mind about the day, just the faintest tint of blue peeking over the horizon. The world was barely stirring. But Reed Ashland had already touched something raw.

Somewhere above him, a toilet ran; somewhere below, a baby coughed. The hallway's fluorescent hum bled under the door, a thin, needling sound. The world was quiet, but not still.

He stood just inside the doorway for a while. Jacket still on. Shoes still damp with the dew of an in-between hour. The quiet was too loud. His ears rang faintly from adrenaline.

"There's a killer in your city, Reed." He could hear Mr. Morrow's words reverberating in his head.

Mr. Morrow's voice: calm, smooth, precise. It looped in his mind like a record caught on a scratch. No matter how many thoughts he tried to stack on top of it, it would not be buried.

He tossed his keys onto the counter and missed. They hit the tile and scattered.

One key skittered under the stove and vanished. His body moved on autopilot. Jacket draped over a chair.

He opened the fridge, stared into the light, then closed it again. Reed walked straight to the kitchen counter, grabbed a bottle of gin, maybe a quarter left, and slammed it down until the burn went quiet. He let the empty bottle hit the tile and staggered into the living room.

He made it to the couch and sat, elbows on knees, hands clasped, head bowed.

On the bookshelf, a frame lay face down. He didn't turn it over. He knew the photo by weight alone. How it always felt heavier than glass should.

The faint ringing in his ears rose, then thinned, a signal trying to lock in. He stood again.

Pacing. Living room to hallway. Back again. A loop. A strange ritual to keep his thoughts from forming teeth. He must've paced the entirety of his apartment a dozen times. By the tenth lap, even his shadows looked tired.

He stopped in front of the window, peering outside. The streets were empty. He moved his hand to the pane. His fingertips met the glass, and a hum rose through him. Not cold but mechanical.

It spiked into precognition: streetlights stuttering, a door opening where no door was. He tore his hand back. He stared at his fingers, half expecting smoke. What was that?

Reed yanked out his phone to look up the news.

He frowned and opened the browser. Maybe grounding himself in the real world would shake the feeling loose. The page loaded in stutters, letters assembling out of order before they snapped into sense.

He flipped to where he wanted to be, his thoughts way ahead of his actions and the connection.

Local news. Crime reports. He skimmed. A robbery gone wrong. A domestic dispute that turned fatal. A drug bust in the South Loop. All tragic. None of them felt relevant. Not to this.

Then he found it. A headline buried under others.

"Woman Found Murdered in Lincoln Park Home. Authorities Seeking Information."

He didn't click. He knew what was under it the way you know a stove is hot before your hand gets there.

His thumb froze above the screen.

Mary Johnson, 43.

There it was. That name.

Mary.

A tremor crawled across his shoulders, slow and certain. His pulse quickened in a way that let him know this was what he was supposed to be looking for.

The Man in the Charcoal Suit. His words echoed from a distance, burning into Reed's brain, straight down to his core.

"There are always two Marys."

The words didn't arrive as thought so much as temperature. A change in the room, a draft from a door he hadn't opened. They crawled from the back of his mind and into the front. He swallowed.

It was nothing. A coincidence. Mary was a common name. Johnson even more so. He tried to reason with himself, to stay rooted.

But the feeling in his chest didn't budge.

That hollow, widening thing; a door was opening inside him.

And something was stepping through.

The floor didn't tilt. The air did. The ringing sharpened to a thread. He took a breath that never finished.

Then he fell and never hit the ground.

***

Reed was plunged into an illusory chasm. It was like living inside a ghost.

He was falling.

Not fast.

Not violently.

Just… falling.

The dark around him had no shape, no texture, no end. He didn't scream. He didn't even try. There was no fear in the fall. Just the sense that something swallowed him up.

Then, slowly, the fall softened. His body no longer dropped, but floated, suspended in something not quite air. He drifted through layers of something thin and brittle.

Reed Ashland had been on a seventy-two-hour bender, which would have been bad enough if it weren't for the insomnia. Had he dropped into an abyss of deep sleep that he so badly needed? Or was this something else?

Then the images came. It was impossible to describe. It was as if a slideshow of memories was playing out all around him but also inside his head. Inside his soul.

A streetlight flickering over a wet curb.

A child's shoe in the grass.

The sound of his daughter's laugh: high, clear, sharp as glass.

Then: the hospital room. White walls and fluorescent light.

Her tiny face, red and wrinkled, pressed against his chest.

The soft, heartening coo of a newborn.

His hand trembling as he touched her cheek.

A warmth.

Then the warmth turned.

The front door slamming.

A bottle smashing.

Her voice, broken by tears and fury, "I can't do this anymore, Reed!"

Suitcase. Hallway. Silence.

He kept floating.

An empty diner booth at 2 a.m.

A coin spinning on a countertop.

A deer frozen in headlights.

A choir singing a haunting hymn in reverse.

A mirror fogging with breath that wasn't his.

A clock face stopped at 3:33.

The clock swelled until the hands and numbers lost their edges, sliding into one another and congealing into indecipherable figures.

Then the blur resolved into the black shadows of trees, perfectly still, until a wind no one could see or hear slipped through and set them whispering.

The image was clearer than the others. A narrow road. Gravel crunching under tires. The moonlight slicing through the maples and the elms.

The scent of cold earth and gasoline.

The wooded property. A place he didn't recognize yet knew.

Somewhere in Northwoods. Near the edge of the map in his mind. An old green road sign leaned at an angle, the last two letters peeled: —ds. Beyond it, a chain-link gate with one diamond cut out—a missing shape he could find again.

A woman's body.

Twisted, still.

The clearing bathed in pale blue.

The symbol cut into her skin.

Reed didn't wake, but he knew.

He didn't question how he knew. He just did. When the images thinned, he tasted metal. His hands were clenched so tight the knuckles shone. Something in him had been used.

He knew where it had happened.

He was already on his feet, reaching for the one key he could still see.

He knew where to go.

12

CHAPTER TWELVE

The Second Set of Eyes

Maria drove north on I-355. The white paint of the road was a metronome. Tick. Tick. Tick.

Maria kept the car between the lines. Mostly. She blinked. The road blinked back.

"Stay with me," she demanded. "Eyes up," she told herself. "Hands steady."

The windshield seemed like a second set of eyes staring back at her, reflecting every blink she fought to keep open.

To her right, the skyline of Chicago glittered against the night. The glass towers lit with cold fire.

It was a city of promise and rot. Beautiful from a distance, poisonous up close. The kind of place that could swallow you whole and never bother spitting you back out.

The city thinned. The lights grew farther apart. Suburbs gave way to black fields rimmed with skeletal trees and the kind of warehouses that go quiet at night and whisper to themselves.

Her lids grew heavy. Not sleep-heavy, but dream-heavy. The kind that pulls from behind the eyes. Her fingertips tingled like static had crawled under her skin. The air around her felt too thick, as if she were trying to breathe soup instead of oxygen.

51

The low rumble of the engine blurred into a hum, until she couldn't tell if the sound came from under the hood or inside her skull.

She tightened her grip on the wheel. Her boys were at home, probably asleep now. Eli. Tommy. Two anchors keeping her from drifting too far into the dark. She hated leaving them. Hated the job for pulling her away again and again. Yet she loved it too. She loved the work, loved the fight. Protect and serve, they said. Corny words, sure, but she'd built her life on them.

But the city she protected rarely gave a damn about her. Not the brass. Not the crowds. Only her boys did. Didn't she owe them something more than this endless grind? A vacation, maybe. She pictured a beach. Sunlight spilling gold, Eli and Tommy laughing as they chased waves. The smell of salt instead of gunpowder, sand instead of blood.

A majestic scene, but something was not quite right. The waves didn't crash forward; they recoiled, sliding back into the horizon as though time itself had reversed.

Puncturing the idyllic backdrop, the dead followed. Pale bodies washed up on her private beach. Faces slack, eyes clouded. She shoved the thought away and forced herself to return to Eli and Tommy, building a sandcastle. She imagined the inevitable argument between them: Tommy insisting on towers, Eli on trenches. That was real. That was hers.

The dead pressed back in. A body in the sand. A forehead marked by the carved mirror symbol, blood dripping, flowing and curling until it formed that jagged geometric design. The smell of iron filled her nose, sweet and metallic. Shadows moved in the lilacs, an ominous backdrop to Maria's visions.

The sound of distant laughter rose.

It echoed from everywhere and nowhere, bouncing through her skull. Another corpse glowed unnaturally bright, its light cutting through the dark.

It sat up. Stiff and slow. Lips parted in a scream. But no sound came. Only the horrible stretching of flesh, the dry click of a jaw unhinging too far.

Only silence.

And then the silence shifted. It thickened, pressed against her eardrums until they felt like they'd burst. Her teeth ached. A hum threaded through the silence.

The corpse's mouth stretched wider, impossibly wide, trying to swallow the silence itself. The hum grew louder, splintering into static, into broken voices. A child's giggle. A church bell tolling.

And then her stomach dropped. One of the bodies wasn't faceless anymore.

A woman lay in the sand, her hair matted and wet, skin pale as porcelain, lips twitching into the beginnings of a smile: sweet, familiar, devastating. A faint scent of lilacs reached Maria, impossibly delicate amid the reek of blood. The color of her dress was blue, too vivid against the gray sand. It stabbed at Maria's memory like a knife twisting.

Maria reached unconsciously for the chain under her shirt.

It wasn't there.

Her chest seized as the air vanished from her lungs. The blue of the dress burned in her eyes, too vivid, the exact shade of a memory she'd buried so deep she thought she'd killed it. Her hands twitched toward the body without her consent.

Heat burned in her palms. Her heart stuttered and raced all at once, panic lancing through her with surgical precision.

She wanted to cry out, but no sound came. All she could do was feel: the undertow of grief and the taste of salt she couldn't swallow away.

The woman's body sat up, jerking stiffly. Her eyes opened wide, milky and unblinking. The voice that came from the corpse's mouth wasn't hers. It was distant and warped, like an old cassette tape played backward.

The words were unintelligible, but Maria knew, with the certainty of a wound reopening, that they were meant for her.

The static swelled. The laughter roared. Blood dripped in patterns, curling across the sand to form the mirror symbol again and again, until the ground was covered. The symbols began to pulse.

The silence became sound, blaring in her skull, a car horn in the night.

Screaming her back into the world.

A horn.

Maria's eyes flew open. Her car veered toward the lane divider. She jerked the wheel, tires screeching as she swerved onto the shoulder. The horn of a passing truck roared by, rattling her bones. For a split second she couldn't tell if the sound belonged to the truck or the corpse's mouth still stretched wide in the sand.

Heart hammering, she braced both hands on the wheel, sucking in air as if she'd just surfaced from deep water. Adrenaline pulsed through her veins, hot and jagged. She stayed there, engine idling, breathing hard in the darkness.

Definitely awake now.

She breathed. She remembered how.

"Okay," she said. The word had no force. She tried again. "Okay."

"Stay with me," she said again.

Up ahead, a narrow road bent off the main one at a stingy angle. The kind of turn you miss if you don't know it's coming. A small green sign leaned, its last two letters peeled: —ds. The gate beyond it held a chain-link diamond like a missing tooth.

Maria flicked the blinker. The click sounded too loud in the car.

She turned, and the night turned with her.

Next time, she thought, she'd just bring the damn coffee.

13

CHAPTER THIRTEEN

The Mirror Tells Nothing

The woods weren't supposed to be alive at night. Not like this.

Detective Maria Voss approached the scene in her car and pulled it into park. Her hands were still trembling on the wheel, the memory of headlights bearing down on her and that half-dream, half-vision clinging to her thoughts. She forced herself to breathe, to shake it off, to silence the icy whisper working its way up her spine.

The rural serenity known as Northwoods was alive with activity. Crime scene tape fluttered in the breeze like ribbons at a parade no one asked for. Flashbulbs blinked from evidence cameras. Boots shuffled, markers were placed, bags were sealed.

Above the yellow tape, two crows perched on a bare limb, heads tilted. They didn't caw, didn't stir. They just stared with unblinking patience. The forest seemed to breathe with them, holding its secrets close.

Amidst the maples and the pines lay a woman, lifeless in the center of all the police routine. She was the cold, stiff headliner of a morbid revue.

She stepped out of her car, the autumn air hitting her. The forest smelled like rot, pine, and the last warmth of summer dying in the soil.

Captain Solomon Bryans stood near the perimeter of the scene, waiting for her with two coffees in hand.

"Figured you'd want it black," he said, handing one over.

Maria took it without a word. Sipped. Winced. "It's hot."

"That's how coffee works."

Maria didn't respond.

"What do we know?" she asked, a mixture of anticipation and exhaustion.

Bryans motioned toward the taped-off clearing. "Nevin Sauers, the old coot who owns this land, found the body around 6:45."

"The same symbol?" Maria asked, though she already knew. That's why she'd been called out here at this time of night.

"Exactly the same."

Maria stared through the trees at the swarm of forensic suits moving with precision. "Positioning?"

"Lying on her back. Arms folded. No signs of restraint. Body looks posed."

"Injuries?"

"Some bruising. She was struck in the face several times and then held down and strangled, by the looks of it. But the cut on her head was clean. Same knife maybe."

"We'll want Rose to examine her. She can confirm if the symbol was carved while she was alive, and if she let it happen. Like the others," Maria said, her voice low but certain.

Maria sighed. "What else?"

"No ID. Looks like she was dumped late last night. No signs of struggle here, so this wasn't the kill site either. Gravel's terrible for tire tracks."

"That was probably the point," Maria interjected.

Bryans grunted in agreement.

They walked under the tape. Maria ducked and stepped into the clearing. The ground was damp, the air thick. Press gathered behind the police lines, their long lenses aimed like rifles. Civilians too, craning necks, murmuring guesses. Rubberneckers.

Maria scanned the crowd instinctively. A seasoned investigator, she knew to take in the entire scene. Not just what had happened, but what was happening now. Many killers return to the scene. They get their jollies from it.

One bystander stood out in particular. Easy to spot. Disheveled. Pale. Nervous energy radiating from him. He stood at the edge of the crowd, eyes fixed on the clearing. Frantic might've been an overstatement, but not by much.

He didn't look dangerous. Just… misaligned. A radio tuned a half-click off station.

Maria stared. Just for a moment. A mental note. Nothing more.

Then she turned back to the scene.

The sheet covering the victim rustled as a breeze swept through the trees. One of the techs nodded at Maria. "You want to see her?" She returned a nod in the affirmative.

Maria crouched beside the body. The sheet was lifted.

She didn't breathe.

A chill spread through her chest, equal parts dread and disbelief. It wasn't just recognition. The rational part of her mind screamed for logic, but something deeper, more primal, whispered that she was staring at the impossible.

Mary Johnson.

Same build. Same face. Same hair. Same tired eyes caught forever in that expression of quiet horror. She looked exactly like the Mary Johnson from Lincoln Park.

But that wasn't possible. Maria had done her homework after the previous body was found. Mary Johnson didn't have sisters. Certainly not a twin.

She stood. "That's Mary Johnson."

Bryans frowned. "No, it isn't. We don't have an ID yet."

"No. I know her. That's her. She's identical."

He shook his head. "Voss, Mary Johnson didn't have a twin. And even if she did, this woman's at least five pounds heavier."

Maria blinked. "Are you hearing yourself?"

He looked back at the body. "They're similar, sure. But not a match."

Bryans's expression wasn't stubborn so much as tired. He wasn't trying to win an argument. He genuinely thought she was seeing shadows where there were none, worn thin by the weight of the case.

Maria turned to one of the younger officers nearby. "You!" she barked. A uniformed cop looked up, startled.

"You saw Mary Johnson. Do you see it?"

The officer hesitated, then said carefully, "Uh… not really, Detective. There's a likeness but… I wouldn't say identical."

Maria's jaw tightened, her pulse pounding in her ears. The more they denied it, the more certain she became. Something was profoundly wrong here.

Maria's voice cracked, low and furious. "This is insane. Look at her. That's Mary Johnson."

Her words fell into silence. Nobody agreed. Nobody even looked long enough to really see.

She steadied herself. "I want DNA samples run. I want a comparison with Mary Johnson from Lincoln Park."

Maria's frustration was turning into determined focus. "I'll get Rose on it."

Bryans gave her a look that tried to be soft but landed just left of pity. "Voss, maybe you should go home. You've been running hot for days."

"I'm fine," Maria snapped.

Bryans sighed. "Alright. Have Rutkowski run the tests. But get some rest. You're chasing shadows."

Maria didn't answer. She turned away and walked to the edge of the woods, where no one was paying attention. Her coffee was still warm in her hand. She hadn't even realized she was still holding it.

She stood alone for a long moment, thoughts swarming in her skull. The noise of the crime scene faded, replaced by the dry rasp of wings. A half-dozen crows had gathered in the trees above, their silhouettes sharp against the thinning sky. Their caws were not normal. They clicked, almost chattered, arguing in a language meant for no one human. Their black eyes followed her, unblinking, curious—or conspiratorial. For a few seconds, Maria found herself almost hypnotized by them.

Her pulse quickened. The woman on the ground was Mary Johnson, down to the eyes and hair and the tired curve of her mouth. Impossible, absurd.

Yet undeniable. And that impossibility tugged at her thoughts, dragged them toward the thing she least wanted to consider. If this was connected, if this duplication wasn't coincidence, then maybe the mirrors weren't just tricks of the imagination.

She hated herself for even letting the thought breathe. But she had to know.

The mirror.

With determination, she tossed her coffee and hurried back toward her car, head down, hoping no one noticed.

From the outskirts of the crowd, Reed Ashland did.

He'd been transfixed on Maria ever since she'd raised her voice, insisting the body was Mary Johnson's. Given the things he had been through and known, how could he not take notice and fixate on this agitated and brazen detective?

Reed watched her burst into her car and start tearing through the glove box. Her bag. The center console. Tossing everything aside in frantic urgency. Every motion said the same thing: whatever she was looking for, it mattered more than anything else.

She found it.

A small compact mirror.

Ashland's stomach dropped. He had carried a mirror once, too. He knew what it meant to want a mirror's perspective on reality.

Reed watched intently, Maria's hands trembling as she walked back toward the clearing. She looked around. Everyone was working. Bryans had his back turned.

Good. She didn't want him asking questions he wouldn't like the answers to.

She crept closer to the body, compact trembling in her grip. The absurdity of what she was about to do hit her. It felt like she was about to perform a magic trick at the worst possible place. She whispered a prayer she didn't believe in.

She opened it.

Turned the mirror toward the body.

Nothing.

The mirror reflected the grass, the trees, the clearing. But not the body.

Her heart was beating hard, trying to break its way out. She snapped the compact shut with a sharp click. Her breath caught. Eyes squeezed shut, a plea to the universe: don't let this be real.

Behind her eyelids, afterimages shimmered. Branches bending in unnatural angles, faces in the bark that weren't faces at all. The silence pressed in, heavy and absolute, though she could still feel the faint pull of the crows' gaze from the tree line. For one awful second, she thought the absence in the mirror had left a hole in the world, and she was teetering on its edge.

Her stomach twisted, confusion boiling into dread. Every instinct told her she had seen something impossible, yet the detective in her tried to frame it in logic, to pin the unexplainable into evidence bags. But anxiety gnawed at her ribs, whispering that she had glimpsed something truer than fact.

Maria exhaled. The breath left her chest as if it had been trapped for hours. She looked down at her hand clasping the compact, her heart pounding and thoughts racing. She took one deep breath.

She opened it again.

The body was there. Clear. Whole. Present.

She shut the compact. Closed her eyes.

The weight of it pressed down on her chest; too many symbols, too many impossibilities, each event gnawing at the edges of reason. She was tired of chasing the unexplainable, yet every step forward seemed to drag her deeper into it.

From the crowd, Reed's gaze never wavered. His eyes weren't shocked, not even disturbed. They were only intent, studying her.

She was not okay. And from the trees, the crows laughed in a silence only she could hear.

14

CHAPTER FOURTEEN

Demons in the Bottle

Reed Ashland lumbered into his apartment. The door still swinging shut behind him with a tired creak. The place smelled of stale air and dust, lit only by a single lamp in the corner casting shadows that swayed when he blinked. Tonight, sober for once, the room felt less like a home and more like a holding cell. Maria's voice still echoed in his skull: "Mary Johnson!"

She'd seen it too.

He didn't know her, had never seen her before tonight. But something in the way she moved, the way she demanded answers, that frantic insistence. It was as if someone had taken his own unraveling thoughts and given them another pair of eyes.

She knew something. Maybe not everything. Maybe not even the worst of it. But she was on the path. The same trail Reed had been staggering down.

He sat on the couch, staring up as though the ceiling might split and deliver him an answer. His gaze slipped to the kitchen cabinet.

He didn't want to look. But he did.

Several unopened bottles of gin stood behind the doors. Cold, clear, smooth. All of them promising silence, promising the sweet blur of not caring anymore. That was the deal alcohol always offered: numb the edge,

61

erase the noise.

Reed rose slowly, approaching the cabinet.

He wanted this. He didn't. All at once.

It was an easy answer. A drink to the lips and drift away. Everything's okay.

His hand hovered over the knob. Fingers twitching. Jaw clenched. He hadn't gone a day without drinking in years. Some mornings, even crawling out of bed required a nip from the bottle. He knew it was killing him, but at least it let him function.

He yanked a bottle of gin from the cabinet and slammed it on the counter. Then he spread his feet and crossed his arms, glaring at it like it was a gunslinger across ten paces.

The setup was comical, the reality was tragic. The thought of not drinking made his chest tighten with real fear.

How am I supposed to handle any of this?

He told himself no. Just one day. One goddamn day. He could do that.

But Maria's voice rang in his head again: "Mary Johnson!" And the pressure built inside him.

His hand moved before his mind did.

The bottle felt heavier than it should have. Or maybe he was lighter than he'd ever been. He stared into the clear liquid. It didn't blink.

Moments passed.

The cap twisted with a click like a loaded chamber.

And then, his head filled with the sound of his daughter's laughter.

The memory hit hard. Emily's first steps. The wobble of her bike without training wheels. Her little voice calling, "Daddy!" Arms stretching up in silence, the universal plea to be lifted and loved. And unexpectedly, the faint scent of her shampoo, the one that always lingered on his shirt after she hugged him.

Reed leaned hard against the counter, eyes squeezed shut, throat thick. When he opened them, the floor swam into view.

Words glistened in blood across the linoleum: *She would be disappointed.*

The letters gleamed wet, metallic, fresh. He blinked and they were gone.

He blinked again. Still gone.

But the emptiness left behind cracked something open. Memories rushed in, unbidden, floodwater breaking a dam.

The classroom first. Students' eyes wide, unblinking, their faces blurred at the edges. His words slurred mid-lecture, the chalk breaking in his hand like brittle bone. Dr. Desmond Edwards appeared at the back of the room, stone-faced, stepping forward with each blink until he was suddenly inches away. His voice low, sharp, final: "You can't keep teaching with the state you're in, Reed. You're done here."

The hallway behind Edwards dissolved into a bathroom mirror. Claire's reflection was there before Claire herself, her face split by the glass into fragments of fury and grief. Bottles clinked in her hands, multiplying in the reflection until they filled the sink basin, the tub, the whole room. Her voice ricocheted around the tiles: "Do you ever think about anyone but yourself?" When she turned away, the reflection stayed, still screaming, even as the door slammed and he was shoved into the night.

Darkness. Then grass. Damp earth pressed against his knees, cold stone beneath his palm. He knew this place before he even looked down. Emily's name carved into granite, the letters shifting in and out of focus. In his other hand, the bottle, sweating against his skin, the gin dripping into the soil. But the sound wasn't a pour. It was weeping. His own sobs mingled with it, raw, wordless, endless.

Reed turned to the sink. Without a word, he poured.

The gin hit porcelain with a hollow splash. Sharp fumes rose like ghosts, stinging his nose. He didn't stop. His hands shook as the drain swallowed the poison, spiraling away.

He stomped back to the cabinet, more bottles. He opened the fridge. Beer, cheap wine, one lonely hard seltzer. He grabbed them all.

From beneath the sink, he dragged out a black trash bag. Bottles clinked as he loaded it, tied it shut, and slung it over his shoulder.

He stood there, the bag heavy on his shoulder, staring at the window. The glass glowed faintly with city light, a pale rectangle cut into the darkness.

His legs resisted, wanting to sink into the comfort of surrender, but his chest burned with the memory of blood-written words on the linoleum. She would be disappointed. He closed his eyes. He could almost taste the gin still waiting in his throat, phantom and insistent.

Slowly, deliberately, he marched toward the window. Each step heavy, ceremonial. He pulled the latch with trembling fingers and pushed the pane upward. Cold air spilled inside, sharp as judgment, making him shiver.

He stood before it, the bag dragging at his arm, his heartbeat drumming in his ears. A drink would soothe him. A drink would kill him. And he knew. He had to choose.

He heaved the bag out.

He stood with his head tilted back toward the ceiling, eyes closed, breathing deep. Therapeutic. Punishing.

A crash. Glass against metal. And a distant voice shouting:

"HEY! What the hell?!"

Reed froze at the sill. Breath tight. Triumph shattered on someone else's hood. He almost laughed. Almost cried. Instead, he shut the window with a sharp click, turned, and bolted for the door, comically fleeing the scene of his own catharsis.

He felt… better. Not healed. Not fixed. But better.

And in the cold night air behind him, faint as a whisper, Maria's voice lingered: "That's Mary Johnson…"

15

CHAPTER FIFTEEN

Reflections After Midnight

Maria Voss arrived home well past midnight. Her house smelled faintly of lavender laundry detergent and stale cereal. Familiar, warm smells that felt alien against the cold storm of her thoughts.

She set her keys on the counter and pulled off her jacket. Her movements were slow, drained. Her mind, however, wouldn't stop racing.

The body.

The resemblance.

The mirror.

She lived in a world where dead was dead and mirrors reflected what was there. And yet...

She'd seen it.

She hadn't seen it.

Maria rustled through her bag and found the picture of the symbol carved into all three victims. She sat with it in her hands, staring until her eyes burned. The crude carving was nothing more than lines and angles on paper, yet it carried the weight of something older, something deliberate.

Her mind reeled back through the day. The body in the woods, wearing Mary Johnson's face. What was she supposed to make of it? A copy of a living woman, murdered. A mirror that lied. A symbol etched into skin, repeating like some obsessive mantra.

And still, nothing resolved. Only questions.

Her son's voice startled her.

"Mom?"

Maria turned. Eli stood at the hallway's edge in pajamas, rubbing one eye. "Can't sleep," he said.

She smiled softly, walked toward the living room sofa, and gestured for him to follow. "Come here."

He padded over and curled beside her on the couch. She wrapped an arm around him and exhaled deeply. The embrace could make everything go away. At least temporarily.

"Rough day?" he asked, voice muffled against her shoulder.

"Yeah," Maria said slowly, exhaling as she spoke. "Something like that," she added.

They sat in silence for a while. The TV was off. The room was dim. The silence thick enough to breathe.

"Eli… I'm sorry," she said quietly.

"For what?" he asked, blinking up at her.

"For not being around enough. For always being tired. For letting the job eat me alive when you just need your mom." Her throat tightened as the words tumbled out. She wanted to be more for them as a mother. Life had a way of stealing the wind from your sails and leaving you with nothing but exhaustion and regrets.

Eli studied her, serious, perceptive beyond his years. "I know you're trying," he said. "I can tell. Your job is tough. You have a lot to deal with. I get it."

Maria blinked hard. "You deserve better," she whispered, fighting the thump in her throat.

"I think you're doing your best. I appreciate you, Mom."

His words struck something in her. Something deep and fragile. She kissed his forehead and pulled him close.

"I love you, Boogie Bear," she whispered.

Eli leaned back slightly and shot her a look of playful annoyance.

"Seriously, Mom..." he groaned, but his smile softened it.

He dropped the joking sass, then smiled affectionately back at her. "I love you too."

They curled up together on the couch and rested in silence. Only the crickets outside kept time as the day's exhaustion washed over them.

Maria sat in silence, holding him, letting the rhythm of his small breaths steady her own. For a fleeting moment, the world felt simple again.

Then her eyes slipped back to the photo on the coffee table. The jagged carving seemed to lean toward her, as if it wanted to crawl into her skull. She felt the thought, not hers, whispering behind her eyes.

The crickets outside cut off mid-chorus. Silent. Absolute. Maria held Eli closer, pressing him against her to keep the thought from crawling any deeper into her mind.

16

CHAPTER SIXTEEN

Somewhere Between a Dream and an Omen

The park was serene in the way only early morning could be. Dew clung to the grass. Birds chirped in timed bursts from the trees overhead. A jogger passed with earbuds in. A golden retriever chased a squirrel with theatrical enthusiasm. The city hadn't fully woken up yet.

And then there was Reed Ashland.

Reed was sprawled awkwardly on the bench, jacket bunched as a pillow. A pigeon walking across his shoe. He groaned and bolted upright with the gracelessness of a man who hadn't meant to sleep outside.

He blinked at the light as if it were personally offending him. Morning light, beautiful to most, stung Reed's tired eyes.

For a moment, he just sat there.

Then the thoughts came.

The killer. The mirror. Morrow. Emily. The dreams that felt more like memories.

He stood, stretching with a series of pops and cracks that sounded like they should've hurt more than they did.

Reed gathered himself and scanned the park, unsure what to do now that he'd hauled himself off the bench.

He did what most people do these days. Out of habit, he dug into his coat pocket and pulled out his phone and tapped it.

3:33 a.m.

He blinked and pushed his glasses to a resting position on his brow to get a better look at what he was seeing.

He tapped again. Still 3:33 a.m.

Confused, Reed looked up. He turned his head at different angles, taking in the fact that it was clearly morning outside. And not the middle-of-the-night kind of morning. The light, the activity, the sky. It was at least 7:00 or 8:00 a.m.

He looked around. Squinted at the sky.

Then a realization hit him.

"…Oh, shit."

The bench behind him shimmered.

Before he could turn, it pulled him backward. Wood and metal folding around his body. No sound. No warning.

And then Reed was gone.

***

Reed was swallowed without chewing. He blinked, and he was already falling sideways into a cathedral made of fingernails and apologies. Its air reeked of acetone.

Time stuttered like a bad connection.

Reed wasn't standing. He wasn't floating. He was suspended in existence amidst an inky abyss.

From below came a voice in a strange mechanical tone: "You forgot your exit. Please remain fictional until further notice."

Within the blink of an eye, everything had changed.

Reed turned and found himself sitting at his desk, back in the apartment, now wearing three watches and none of them ticking.

His fingers typed on a laptop with no screen. Just glass. His reflection typed back. Different words. It was smiling. The smile had a peculiar and suspicious look to it. Like when you can tell someone has a dark secret, but they won't tell you.

Reed glanced down the side of his desk for some unknown reason. Abruptly, the gin bottle in the trash can whispered.

The words stabbed his eardrums with mystery: "Pay attention to the curtains."

Reed turned. This time it was curtains. Heavy red velvet, impossibly tall, their folds rippling without air. A theater stage framed before him.

The curtains shivered, then slowly pulled back. Reed braced himself for horror, revelation, anything that might justify the warning.

What lay beyond was a fast-food restaurant.

Overhead lights buzzed. Plastic booths gleamed in neon yellow and teal. A half-dead ficus slumped by the soda machine. A fry cook in a paper hat dropped baskets into oil with a sullen expression. Somewhere, a timer beeped.

Reed blinked. The absurdity rattled him more than terror would have.

He took a step closer. The smell of grease wafted through the curtain. A family laughed at a corner booth, though their faces were blurred, melting into static as he tried to look. The menu boards above the counter flickered. Not with food prices, but with jagged lines forming, reshaping.

The laughter cut. The lights went out.

On the glowing boards, a single image burned through the darkness: the mirror symbol. Black carved into white, stark and pulsing.

Then the symbol itself snapped, vanishing. The curtains closed again, leaving only silence.

The silence was then pierced by a voice.

"Behold the home of the two Rs."

Reed staggered backward, chilled. The warning lingered in his ears, cryptic as ever.

Another blink. Another change.

He stood. No—hovered—above a spiral staircase that turned inward into itself. Each step was a day he regretted.

The steps didn't just creak. They flickered.

On one step he saw himself slamming the apartment door on Claire, her voice breaking in the hallway while he drowned her out with another drink. The image dissolved before he could reach for it.

Another step showed Emily. Five years old, dancing barefoot in the kitchen, hair a messy crown. He reached down, but the memory burned to white, gone as quickly as it appeared.

The memories didn't just sting. They hollowed him out. Each flicker of loss was a reminder that his life wasn't a narrative; it was debris.

Reed's attention snagged on something enormous fused to the wall of the spiral. A grandfather clock, bent sideways, warped into the curvature. A tumor in the architecture. Its glass face was cracked, the numbers smudged into unfamiliar symbols.

The hands twitched backward in uneven jerks, fighting the direction of time itself. Each tick wasn't sound, but a shudder he felt in his bones. And with every pulse, a droplet of black ink bled from the clock's fractured center and fell upward, vanishing into the ceiling. Rain in reverse.

Books were everywhere. Floating like dust.

Reed reached for a book. An outlandishly shaped geometric object floated by. It knocked the book out of reach.

The figure then contorted in an indescribable way and slithered around Reed's arm and wrist. It became malleable, engulfing his entire arm and subduing him completely. Cold spread from his arm until his whole body felt frostbitten. Reed panicked and tried to scream, but he had no words.

He wasn't silent out of fear. It was as though language and sound didn't exist for him.

Inch by inch, Reed was forced to succumb to the will of the pliable substance. The evolving geometry had covered him head to toe.

He became a man of stone. A statue. Frozen in time and space. Floating.

In the stillness, Reed saw himself displayed in a hall of statues. Dozens of Reeds lined up, each carved in a different pose of failure: one with a bottle clutched in his stone hand, one on his knees, one with Emily perched on his shoulder, whispering in his ear. The hall went on forever, a gallery of inadequacy, frozen mid-regret.

Hairline cracks began to spread across his stone skin. Each fissure hissed out pieces of Reed's life, and they vanished into the abyss around him, swallowed by a silence that refused to echo.

Blink. Change.

Reed was inside a classroom with no doors. Children made of fog sat attentively, waiting for him to teach. He opened his mouth to speak, and bees flew out. The chalkboard read:

REALITY IS A MIRROR BROKEN INTO LANGUAGE.

Then the lights flickered, and he was underwater.

A woman swam by with a rotary phone for a head.

The phone rang: shrill, impossible, muffled through water yet piercing straight into his bones. Reed's hands trembled, but he couldn't stop himself. He lifted the receiver.

"Hello?" he thought rather than spoke.

A pause. Then static. Out of it came a child's voice, fragile and thin: "Daddy? Come home."

Reed's lungs seized. His chest hollowed.

No. The voice was too young. Not her voice, not really. He tried to answer, but all that came out of his mouth was a black, oily substance.

The line cracked sharply; the rotary dial spun, clicking over to the next call.

A gravelly baritone erupted, jagged, mocking: "There's a killer in your city, Reed. One who carves the memory of himself into others. Can you feel him? He's already closer than you think." He tried to rip the receiver away, but it clung to his ear, the cord tightening.

Another mechanical snap. Another line.

A woman's whisper. Soft. Trembling. Familiar. "You left me. You left me in the dark."

His mind spun. His throat burned with unscreamed apologies, but bubbles rose instead of words.

Click. Silence. The phone woman dissolved into shadow, her rotary dial spinning one last time.

***

He snapped awake on the floor, his hands covered in ink and something else. A journal sat nearby, the mirror symbol on the front taunting him.

Reed stared at the words as they formed, letter by letter, like veins crawling across the page.

REED: Your fiction has become self-aware. It wants to leave. What should we tell it?

He read it once. Twice. His pulse climbed.

His fiction?

His philosopher's training rose unbidden: the problem of identity, the blurred line between author and text, the nightmare Lacan hinted at when the mirror no longer reflects but devours.

Reed's breath quickened. His own name glared at him from the page. He couldn't even read it properly, the letters R-E-E-D writhing into nonsense the longer he stared.

"Am I recording this," he whispered to no one, "or is something recording me?"

A descent into madness would be a welcome vacation.

A flutter of the eyelids. Reality bent once more.

Reed was now sitting in a chair that seemed to have been built centuries before—and felt just as comfortable.

He was in a field. A dark landscape of melancholy and revelation.

The chair beneath Reed felt like it had been carved from sorrow itself, ancient wood pressing into his back. He stared across the black field. At first, a shape was barely visible, a smudge against the horizon. The dark blurs formed into a shack in the distance.

It was too far away for detail, yet Reed swore he could see the frame of a window. The shape of it. The darkness within. And in that darkness, something stirred.

The closer he tried to look, the less the world around him obeyed. The field stretched and shrank in pulses, like a lens focusing wrong. One breath, the shack was a hundred yards away. The next, it pressed against his vision. He felt he could reach out and touch the peeling wood.

Reed gripped the arms of the antique chair. His knuckles blanched. The grass around him whispered, rustling without wind.

He half-stood, half-stumbled forward, but the chair clung to him. His legs refused to carry him. He strained against invisible gravity, drawn toward the shack, yet nailed to the spot.

And then—light.

A weak glow flickered in the shack's lone window, pale and sickly at first. A candle burning through fog. It brightened, too quickly, flaring white until it hurt to look at. Reed flinched, covered his eyes.

Something moved in that light. A shadow framed by the window. Watching.

The glow swallowed the shack whole. The field bent sideways.

And Reed was gone.

***

Reed Ashland woke up in his bed with the slow, careful suspicion of a man who no longer trusted mornings.

He kept his eyes half-closed, intentionally avoiding the clock on the nightstand. A faint breeze from the cracked window stirred the room. Everything looked normal. Too normal.

His head pounded. He knew the feeling better than anyone. A hangover.

"Not possible," he muttered to himself. He hadn't been drinking. But he knew a hangover when he felt it.

Shrugging off the phantom headache, he swung his legs over the edge of the bed with the exaggerated caution of someone trying not to trip a wire. He crept through the apartment on tiptoes.

His apartment was, as always, empty. But that didn't stop him from peeking around corners as if someone might be hiding.

He made it to the kitchen. Still no sign of doom.

He stood in the kitchen doorway, eyes darting. The refrigerator hummed. The overhead light flickered. He scanned the countertops and then, dropped to his knees.

The lower cabinet squeaked when he pulled it open. He winced, then contorted himself inside. Knees jammed to his chest, elbow banging a pot and hinges creaked shut.

For a moment, Reed Ashland, ex-professor and alleged grown man, crouched in his own kitchen cupboard like a child hiding from monsters. The air smelled faintly of dish soap and old wood. His pulse banged in his ears.

And then his phone blared.

An alarm. Shrill. Annoying.

Reed didn't set alarms. He knew what time his phone inevitably had on its screen without even looking.

In disbelief, Reed asked the universe, "Are you fucking kidding me?"

The moment the words left his mouth, the darkness of the cabinet enveloped him.

He didn't fall. He folded. The kitchen bent in on itself, colors draining, angles twisting. And Reed was gone, swallowed once more.

*****

Reed stood barefoot in a hallway made of velvet and bone. From somewhere far off, the sound of a ticking clock echoed.

He tried to move, but his body floated instead, drawn forward remembering a direction he had never learned.

The air buzzed.

From the corner of his eye, a child watched him. The child had no mouth, only eyes. Familiar ones.

A door appeared in the wall. It was frameless and knobless. It opened anyway.

Inside: a chair, a mirror, and a figure sitting with its back to him. The mirror did not reflect the figure.

Reed stepped forward and the lights dimmed. The mirror turned, and the figure remained facing away from Reed. It spoke in his voice:

"We blink. We live. We blink. We die."

He reached out.

The room collapsed in on itself and Reed.

***

The park was alive with motion. It was unseasonably warm and the afternoon sun poured through the canopy of leaves.

Children screamed in delight as they ran through fountains. Cyclists zipped by with the confidence of practiced routes.

Vendors sold popsicles, hot dogs, and soda. The air smelled of sunscreen and fresh-cut grass. A jazz trio played near the gazebo. They were playing something old and swingy, the kind of tune that made you forget time.

If time were real, that is.

Reed walked through it all as a man who had nowhere to be and all the time to get there.

He took in the buzz of humanity. It was the kind of day you could almost believe in.

He felt a sullen envy of everyone around him.

And then, the jazz trio's melody cut mid-note, and silence followed. No warning. No fade-out. Just a clean, total stop.

Reed blinked. His feet continued walking. One step, then another, while every single other thing in the park had frozen.

A jogger hung in mid-stride, ponytail suspended mid-swing. A pigeon floated mid-wingbeat above the path. A child's balloon paused in its rise like it had forgotten how helium worked.

Reed stopped. The hairs on his arms lifted.

Then he heard it.

That hum. Low and distant at first, vibrating just beneath perception, but unmistakable. A sound he hadn't heard since that impossible night in that not-so-enchanted pasture—and would never forget.

The sound stitched itself into his bones and hummed in the gaps between thoughts. His head tilted upward instinctively. The hum grew louder, but he couldn't place a source.

The sky was blue and cloudless, impossibly still.

Then he looked back down.

Everyone in the park turned to face him at once. Silent, rigid, eyes empty. An army of mannequins, frozen midway through life.

Reed didn't move.

Above him, something shifted. A gust of wind that didn't touch the trees and didn't belong to this Earth. A shimmer in the air.

A triangle. Metallic. Silent. Close.

So close it seemed to warp the sky around it. It wavered, like something staring at him from underwater.

Reed craned his neck to look up.

Then, a voice. Low and mechanical but layered. Speaking in reverse and echoing before it began.

It was coming from every single person in the park who was now staring at him. But it was one voice. "Welcome to the Fold."

17

CHAPTER SEVENTEEN

Morning Rush

Maria woke up with a start, and the stiffness in her neck gave away the fact that she hadn't made it to her bed. Her arm was draped protectively over Eli, who was curled into her side beneath a throw blanket on the living room couch.

The house was still, caught in that fragile quiet of early morning. The hum of the furnace. A neighbor's dog barking faintly down the block. For a brief moment, it was tranquil, almost peaceful. Until she sat up.

"Crap. Crap, crap, crap."

Still dressed in yesterday's jeans and shirt, she gently shook Eli awake. "We're late," she muttered.

Eli stirred and blinked at her. "How late?"

"Bus-leaving-without-you late."

Chaos ignited. Maria darted into the kitchen, flipping on the coffee machine with one hand while digging through the laundry basket for a barely passable shirt with the other.

Eli shot off the couch, pulling clothes on at lightning speed. "I can't miss dodgeball again," he grumbled, toothbrush jutting from his mouth.

"Tommy! Get up!" Maria called. No answer.

"Tommy! You're going to miss the bus!"

Still nothing. Eli yanked a hoodie over his head, hopping on one foot to jam his shoes on. "Tommy! Get up!"

That got a groan. "Shut up, Eli."

"Don't tell your brother to shut up!" Maria snapped from the hallway.

Tommy eventually emerged like a zombie from his room, dragging his feet. His shirt was backward and he was carrying two mismatched socks.

Maria's temper flared. "Shoes. Backpack. Now."

Tommy blinked slowly, muttering something under his breath as he began the world's slowest attempt to match his socks.

Eli stood at the front door, already laced up, arms folded.

"Why do you always wait until the last second?" Eli snapped.

"Eli! You're not the boss of me!" Tommy jabbed a finger at his brother.

"Okay, stop. Both of you." Maria spun, torn between mom mode and detective mode: keys, hairbrush, phone. Where the hell was everything?

Eli stood in the kitchen calmly, the only one who was ready to go. His eyes drifted toward the crime scene photo Maria had negligently left out on the counter the previous night. He didn't seem to recognize the weight of it, only studying the lines the way a kid looks at shapes on homework.

Maria finally had everything she needed. She thought. And just as she reached for her jacket, Eli's voice cut through the frantic air.

"Mom!"

She didn't answer.

"Mom!"

Still brushing her hair in the hallway mirror, she called back, "What?!"

"You have geometry in your picture."

That made her stop. "What?"

Eli's gaze stayed on the photo. The one of the symbol carved into the victims' foreheads. She marched over, annoyed with herself for forgetting to put it away.

"You shouldn't be looking at that."

"It's geometry," he repeated.

She was halfway through zipping up her jacket. "Eli, please, we don't have time for—"

"It's symmetrical," he said, tapping the image with casual certainty. "Like in my geometry class. Both sides are the same. See? They're mirroring each other."

Maria froze.

The words were so simple, so offhand, but they cut through the noise of the morning sharper than any alarm clock.

"Mirroring?"

"Yeah," Eli said simply, already reaching for his backpack.

She leaned in slowly. The house noises dulled, the rush of the morning falling away.

She saw it now; two halves, not random scratches, but a precise, deliberate symmetry.

The clock ticked, steady and merciless, and Maria realized that she hated the sound now.

Her boys bickered in the background, reflections of each other's stubbornness.

"Mirrors," she whispered to herself.

The bus. The rush. All of it faded. What mattered was that word. Mirrors. And the way the symbol stared back at her, daring her to look deeper.

18

CHAPTER EIGHTEEN

Time and Reflection

Maria pushed through her department's swinging doors. Her steps echoed against the linoleum, but the noise did nothing to drown the storm in her mind.

"Mirrors…" she muttered, the word tasting bitter and hollow.

The station was alive in its usual way: phones jangling, keyboards clacking, laughter rising too loud in one corner and dying too quickly in another. The air carried the sour tang of burnt coffee and the faint musk of old sweat. Everything felt both ordinary and wrong, as if the place itself were pretending to be normal.

She found her desk amid the hive of worn-out cops and scattered files. Yet inside her head, the noise was silence. Her thoughts spun faster than she could follow.

Part of her was proud that her son had figured this out, but another part was unsettled that it hadn't dawned on her. Of all people, she was the one who had the odd encounter with the mirror in the first Mary Johnson's bedroom.

She sank into her chair, the creak oddly grounding. Her eyes flicked to the photo taped to her cubicle wall. The symbol carved into the victims' foreheads.

Mirrors. Symmetry. Reflection.

A shake of her head. No. Not now.

She pushed herself up and made a beeline for the coffee station. Maybe the ritual would steady her. Coffee was the only constant she trusted these days: black, bitter, real.

She poured the dark liquid into a chipped mug with a half-faded "World's Best Mom" painted across the side. Her hand trembled slightly as she lifted it. Sipping slowly, she closed her eyes and let out a long sigh. For a moment, the chaos faded. The world felt almost normal.

Maria started back toward her desk, letting the coffee carry her as long as it could.

It wouldn't be very long.

Captain Bryans was hovering near her desk, a man clearly debating whether to speak or stay quiet.

Maria sat down without enthusiasm. Bryans let her settle in, but only for a second.

He scratched the back of his neck, then finally set a file folder down with a muted thump.

"You're not gonna like this," he said.

Maria looked up, sipping coffee gone cold. "That's one hell of a way to start a conversation."

He opened the folder. A crime scene photo. The woman from the woods. Pale, eyes closed, the strange symbol carved into her forehead. Below the image, the victim's name printed in block letters.

Maria felt the air drain from the room. It wasn't just familiarity. It was a name that shouldn't echo, but did.

Her brain stalled, refusing to process it. Two Mary Johnsons. Two identical names tethered to two carved foreheads. She wanted to laugh at the absurdity, but her stomach turned instead. It wasn't coincidence. It was reflection.

"Johnson?" she whispered.

Bryans nodded. "Mary Johnson."

She sat up straighter. "Same as the soccer mom from suburbia?"

"Mm-hmm," he grunted.

"And listen, this Mary Johnson? We talked to her husband. He reported her missing yesterday morning. This Mary Johnson also has three kids at home. Works as a secretary for a law firm downtown," he elaborated.

Maria's stomach lurched.

Two Marys.

Mirrors of each other.

For a moment, she imagined their lives laid on top of one another like transparent film—the same name, the same domestic anchors, the same carved fate.

"No relation," Bryans added quickly, steering her away from the thought before it rooted too deep.

"You sure?" Maria pressed.

"Confirmed. Different families. Different parts of the city. No connection. I triple-checked."

Maria's eyes darted around. Then she declared, "I still want Rose to look into this. This is too bizarre."

Bryans shrugged and threw his hands up. A silent gesture that seemed to say "Go right ahead."

Maria leaned back, brow furrowing. "Kids. Name. Job. Symbol. Killed in the same week," she said, voicing the thoughts racing in her head. Trying to piece together an impossible puzzle.

"That's why I hesitated telling you," Bryans admitted. "You were acting… different at the scene."

She didn't deny it. "This isn't coincidence."

Bryans sighed, the sound of a man just proven wrong by his own kid.

"I know how it looks," he said carefully. "But we can't build a case on weird feelings."

He rubbed at his jaw, trying to massage away his own doubt. "Mary Johnson's a common name. Generic as hell. Second only to Jane Doe." He laced it with snark, hoping to snap her out of the strange spell she'd been under.

Maria's eyes stayed locked on the photo.

"It's not a feeling," she said quietly. "It's something else."

Bryans hesitated. "You think there's a pattern."

"I think we've only just started seeing it," Maria murmured.

They sat in silence, both marinating in the weight of the case.

Bryans's brow furrowed deeper. A cauldron of emotions churned: confusion, disbelief, irritation. On top of it all, he was stumped, and he hated that.

He flipped a few pages, pulling out more photos. "And, get this: the second Mary's place? Same story as the first."

Maria looked up sharply.

"Broken mirrors. Shattered clocks. Everywhere," Bryans said, his voice like someone finishing a puzzle only to discover missing pieces.

Her mind snapped back to the first Mary Johnson's house. The mirrors fractured in ways that felt deliberate, not random.

"And…" Bryans continued, reluctantly feeding her fire. "It wasn't the killer who did it."

Maria stood, pulled forward by her morbid curiosity.

She leaned forward, both hands pressed to the desk, eyes locked on him.

"I had Darnell talk to the husbands and kids of both victims." He rubbed at his forehead, exasperated. "Both Mary Johnsons apparently did this themselves. Husbands said the same thing; their wives were acting very 'off' in the days before the murders."

"Any reports of stalking? Someone following them?" Maria shot back.

"Nope," Bryans answered just as fast, cutting her off.

Maria narrowed her eyes. "What does that mean?" She almost brought up the mirrors and vanishing victims but thought better of it—for now.

Bryans straightened, hand lifted in concession. "No obvious connection, but the signs are all the same."

"Speaking of signs…" Maria rifled through the crime scene photos. "You can thank my son's aptitude for geometry for this, Captain."

Bryans leaned in, curious.

She held up a photo of the carved symbol.

"This…" she paused, tracing it with her finger. "is a mirror."

Bryans shot her a look that said What?!

"They're symmetrical," Maria explained. "The shapes mirror each other. It's a symbol for a mirror."

Bryans looked down, astonished at how simple it was, and more astonished he hadn't seen it. He looked back at her, blurting, "What the fuck?!"

"Yeah," Maria replied right on cue. "I kicked myself too."

She sat back and let the silence stretch. Then came the smirk. Not for him. For herself.

Bryans scoffed and turned to leave. He stopped, then glanced back just enough for one last jab.

"Even a broken clock is right twice a day."

He walked off, hiding the grin tugging at his face. He knew she was good.

Maria let a short laugh escape her and sank back into her chair.

Her eyes fell to a photo of a smashed clock. She held it up, studying the frozen hands. The silence pressed in on her ears, the absence of ticking louder than any sound. Her fingers tightened until the paper nearly bent. The number leapt into her mind.

3:33.

"Bryans," she called, sharper than intended. "Do we know what time the clocks were broken at the second Mary Johnson's house?"

He looked back, brow raised. "No idea. I can find out."

Maria lowered the photo, her mind looping back on itself. "I'd bet anything they all stopped at 3:33."

Her gaze drifted toward the window, not for comfort but for calibration, hoping to find the answer written in the sky itself.

True wisdom is knowing that you know nothing. Socrates had said that centuries ago, and here she was, living it in the ugliest way possible.

In an instant, her pulse quickened, though she didn't know why. A sudden chill traced her spine. The fluorescent lights above flickered once, perfectly timed with the hollow tug in her chest. For a moment she thought she heard someone whisper her name, though the room buzzed on as always.

On the empty desk behind her, a blank piece of paper began folding on its own.

19

CHAPTER NINETEEN

Backwards

Reed woke in his bed. For a moment, he didn't recognize it.

Not because it wasn't his, but because it was too perfect.

The sheets were tucked with military precision, the comforter smoothed flat, the pillows fluffed and squared. It looked staged, like something from a glossy catalogue.

He blinked into the stillness. His pajamas, clean, crisp, and freshly pressed, clung to his skin, carrying a faint smell of starch.

For most people, that would have been reassuring. For Reed, it was unsettling. He wasn't used to waking in order.

The grogginess was different too. Not the sour fog of gin, not the thumping migraine of a bad night. Just a weight behind his eyes, a heaviness that had nothing to do with chemicals.

It had been… how long? Years? Since he had opened his eyes without alcohol dragging his body down. Sobriety itself was the strangest drug of all.

He pushed himself upright. That's when he noticed. The buttons on his pajamas weren't where they should be. His shirt was reversed, perfectly tailored down his back.

The whole set was backward. Snug, meticulous, wrong. And beneath the

86

starch, the fabric carried a faint metallic tang, sharp and sterile.

Reed stared into the air, blank, bewildered. "What the hell…?"

Who had been in his apartment? How long had he been out? The questions cracked across his mind, sharper than the confusion itself.

He glanced back at the bed, sheets tucked crisp as a hotel advertisement, then down at the backwards pajamas clinging neatly to his frame. A brittle laugh escaped, dying in his throat.

"Must've been housekeeping," he muttered, though the sound of his own voice didn't convince him.

Something pulled his attention sideways. On the dresser. Against the backdrop of his unkempt apartment, the shape stood out. A mound of earth. Soil, loose and dark, piled neatly.

And perched atop it was a knot. Twisted with careful symmetry. A wisdom knot, braided from coarse rope. It looked damp, as though it had just been pulled from the earth.

Reed's senses prickled. His breath caught. The air felt heavier, like the room itself was waiting for him to understand.

Reed swung his legs over the side of the bed and tried to stand. His knees buckled. He collapsed back down with a graceless thud, the room pitching sideways as if he'd just stumbled off a carnival ride.

He pressed his palms against the mattress, fighting the blur in his vision. Even focusing on the dresser took effort; his gaze slid away from the mound of dirt.

He tried again, pushing to his feet more carefully this time. His balance wavered. Even turning toward the dresser felt strange. His body and his center of gravity weren't in agreement.

A shaky grin touched his lips.

"Maybe I am hungover," he muttered to himself. Then, after a beat: "Maybe I just got back from space."

The joke fell flat in the silence of the room, but it steadied him.

Step by uneven step, he crossed to the dresser. The mound of soil sat there, damp and dark, the kind of dirt that clung to your skin when you touched it. And on top of it, the knot. Twisted, deliberate, patient.

Reed stared. His throat tightened. The coarse rope seemed to shimmer in his vision, every bend and cross of its weave pulling his eyes deeper. The longer he looked, the more he felt it wasn't an object at all, but a thought waiting to be completed.

His hand rose slowly, almost against his will. Fingers curled around the knot, the rough weave biting into his palm.

The instant he lifted it, something clicked in his chest that was sharp and undeniable.

Like a compass snapping north, he knew where he had to go.

20

CHAPTER TWENTY

Ride or Die

The halls of the precinct's medical examiner wing hummed with low incandescent light, sterile and faintly metallic. Maria's boots echoed as she wandered past half-open doors and empty exam rooms. The air was antiseptic, but it couldn't scrub away the weariness that clung to her.

She turned a corner and found Rose's office. It was a broom closet masquerading as a workspace. Files leaned, coffee mugs nested in one another, and a battered Bears blanket had been shoved across the back of a chair. It looked less like an office than someone's entire apartment had been poured inside and left to settle.

Behind the desk sat Dr. Rutkowski. Rose.

She was half-chewing a glazed donut, coffee cup balanced dangerously close to her keyboard. She froze mid-bite when she saw Maria in the doorway, cheeks puffed. Then she grinned.

"Hi," Rose managed, muffled by dough.

Maria laughed. "Breathe, Rose. Eat. Nobody's about to snatch it from you."

Rose swallowed with theatrical effort, then reached behind her desk without breaking eye contact. When she came back around, another donut was in her hand. She slid it across the desk toward Maria with mock solemnity.

Maria blinked, touched and starving. She hadn't had time to eat since yesterday evening.

"Knew you'd be in," Rose said, wiping sugar from her fingers. "Heard we've got ourselves another Mary Johnson."

Maria started rattling off everything she needed: DNA comparison, toxicology, the same cuts, the same symbol.

"Whoa…" Rose cut in, raising a palm.

Maria stopped, surprised.

"I had a nice night," Rose said, leaning back in her chair. "Slept like a rock. Coffee's good this morning. And how are you, Maria?"

Maria blinked again, then smirked. She knew when she'd been caught. "Good morning, Rose. How are you today? How was your night?"

Rose nodded approvingly. "Not as bad as yours, judging by this latest body. So. Talk to me, Hoss."

Maria smiled despite herself.

She laid it out; the new Mary Johnson was identical to the last. Same name, same life, even the same face. Rose raised her brows, chewing slowly on the inside of her cheek.

"I haven't seen her yet," Rose said. "Let's take a look."

They walked together down the hall. Rose handed Maria her donut back when she noticed she hadn't taken a bite yet.

Inside the exam room, Rose pulled back the sheet. The body lay pale and still beneath the harsh lights.

Mary Johnson lay stretched out on the steel like a mannequin abandoned mid-display, her stillness daring recognition. Her skin had the waxy pallor of old candles, smooth in places, cracked in others.

The carved symbol on her forehead broke the stillness. A jagged geometry that seemed to pull the light toward it, a wound and a message all at once.

Maria's nostrils filled with the faint mix of antiseptic and something earthier, the copper ghost of dried blood. The room felt too cold, though she knew it was only the vent rattling above.

Her gaze lingered on the face. The mouth slack, lips parted in the faintest suggestion of a word that never arrived. The eyes closed but restless.

For Maria, the sight was unbearable and magnetic. Every detail screamed familiarity.

It wasn't just resemblance. It was reflection.

Rose slipped on her glasses and circled the table. She checked the limbs, the curve of the neck, the hands with chipped nail polish. Finally, she leaned over the face.

"Identical?" she asked.

Maria, already chewing her donut, nodded firmly. "Yes."

Rose squinted closer. "Well, I know one thing for sure. You're cleaning éclair crumbs off my exam table."

Maria laughed, brushing sugar from her coat. "If only you kept your office this tidy."

"Appreciate the input, Mom." Rose shot her a look.

She tugged the glasses off and sighed. "Well, they do look similar."

Maria froze. She stared at her, incredulous. "Seriously? You don't see it either?"

"Sorry, Hoss."

Maria tossed the rest of her donut in the trash, slumping into a chair. The frustration finally cracked her.

Maria pressed her palms against her knees, willing herself to hold still, but her chest ached.

The case was piling on her: bodies that shouldn't exist, names that echoed, mirrors refusing to reflect what was right in front of them.

And then the other weight, the heavier one: Tommy's scraped knee she hadn't been there to kiss, Eli's lopsided grin she only caught in the sliver of an hour before bed. She felt like she was watching her own life through glass, close enough to touch but always a step removed.

She bit the inside of her cheek to keep it in, but the fatigue showed anyway, lining her eyes, dragging at her mouth.

Across from her, Rose leaned against the exam table, arms folded, glasses dangling from her fingers.

She didn't say anything at first. She just studied Maria. The restless tap of her foot, the rigid angle of her shoulders, as if she'd been expecting this collapse.

The sympathy in her gaze wasn't pity, but recognition. She'd known Maria long enough to read the cracks and trust they wouldn't break her.

Rose sat down beside her. "Alright. What's going on?"

Maria rubbed her forehead, words tumbling out in a rush. "I don't see the boys anymore. Not really. Dinner's an afterthought. I'm always running out the door, back after midnight. This case. These victims, these symbols; it's insane. It doesn't add up, it can't add up. And I'm just… I don't know how to do this anymore. As a cop. As a mom."

"Hey." Rose's tone softened, serious. "First, you're a great mom. Those little cracks love you. And you love them. And they know it. They're smart, they're healthy, they're fine. And second, you're the best cop I know. Which, granted, is an easy bar to clear in this town."

Maria laughed, a choked little sound.

"Seriously, Maria." Rose only used her real first name in these moments. "You're an insanely good detective. This is just one of life's perfect storms. Too much all at once. It passes."

Maria's eyes warmed, a rare break in her armor. "Thank you. I needed that."

"Anytime. Ride or die, remember?"

Maria chuckled. "Yeah. But do we have to die?"

Both of them laughed at their running inside joke. The sound bounced strangely against the tiled walls.

It was the kind of laugh that knew it didn't belong here. An intrusion into the morgue's hush.

Maria's smile lingered, thin but genuine, before it settled back into something quieter. The tension in her chest loosened, just enough to let her breathe. Rose smirked at her, that familiar glint of mischief in her eyes, but Maria could see the worry tucked behind it.

Then Maria went quiet. Her voice dropped low, almost conspiratorial. "The victims *disappear* in mirrors."

Rose tilted her head. "Okay. What now?"

Maria took a deep breath and let out a long exhale.

The weary detective began to explain. "The first Mary Johnson … one moment she was in her bedroom mirror, the next she wasn't. Gone. And last night, at the scene? I pulled out my compact. This one wasn't there either. And then, just like the first Mary, she came back. In the reflection. I looked. I really looked. This wasn't just something I thought I saw out of the corner of my eye. They were *gone*."

For once, Rose had no comeback. Her face went slack, mouth half-open.

"I know," Maria said. "Imagine how I feel."

Silence stretched between them. Rose blinked, trying to find words and failing.

Finally, she cleared her throat. "How about I bring sushi over tonight? We hang with the boys, watch something dumb. You sleep a full night and reset. Come back as refreshed as you possibly can tomorrow."

Maria's face lightened. That sounded good—until reality took it back a few beats later.

Her gaze drifted to the still form on the table. Her reply was soft, cryptic: "I'd love that. But what if this is just the beginning?"

The lights overhead flickered. Their hum filled the room.

Maria's eyes flicked to a steel tray on the counter. For half a second, she thought the reflection staring back wasn't hers at all. Then the lights steadied.

21

CHAPTER TWENTY-ONE

Cream Cheese Bananas

Reed Ashland walked through the city with sleep still heavy behind his eyes.

Morning light draped itself over downtown Chicago, pale and reluctant, turning glass towers into dull mirrors. The streets already carried their weekday pulse of horns bleating, buses wheezing at their stops, a river of suits and backpacks moving with the efficiency of habit. Baristas shouted names into the air, steam fogged café windows, and newsstands stacked with tabloids.

Yet to Reed, it all felt misaligned. The tempo of the city moved briskly and mechanically, but he trudged through, each sound arriving a second too late.

He didn't know how long he'd been walking. Maybe an hour. Maybe all day.

In Reed's existence, time didn't behave.

His sense of scale had warped too. Streets were corridors, the sky a ceiling. Ever since the lights, the missing hours, the backward pajamas… he couldn't tell what was real and what had only borrowed reality for a while.

Thoughts circled his mind. The victims. The symbols. The dreams that weren't dreams. The detective at the crime scene. She'd looked at him like she'd seen it too. Whatever it was.

He didn't know her name, but he knew the look: haunted, searching, as if reality had betrayed her the same way it had betrayed him.

He followed East Washington Avenue, the October air brisk against his face. The Staypineapple Hotel rose on his right, all bright windows and cheery branding.

Then, the Museum of Illusions advertised its tricks in bold colors, an almost mocking reminder of how fragile sight and sense could be.

A bus hissed at the curb, brakes shrieking, before swallowing up a line of passengers.

At Michigan Avenue, he didn't wait. He simply stepped into the chaos. Horns flared, tires skidded, but somehow the cars flowed around him without touching.

He crossed into Millennium Park, the city's roar dimming as he slipped onto a winding path flanked by rustling trees and steel benches that gleamed in the pale light.

He turned a corner and paused.

Grainger Plaza.

Cloud Gate, the great silver curve rising like it had been dropped there by something not human.

Its surface bent the city around it, swallowing towers and sky into a seamless skin of steel.

Tourists pressed close, grinning, snapping photos, but to Reed it radiated wrongness.

The reflection didn't just mirror. It absorbed, pulling faces and buildings into its belly until they looked stretched and unfamiliar. The sheer weight of its silence made his chest tighten. He didn't know why, but he knew it mattered.

Reed didn't move.

It shimmered.

Not from the sunlight, but from within.

The reflection warped. Twisting into a spiral, then a black hole, then something that didn't make sense. People kept walking by but Reed stood frozen, transfixed.

The surface no longer reflected the skyline. It devoured it. Skyscrapers folded into themselves. People's reflections stretched into long, unnaturally thin silhouettes, then bloated into grotesque bubbles of skin and fabric.

A faint, low-frequency hum vibrated the air. It was felt more than heard.

The spiral in the metal tightened.

Then the Bean buckled, and for one moment, it spat. Something black and tall fell out of the Bean's side, vomited by the sculpture's impossible curve.

A Man in a Charcoal Suit. Hat low.

Dark. Silent. Enigmatic.

Mr. Morrow.

He moved toward Reed like a dream moves toward its recipient in the dark.

He floated through the crowd without ever adjusting his path, as if he already knew each step they would take before they did. The crowd parted around him without noticing. He never broke eye contact. A stare that should have felt aggressive instead carried a strange calm.

He walked right up to Reed, smooth and silent.

For a long moment they stood there, the city moving around them.

Reed felt the air shift. It was cooler, denser.

The crowd blurred at the edges of his vision, their chatter dissolving into a low hum. He didn't feel fear. What washed through him was stranger: a calm so complete it left him weightless.

Reed's chest rose and fell in rhythm with something larger than him, some hidden metronome ticking behind the world. He didn't know what was coming, only that it mattered.

The Man in the Charcoal Suit didn't speak. He simply held out a business card.

It was blank. Except for a phrase in neat type:

Time eats truth.

He handed Reed another:

Another awaits their fate.

Then another:

CHAPTER TWENTY-ONE

The mirror knows your shape better than you do.

Reed felt cold.

Mr. Morrow extended one final card. He didn't hand it over. He placed it in Reed's palm, closing his fingers around it.

Their eyes locked, and the world collapsed into the space between them.

Morrow's gaze wasn't stone after all. It shimmered, vast and endless, like staring into a sky stripped of clouds.

Reed felt something move through him that wasn't thought, but a pressure in his chest and a ringing in his ears that carried meaning.

This matters, Reed could feel the Man in the Charcoal Suit saying rather than actually hearing.

"You are chosen. There is no turning away."

The messages weren't words, but Reed understood them as if they had been carved into his bones long ago.

His pulse slowed, his limbs grew weightless, and the plaza's noise fell away until there was only that gaze: bright, depthless, infinite.

The importance of it landed on him all at once, crushing and exalting: the certainty that whatever came next was his alone to bear.

Reed looked down. His fist was still clenched tight around the message card Morrow had pressed into it.

For a moment, he couldn't bring himself to move. Feeling that opening it too quickly might scatter whatever power had been sealed there.

His fingers uncurled slowly, one by one, his anticipation thick as the air around him.

In his palm lay only another business card, plain and weightless, but the sight struck him. It wasn't his hand, not really. It was a lectern holding a prophecy, a fragment of some truth older than language.

Reed's breath caught as he braced for what the message would demand of him.

He exhaled slowly and read to himself.

Cream Cheese Bananas.

Reed blinked.

He tilted his head and read it again. *Cream Cheese Bananas.* He hadn't misread it even though he thought he had.

He blinked again.

The plaza tilted.

Not the ground, but the air itself.

Colors thickened, edges blurred; the laughter of tourists slowed to a warped crawl, each syllable stretched thin as melted tape.

Reed's ears rang with a high, glassy tone that seemed to come from inside his skull.

The Bean no longer reflected the city. It showed him. A thousand versions of his face stared back, blinking out of sync, mouths twitching in half-formed words. One smiled. One wept. Another mouthed something he couldn't hear but somehow knew: *it isn't yours anymore.*

The smell of ozone burned in his nose.

The light overhead fractured, shattering into prisms that bent across the plaza. Reed swayed.

Then, just as suddenly, everything snapped back. The tourists were laughing, snapping selfies. The Bean was only steel. His own breath rasped loud in his ears, proof that he was still here.

Wherever here was.

Morrow was gone.

Reed didn't realize he had been clenching his fists so hard.

He opened his hand and looked at Morrow's card.

The letters were smudged.

Then they were gone.

The words lingered anyway.

Cream Cheese Bananas.

They pulsed through his skull like an echo that refused to fade, ridiculous and terrifying in equal measure. Reed shut his eyes, but the phrase scrolled across the dark behind his lids, looping, insistent.

What the hell was this? A hallucination? Some fracture in his already battered mind?

He almost laughed at himself, standing in the middle of Grainger Plaza, haunted not by prophecy or scripture but by nonsense.

Yet the nonsense carried weight. The words felt planted. They were absurd, yes, but deliberate. A code he couldn't crack.

Cream Cheese Bananas.

"Uh… okay…" Reed lingered in bewilderment.

He had picked one hell of a time to quit drinking—he thought.

Somewhere in the sky over Grainger Plaza, unnoticed by all, a shimmering triangle blinked in and out of existence.

22

CHAPTER TWENTY-TWO

What We Don't See

Captain Bryans nursed the last inch of lukewarm coffee from his paper cup, leaning back in his chair just long enough to pretend the day wasn't swallowing him whole. Through the smudged squad room window, the city moved in its usual rhythm: cabs honking, a delivery truck double-parked, pedestrians arguing at a crosswalk. For a rare few beats, he let his shoulders loosen, pretending he could step outside that grind.

Then movement near Maria's desk caught his eye. A man stood waiting there, still as a coat rack, FBI credentials clipped to his sweater. Bryans set his cup down, suspicion rising halfway as he pushed off his chair and made his way over.

"Can I help you with something?" Bryans asked.

The man looked up and smiled, already knowing the question.

"Looking for Detective Voss. Agent Felix Harlan." He reached out a hand. Bryans shook it.

Bryans blinked. The name hit something, but not hard enough to draw a face.

"I've… heard that name," he said slowly, scratching the back of his head. "Didn't we meet once at… a fundraiser? Or a crime scene? Hell, I don't know."

100

Felix shrugged good-naturedly. "It's possible. I have one of those faces. Too average to stand out, but unsettling when you look at it too long. An AI-generated school photo," Felix said and then laughed lightly at his own joke.

Bryans didn't. He was staring at him, seriously kicking himself for not being able to place this guy.

Felix stared awkwardly, and then quipped, "It wasn't me, copper, I swear!"

Bryans chuckled despite himself. "Yeah. Now I remember why Voss likes you."

A phone rang three desks over, clipped voices overlapping in the squad room's constant hum. Just then, Maria came through, coffee in hand and detective brain already mid-spin. She stopped when she saw him.

"Felix!"

"Maria!"

They hugged quickly, the hug you give to someone who's been in your life forever, even if you hadn't seen them in months.

Felix Harlan looked exactly how Maria remembered him. The kind of guy who organized his sock drawer by emotional attachment. Tall, slightly hunched, with a mop of curly hair that seemed to defy combs out of principle. His wire-rimmed glasses were fogged from the humidity. He kept nudging them up with a restless finger.

"You look tired," he said, eyes scanning Maria's face. "But, in a philosophical sort of way. Existential fatigue. I get it. I read the news too."

Maria smirked despite herself. Felix was brilliant. An expert in behavioral patterns, criminal profiling, and obscure trivia no one ever asked for. But he also had the uncanny gift of being disarmingly kind. The kind of man who could psychoanalyze a serial killer one minute and bring you soup the next.

They'd met years ago in a college philosophy class, a serendipitous friendship sparked by late-night debates about free will and the nature of reality. Even when Maria lost touch with most people, Felix was a constant; babysitting her kids when she needed a hand, popping back into her life after long stretches apart as if no time had passed at all. Their bond was rare and steady, a quiet tether in the chaos.

Bryans snapped his fingers. "Agent Harlan. That's it. You babysat her kids once, didn't you?"

"Guilty," Felix said. "They tried to stage a coup. I barely escaped with my dignity."

"Barely," Maria added, sipping her coffee and smirking.

They all laughed. Different energies, but mutual respect. Bryans was rougher around the edges, Felix smoother but less interested in asserting it. The dynamic just worked.

Bryans watched, not jealous, but aware of a bond older and deeper than the precinct. He filed it under things he couldn't control.

Maria gestured toward the hallway. "Let's go to Bryans's office. We've got some catching up to do."

A detective walked past carrying a stack of crime scene photos, faces flickering in the overhead light.

Once inside, Felix pulled a neatly folded packet from his messenger bag and slid it across the desk. "I put together a preliminary profile based on what Maria sent me."

"Callin' in the feds before the press? I like how you think, Voss," Captain Bryans said as he picked up the perfectly organized file. Normally, Bryans would be wary of federal help, but he trusted Detective Voss.

Bryans opened the file while Maria leaned in behind him, scanning the bullet points.

"Thanks. Felix is practically a psychic with these sorts of things," she replied.

Bryans responded with silence that seemed to say I'll be the judge of that. As captain of one of Chicago PD's toughest precincts, being hard to impress came with the job.

Felix explained. "Okay, so this guy…" he trailed off in an introductory sort of way and then continued. "He's likely attractive, athletic, strong: not because he cares about health—because it gives him control. Beneath that? Deep insecurity. High intelligence, likely self-taught. Autodidactic."

Bryans half-listened, jotting a meaningless line on his notepad just to look busy. Profiles always sounded neat in theory. In practice, it was messy cops chasing the bastard down an alley at three a.m. Still, something in Felix's calm certainty made him uneasy. He was peeling layers off a person Bryans hadn't even met.

"*Auto-diabetic?*" Bryans raised an eyebrow.

Maria and Felix laughed while Bryans smirked, still unsure.

Felix smiled and answered, "Autodidactic. It means a person who learns or has learned a subject without the benefit of a teacher or formal education."

"So, self-taught?"

"Yes," Felix answered quickly.

"Agent Harlan, are you the chief of the Department of Redundancy Department over in Washington?" Bryans asked jokingly. Years on the force in a city full of nastiness had taught him the art of levity.

"They actually just appointed me to that position last week, for the fourth time." Felix smirked.

More laughter.

"Lives alone," Maria returned to Felix's profile, knowing a response to the captain's joke was not necessary. "Let me guess, single, no kids?" she added.

"Exactly." Felix started again with pride in his friend.

"Works from home or keeps a schedule that lets him isolate. Minimal long-term social interactions. Charm wears off quickly. Conversations stay on the surface. Anything deeper, and people get the feeling something's off." Felix leaned forward, fingers drumming the file, impatient for them to catch up.

Maria's knuckles whitened on her coffee cup.

Bryans nodded slowly. "Okay. What about his background?"

Felix hesitated a beat. "Strict father. Impossible standards. Probably physical or emotional abuse. Mother? Gone early. Left or died. I'm leaning toward death. That kind of emotional vacuum doesn't leave by choice."

Bryans shifted in his chair, heavy silence crowding the office.

"Father?" Bryans began. "Not mother? Most of these Looney Tunes have mommy issues, not daddy complexes."

Felix knew this question would come. "Normally, I'd say that's a distinct possibility."

Felix took a deep breath and continued. "But the lack of sexuality in these crimes says no. Most sociopaths who develop 'mommy issues' start with some kind of Oedipus complex in childhood and feel rejected by their overbearing and persnickety mothers.

"In late adolescence, these feelings of hatred and rage usually transfer to all women they find sexually attractive. They are killing the mother in all women in a way and getting off on it."

He paused to let everything sink in and then continued. "This guy, no. These crimes lack any sexual element. They're pure anger. Rage at the world. That usually is derived from an overbearing father who probably beat his son. The killer's antisocial personality likely leads him to take his rage out on his victims in the way his father did to him. With his fists or by strangling them with his bare hands. No blades are used."

"He carved into their heads," Bryans quickly interjected. Not so much challenging Felix as teeing him up for elaboration.

"Ah!" Felix had anticipated this question as well and eagerly continued.

"Not to kill them. It wasn't the murder weapon. He used it to carve the symbol of a mirror into them," he proclaimed.

Another jolt of insight hit Maria. This time it was the image. Or rather lack thereof, in her compact mirror at the wooded crime scene.

"Okay. That's fair," Bryans replied in agreement. "So, what does THAT mean?" he asked eagerly, because Felix had provided many answers but not the most important one.

"Hermann Hesse once said: 'If you hate a person, you hate something in him that is part of yourself or something you fear you might become.'" Felix stated with satisfaction.

Maria beamed proudly. "But Agent Harlan," she professed, having fun with Felix. "It was Michel Foucault who once stated that societal power structures shape individuals' identities and behaviors, arguing that people internalize these and engage in 'self-surveillance,'" Maria continued academically.

Bryans shifted with impatience and snarked, "Christ… grad school pillow talk."

CHAPTER TWENTY-TWO

Laughter again. The kind that made the room feel just a little lighter.

Felix continued, slightly apologetic for the philosophical tangent. "The killer is killing himself."

Bryans furrowed his brow inquisitively.

"He's angry at his father. Yes. He kills to get that anger out. Yes." Felix was now talking to himself more than Captain Bryans.

"But…" he paused for his grand finale.

Felix leaned forward, glasses slipping down his nose, eyes bright behind the fogged lenses. "The killer is all about reflection!" The line came out with theatrical flourish, almost triumphant.

Silence followed. Bryans stared flatly, unimpressed, while Maria just sipped her coffee, unreadable. The reaction Felix had been expecting never arrived.

He shifted in his chair, tugging at the strap of his bag. The confidence in his voice ebbed, leaving him caught for a beat in the quiet, awkward space he'd created.

"Okay," Felix said, trying not to be embarrassed. "After the kill, he reflects on what he's done and realizes that he is his father. He's a reflection of his father, and what he's done is a reflection on his feelings about himself. He realizes that he's become the thing he hates and therefore he hates himself. He IS the mirror. Both sides."

Bryans and Maria regarded him in silence, each weighing the words differently. Their eyes met for the briefest moment across the desk, an unspoken exchange neither of them put into words.

Maria flipped the packet closed. "This is good. It tracks."

Bryans grunted his minimalist approval.

They all stood to leave. Felix gathered his bag, adjusting the strap with absent-minded precision.

"If you need anything else, you know where to find me," he said.

"Thanks, Felix," Maria said.

Bryans gave him a two-finger salute. "Be good."

Felix sauntered out, his footsteps fading into the buzz of the squad room.

Bryans stayed behind his desk, standing but not moving, lost in thought.

The words of the profile clung to him, pieces clicking together even as his instincts kept circling the gaps.

Maria lingered at the doorway, eyes following Felix as he disappeared. He was good. Better than good. She'd always trusted his read on people. Yet as solid as his profile had sounded, a knot of unease twisted in her chest. The logic was there, but something beneath it whispered doubt. She couldn't name it, couldn't grab hold of it. The case was stirring her subconscious again, tugging at threads she couldn't quite see.

And that unsettled her more than she wanted to admit.

Then Felix paused at the doorway, looking back. "You know... some people aren't afraid of mirrors because of what they see. They're afraid because of what they don't see."

He smiled warmly, gave a small wave to them both, and turned away.

Maria stood staring, frozen by his words, the sound of the room around her thinning to nothing. Bryans returned the wave, his voice following with some remark, but to Maria it was indistinct. A background noise she couldn't process.

The only thing echoing in her mind was Felix's line, sharp as glass.

On the far wall, a narrow mirror caught the room in its silvered surface. The reflections inside it bent strangely, as if the glass were breathing. Desks curved at impossible angles. Filing cabinets seemed taller, stretching upward like narrow towers. Bryans's reflection twitched, flickering one frame behind his movement.

Only Maria's reflection stood untouched. Clear, steady, razor-sharp amid the warped surroundings. And as she stared, it seemed her reflection didn't blink when she did. Didn't breathe when she breathed.

It only watched.

23

CHAPTER TWENTY-THREE

The Mirror Doesn't Lie

The bedroom would be completely dark if not for the desk lamp. An antique-looking thing from the 1800s, casting an ominous red light across the room. The glow painted everything in rust and dried blood.

The room breathed no life. No pictures, no books, no trace of a human presence beyond the bare essentials: a dresser hunched against one wall, the lamp, and the bed. And a tall floor mirror standing ominously between the bed and dresser.

The rest was emptiness, heavy and deliberate, as if the absence of things had been arranged with more care than the presence of them.

The walls, bare and colorless, seemed to pulse in the lamplight, expanding and contracting almost imperceptibly. The air was thick and stale, heavy with a quiet hum that had no source. A low vibration that crawled under the skin and stayed there.

Amid the sinister red glow, a man stood before the mirror, face blank, eyes vacant. For now, the glass gave him back exactly what it should. However, the air trembled with the sense that something, at any moment, might shift.

Bathed in crimson light, the man oozed menace.

He was moving his arms up and down methodically, performing some dark parody of yoga. He closed his eyes in a way that seemed to imply he was meditating.

Then they shot open, and he stared at his reflection. But it wasn't him.

He stared, unmoving. But the image in the mirror moved first. Looking off to the left.

He knew what that was. He smirked and moved in an oddly slow, rhythmic way toward the dresser. He tapped a cell phone that sat there with eerie intent.

He leaned his head back, eyes closed, taking in the moment.

"Mother's Gone" by Trouble began to play. The ominous notes of the deranged melody filled the air with a tension that only this sinister being could appreciate.

He started to rock, slowly at first, swaying side to side like a pendulum to the music in the air. His movements lingered in the red glow, languid and unsettling.

As the song built, so did he. The sway sharpened into jerks, his shoulders snapping, his arms cutting the air in sudden arcs. What began as a slow drift turned into a frenzy, his body thrashing and contorting in wild bursts.

It was less dance than a performance. A ritual. Something offered up to the glass.

The mirror only watched. His reflection did not move, did not sway, did not thrash. It stood there, blank and silent, taking him in as if the glass were a one-way screen and he was the subject of an evil peep show.

Only the faintest shift betrayed it. The reflection's mouth curved with curiosity, a devilish calm resting on a face that should have been his own.

He finally stopped swaying to the foreboding music and stared.

A twitch at the corner of the mouth. A ripple through the glass. Not much. Not enough to shout about. But it happened. It always happened.

He smiled slowly. Each fraction of movement deliberate, stretching out in the red light. The smile widened, patient and predatory, the way a serpent lengthens itself before striking, uncoiling not out of panic but certainty.

"The next one," he whispered. The mirror twitched again.

He tilted his head to one side and let out a low chuckle.

His eyes never left the glass. And now the glass began to breathe.

The reflection exhaled fog, though his lips never parted. A soft mist curled across the surface, distorting the image, then retreating.

"I saw his face in the hush between thoughts. Not a face, no. A shape. An outline. Smoke remembering skin."

He blinked, but the image in the mirror did not. The doppelganger in the glass stared back, eyes wide, unblinking. Completely black. No whites in the eyes. They were alive in ways that shouldn't be.

"He is not chosen—*he is*. That's the secret, isn't it? They choose themselves. Every time."

The red light flickered, once, then again. Shadows jumped and stretched across the bare walls, twisting into long, clawed shapes that seemed eager to escape the confines of the room.

The man bent over slightly in a slow, deliberate motion and stopped, hunched over for a moment and then snapped up in a way reminiscent of the way a cobra attacks. His face was right in front of the mirror smiling maniacally, wide-eyed in a way that seemed to say, "*Gotcha!*"

The mirror showed a likeness tilting its head sideways slowly. Its stillness, its silence.

Both the man and his conflicting image in the mirror froze in these poses for several seconds staring at each other like they were sharing some sick inside joke.

But then the hand in the mirror began to press outward.

The man smiled wider. "The hour draws near. Tick, tick, tick."

The clock on the nightstand twitched in an unearthly fashion and began to tick backward.

The reflection began silently laughing in the glass.

He leaned forward, inches from the glass, whispering, "You see him, don't you? I see him too. So small."

"I see him folding!" The dark double barked back.

From the mirror came a soft crack—thin, delicate, almost gentle. The sound lingered in the air longer than it should have.

Another crack joined the first, and then another, weaving across the glass. Soon there were dozens of them. Threads of black and silver crawling across the mirror's face, breathing, writhing, multiplying. They quivered faintly with each pulse of the dying red light. The reflection behind them dissolved into distortion, its features shredded into fragments.

Then, in the blink of an eye, the mirror was whole again. The countless cracks slithered out of existence in a single flash, vanishing quickly.

The dark-eyed reflection stared back at him blankly once more.

Its presence pressed outward, saturating the room, its essence bleeding into reality.

The man facing it tilted his head back, eyes closed with a fervor that was almost religious. He drew in a long, meditative breath, the air rattling through his chest.

When he exhaled, the words came low and raw, carried on the last remnants of air in his lungs.

"I need this." The unsettling music lingered.

Then the red light failed.

Darkness poured in, swallowing the room whole. It was not the darkness of night but of absence, the kind that erases rather than conceals. Walls, floor, ceiling; all dissolved into a void, leaving behind nothing that belonged to any natural plane of existence. Only the echo of hunger remained, stretching out in every direction.

Waiting for its next offering.

24

CHAPTER TWENTY-FOUR

Star of the Show

Reed drifted through the grocery store like a misplaced ghost in yesterday's clothes, his hair uncombed, eyes wide. He had the kind of sleepless wonder that made him look like a man waiting for the universe to leave him a note in the frozen food section.

Every carton, every label, every flicker of light a clue—some hidden cipher pointing back to Morrow's words. He scanned the shelves with the anxious reverence of a man searching scripture for prophecy, questioning if meaning lived in the mundane. And then his hand closed around the cream cheese.

He didn't move. Not really. He just… stared. Slumped posture, crooked glasses, yesterday's clothes. Arms limp at his sides. A paperclip still tangled in the fabric of his shirt pocket. Eyes bloodshot.

Hungover was the only word he could conjure for it. Except he hadn't had a drink in—how long had it been? Days? Weeks?

Time was a soft thing now. Everything after Mr. Morrow and the Fold blurred into a looping fever dream. Wake, wander, whisper, repeat.

He stared at the carefully displayed row of identical cream cheese containers with a comical suspiciousness. As if the cream cheese had something on him that could be used in a court of law.

He leaned in close to the row of containers and whispered, "Tell me your

111

secrets." Reed leaned back.

He thought he was being discreet, but everyone within thirty yards of him could see what was happening.

Someone behind him cleared their throat in impatience. Reed didn't flinch; he just kept staring.

A hand reached past his field of vision and snatched one off the shelf.

"There are recipes on the website," the stranger muttered and walked away.

Reed blinked. Came back to the world. His stomach growled so loudly it echoed off the linoleum. The sudden craving made him feel human again, tethered by hunger. It made him forget he had just tried to have a confrontation with a very small container of cream cheese in public.

He needed to eat.

Fast food, the kind that had the taste of childhood and sin.

He left the grocery store, trying not to get too emotional about dairy products.

Reed wandered the streets with no map, no destination, just the compulsion gnawing at him. A splinter under the skin.

The city breathed in static rhythms: neon flickers, passing cars, voices chopped into fragments. Reed let it all wash over him, scanning every corner.

And then it appeared.

A building that had no business being there.

Yellow and teal blazed across its façade, colors so loud they bordered on hostile. Curtains in the wide front windows shivered, unveiling the place exactly as he'd seen it in his dream.

His vision.

Whatever it was.

The employees inside wore old-fashioned paper hats, the kind of thing that belonged in a cartoon or a memory, not a real city street.

Reed stopped dead on the sidewalk.

The sign above the door glowed with a garish smile: *THE ROCKET ROLL.*

His stomach sank as the words collided with the memory of a voice that had not spoken but entered him. Searing, intimate, undeniable:

Behold the home of the two Rs. This is where the moment shall happen.

The hairs at the back of his neck prickled. He'd never seen this place before. If it was a chain, it belonged to some universe other than this one. And yet, here it was, waiting.

He stepped forward, the certainty absolute. He had to go inside.

The door gave way too easily, bells chiming with a cheerfulness that mocked the dread tightening his chest.

Plastic booths gleamed under buzzing lights, teal tiles casting a jaundiced glow.

The air reeked of fryer oil and something sweeter underneath.

Reed scanned the room with the wide-eyed curiosity of a man certain he was about to watch a bomb detonate. Every detail begged for interpretation, demanded to be part of the message.

Then his body betrayed him.

Hunger rose sharp and insistent. His stomach growled with such force it nearly startled him. Against the tension coiling his nerves, the need for food took over.

He walked to the counter, hands trembling, and decided to order.

Five double cheeseburgers. They weren't food, not really. Just something to fill the space where alcohol used to live. Chemicals and salt. The best hangover cure for a hangover that wouldn't leave.

Across the room, a family came in. Normal. So normal it hurt.

Mom. Dad. Toddler.

Like a Norman Rockwell painting. If Rockwell had ever painted air so thick with fryer grease it could choke a ghost.

The parents stepped up to the counter and ordered the old-fashioned way. Cheerful. Familiar. The kid was a blond mop of hair, cheeks red from the summer heat. He clung to his mom's leg.

Then came the moment. The parents nudged him forward, the way people do when their toddler is unbearably cute and they want the whole world to see.

The cashier, a teenage girl with pink hair and a name tag that said SIERRA, leaned forward and asked gently, "And what about you, buddy? What do you want?"

The boy, Colin, put one finger to his lips. His whole body went still. He stood there, thinking deeply, a tiny replica of Rodin's Thinker.

Everyone near the counter turned to look. People chuckled. Smiles formed, slow and genuine.

Then, he lit up. A light bulb clicking on behind his little eyes.

"Cream cheese!" he shouted.

Laughter. All around.

Reed didn't react. Cream cheese. His mind perked up.

The mom laughed, eyes crinkling. "Cream cheese, huh?"

Sierra giggled. "What else would you like with your cream cheese, little man?"

Colin went back to the Thinker pose. People in line exchanged glances and grins. The kind of simple communal joy that rarely survives the checkout line.

The dad leaned forward and said, mock-stern, "Come on, Colin! What do you want, little guy?"

Colin stomped his tiny foot and glared. "No, Daddy!... Wait!"

Louder laughter.

Little Colin was the star of the show in this fast food restaurant.

He threw his hands in the air and screamed, "BEE-NANAS!"

Colin had the whole place laughing, strangers united in the glow of his outburst.

The mom, through giggles, said, "Baby... do you want cream cheese bananas?"

Reed's stomach twisted.

His mind, half-lost in a haze, snapped back violently.

His head turned sharply and suddenly. He stared at little Colin like a madman, though it was born of legitimate fear.

Cream cheese bananas.

The card. The final card from the Man in the Charcoal Suit.

Mr. Morrow.

Dammit.

Goddammit.

The child's arms raised up in charming protest and his voice rang again:

"I want… CREAM CHEESE BANANAS!!!"

The walls tilted. Reed shot upright from the seat he was in with the urgency of someone who had lost someone and he knew what this meant.

He could hear Morrow's voice now even though he hadn't spoken.

He could see the cards.

Another. Awaits. Their. FATE.

CREAM CHEESE BANANAS.

No.

No.

No. No. No. No—

He stood up, staggered, then steadied himself and moved toward the family with forced purpose.

Calm. Casual. Or at least that's how it felt in his head.

Inside, his nerves buzzed. He knew how this would look. It was some strange man, unshaven and jittery, wandering up to a family just trying to enjoy their greasy meal. Weird. Suspicious. Dangerous.

He could already see the father's instinct tightening, the mother's protective glance at the boy.

But the knowledge pressed against his skull like a migraine: that boy was going to be the target. He didn't know how, didn't know when, but he was certain. And doing nothing wasn't an option.

His mind scrambled for the right words, the right approach, some clever way to package the truth so it didn't sound crazy. He came up blank. Completely blank.

So, he leaned into urgency instead, his body taking over where his brain failed.

Smile too wide, voice a little too quick, hands gesturing, persuasion willed into existence.

"Excuse me," he said to the father, trying to force a smile. "Do you work from home?"

The dad turned, confused. "Uh… sorry?"

Reed kept the smile. "Just wondering. Do you work from home?"

The father blinked. "I… Who are you?"

Reed turned to the mom. "How about you? Do you work from home?"

She stiffened, pulling Colin gently closer to her side.

"I think you need to—"

"I'm sorry," Reed interrupted. "Look, I know this sounds insane, I know, but I need you to stay home with your son for the next few weeks. Please. Just… just make that happen. Don't let him out of your sight. Keep him safe. Keep him close. If you don't…" Reed swallowed his emotions and continued. "Someone is going to kill him."

Reed knew how he sounded; a lunatic strung out on something, anything. But he didn't care. They had to listen.

Silence.

Dead silence.

Then whispers. Confused muttering from nearby tables. Someone stepped closer.

The mother's hand tightened even more around Colin's shoulder, pulling him closer against her side.

Her eyes never left Reed, wide and trembling, pupils darting. Her breath quickened, audible now in the thick hush that had swallowed the room.

She turned to her husband, voice sharp with alarm, almost breaking.

"Ray…" she said, urgent, pleading. His name carrying all the weight of do something, now.

Colin blinked up at her, confused, tugging lightly at her sleeve, but she held him tighter, her gaze locked on Reed like prey recognizing the predator.

Reed held up his hands, voice cracking. He hesitated because he knew what he was about to say would elicit a strong reaction, but he was overcome with emotion.

"He's going to carve him up. His head. His forehead. Please listen to me," Reed implored.

Those words sounded better in his head.

The mom was white-faced, pulling Colin behind her now.

The dad stepped forward. "Back up."

People were watching now. Phones came out. A man stepped in front of the counter, protective.

Reed recoiled slightly in the face of the father's confrontation. He held one hand up as if to say "calm down, hear me out" in a nonverbal way but Reed's lack of sleep and possible alcohol withdrawals made him incapable of outwardly appearing sane no matter how hard he tried.

Reed's hand hung in the air for a beat too long before he let it drop, his shoulders sagging. He looked down at the floor. His throat worked as he swallowed hard, mind racing through a dozen ways he might salvage this.

None of them fit.

None of them could make him seem sane.

A wave of despair pressed against his ribs, but beneath it something harder flared: urgency, need, inevitability. He realized in a flash that he didn't have the luxury of social awareness, of careful phrasing or subtle persuasion.

Filtering the truth would waste time he didn't have.

He lifted his head again, jaw set, eyes burning with something raw and unguarded. For better or worse, he was going to say it exactly as it was.

"He's going to kill Colin! You have to protect him! Please! You have to stop the mirror!" Reed exclaimed.

"Call the police," someone said behind him.

Reed turned and shouted, "Stop him! Stop this! You have to stop it!"

A hand grabbed his arm. He thrashed.

Reed was sobbing as much as he was screaming, "THE KILLER'S GOING TO GET HIM! YOU HAVE TO LISTEN! COLIN'S GONNA DIE! HE'S GONNA DIE!"

Screaming. Chaos. Heat. Hands everywhere.

"I'M NOT CRAZY! I'M TRYING TO SAVE HIM! CREAM CHEESE BANANAS! IT MEANS SOMETHING! IT MEANS SOMETHING!" Reed shouted through sobs that made him sound deranged.

His voice cracked and broke as the crowd pinned him, breathless, face pressed into the cold tile floor.

He could still hear Colin's laugh echoing in the air as darkness swallowed the edges of his vision.

Fade to black.

Somewhere unseen, black eyes watched. And snickered.

25

CHAPTER TWENTY-FIVE

What Did You See?

Bryans walked beside Maria down the long hallway, lined with scuffed doors and walls the color of old paper. The whole place carried the stale hush of too many secrets.

Bryans's head was buried in a manila file folder as though it held the answers to the universe. Or at least a decent lead. His brow was furrowed, eyes scanning, lips moving faintly as he read aloud.

"Former professor. University of Chicago. Divorced. Daughter died at ten. Drunk. Lives alone. Neighbors say he talks to himself. The usual cocktail."

He glanced at her. "Sound like our guy?"

Maria didn't answer. Not right away. Something in her resisted the neatness of the captain's summary. It all sounded too pat, too convenient. A mask placed over something stranger she couldn't yet name.

She slowed as they approached the interrogation room and looked through the one-way glass.

Reed Ashland sat alone at the table inside, hunched forward, hands twitching slightly. There was something familiar about him.

A faint ripple across memory. Maria started to remember.

In her mind, she could see Reed's silhouette at the tree line, half-hidden

119

in shadow, his eyes fixed on the scene with an intensity that went beyond a bystander's.

"I've seen him before," she said quietly.

Bryans blinked. "Yeah?"

"The second Mary crime scene. He was there. Watching from the edge of the crowd," she explained, searching for clues in her memory.

That stopped Bryans. "Shit. Well, that's a hell of a coincidence. Killer returning to the scene? That does happen. Probably even more than we know about," Bryans elaborated.

Bryans's mouth set into a hard line; the more he learned about Ashland, the more the man's very existence rubbed him the wrong way.

Maria was lost in her thoughts and uttered, "Yeah. Maybe." Something in her tone said she didn't believe it. Even if the evidence did.

Maria's eyes didn't leave Reed. There was something strange about the way her stomach tightened. A low unease that wasn't suspicion. It was recognition, as if she'd just met someone in a dream and found them in real life.

Bryans grunted. "Look, it's thin, but it's more than we had yesterday. You think he's the guy?"

She hesitated. "Yeah… I don't know."

Bryans gave her a sidelong glance. "Don't get weird on me, Voss."

As they entered the room, Maria muttered to herself, "Too late."

Reed looked up as the door opened. His eyes were bloodshot but alert. He straightened a little, but didn't speak. Anxiety flickered in his gaze. He looked desperate to speak, yet already certain his words would be dismissed as madness.

Bryans dropped the file onto the table with a satisfying thud and took a seat, arms crossed, stare dialed to maximum intensity. Maria remained standing in the corner, arms crossed, studying Reed.

Something about him vibrated on a frequency she couldn't place. Killer or not, he mattered. She was sure of that much.

"Dr. Ashland," Bryans announced. "You asked for a lawyer," he continued. "He's on his way. In the meantime…"

He flipped open the file. "Where were you two nights ago?"

Reed blinked. "I don't know."

Bryans's eyes narrowed; for him, it was the worst possible opening note: an admission. Guilt wrapped in a fog.

"You don't know," Bryans said slowly.

"I don't sleep right," Reed said. "I walk. I forget."

"Convenient," Bryans said, leaning forward. "How about the night of October sixth?"

"I don't remember."

Bryans almost smirked, the pieces falling into place just the way he liked them: drunk professor, memory blackouts, no alibis. Every box was checked in bold red ink. To him, Reed wasn't just a suspect; he was gift-wrapped guilt.

But in the corner, Maria's arms tightened across her chest. On paper, it was damning, sure. But her instincts kept tugging at her, whispering that something about Reed Ashland didn't fit the mold he was being shoved into.

The captain looked down and let out an amused exhale.

"You were seen threatening a child in a restaurant, Dr. Ashland," Bryans continued, looking back up at Reed. "Said you were gonna carve a symbol into his head."

"I was trying to warn him," Reed said. "Warn his parents."

"By yelling at them in a diner?"

"It was a 'Rocket Roll,'" Reed pointlessly corrected him.

The correction threw Bryans off for half a beat. His brow furrowed.

He gathered himself quickly, jaw tightening as he pushed past it.

Across the room, Maria almost, almost, let the corner of her mouth twitch upward, the tiniest spark of amusement breaking through her guarded stare.

"You know anything about this?" Bryans asked, impatiently pulling out a printed photograph. It was the symbol. The carved mirror. He slid it across the table in a way that seemed to say 'We got you'.

Reed stared at it but said nothing.

Reed's eyes lingered on the jagged lines of the symbol, recognition flashing.

He lifted his gaze toward Maria, searching her face for even a crack of belief.

The glance hit her harder than it should have. The air tightened in her chest, a sudden ringing in her ears. Her hands curled against her arms, fighting the urge to shiver.

Bryans sighed, annoyed.

"So, you don't remember where you were, but you remember enough to 'warn' a child, and now you've got nothing to say about this?"

Bryans drummed his fingers once against the file, irritation hardening into resolve. He wanted this guy booked, locked down, but he knew he needed one more slip—something solid to nail Ashland with before he could make the move.

"DA's gonna love the 'I don't know' alibi. That's a layup conviction," Bryans said, trying to intimidate the silent suspect.

Bryans opened his mouth to push harder, but something shifted in the room. Reed's eyes had drifted from him back to Maria again.

Locked on her. Watching.

Bryans snapped. "Hey. I'm over here."

Reed didn't respond. He just stared at Maria.

Their eye contact held. Long. Uneasy. The rest of the room faded.

Then Reed spoke.

"What did you see in the mirror?"

Maria blinked. Her mouth parted slightly. Words caught in her throat.

"What?" Bryans said.

Reed ignored him. "At the crime scene. The second Mary Johnson. You pulled out your mirror. You looked at it and saw something."

Bryans turned toward Maria. "What is this guy talking about?"

Reed leaned forward, eyes never leaving hers. "What did you see?"

Maria stepped back like she'd been shoved. Her breath caught.

Bryans stood, suddenly off balance. "What the hell is going on here?" he asked.

"I saw you," Reed said. "You saw something. You thought no one was paying attention but I was."

Maria turned and walked out.

Bryans's face tightened, confusion colliding with frustration in a way that made his jaw clench.

The interrogation had been sliding neatly into place. Until Ashland's words cracked it sideways, that is.

Another damn curveball, another twist in a case that refused to play straight. Bryans hated the feeling of being off balance, of chasing shadows instead of answers, and right now he felt like the room itself was laughing at him.

He followed Maria out the door.

The echo of their footsteps filled the space between words neither of them wanted to say. He caught up to her just before the door to the stairwell.

"Okay," he said, his voice low. "What the hell was that?"

Maria didn't answer right away. Her arms were crossed tight against her chest, eyes fixed on the wall across from her. She was pale. Distracted. Reed's words had cracked something deep inside her.

"Voss," Bryans said again, more gently this time. "Talk to me. What did he mean about the mirror?"

Maria's mind scrambled for an exit. For some half-truth, some dodge that would keep her from sounding insane.

She wanted to shrug it off, to brush Reed's words away. But the pressure in her chest only grew, the memory of those mirrors gnawing at her resolve.

She hated this. She hated having to pull Bryans into the nightmare she couldn't even explain to herself.

Her arms tightened, and after a long, reluctant exhale, she gave up the fight.

Her voice trembled at first, then steadied with grim resolve as she began to explain. "At both scenes," she said. "The Mary Johnsons. There were mirrors."

Bryans blinked. "Okay…?"

"When I looked into them… something happened," she confessed.

Bewildered, Bryans asked, "Something like what?"

Bryans's stomach sank; he already knew whatever came next wasn't going to be good, the kind of answer that made a case murkier instead of clearer.

A feeling he was reluctantly becoming used to.

Maria looked down, then up again. "At the first scene. In the bedroom mirror and then in the woods with the second Mary, I got my compact out to check it…" she trailed off. She really did not want to be talking about this.

Bryans, wide-eyed for a silent moment, finally said, "Voss… what are you telling me?"

Maria exhaled once more and took the plunge. "The bodies were just… gone."

Bryans stared at her. "Gone?"

"Gone," she said flatly. "Like they were never there."

Bryans was dumbfounded, his mind stumbling over the word, and for a fleeting second, he thought about how badly he needed a vacation.

"I looked at the victims and they were for sure there. But the mirror didn't reflect them. Then their reflections came back." Maria said, trying to catch her breath.

He scratched the back of his neck, looked down the hallway, then back at her. "You're telling me the victims disappeared into a damn mirror?"

"I don't know how to explain it," she said. "And now Reed Ashland, somehow, he knows about it. He saw me use the mirror. I didn't even tell you about that part."

Bryans ran a hand down his face and let it linger there for a beat. When he looked at her again, the doubt was gone.

He liked Maria. Trusted her. She was a damn good detective. His best, no doubt about it.

That's what rattled him most. He could brush off weird theories from anyone else, but the fact that she believed… it sank its hooks into him. If Maria Voss thought this was real, then maybe it was. So, how the hell was he supposed to deal with that?

His silence spoke volumes.

"I know." Maria knew her captain well enough to understand what he was thinking.

Bryans let out a slow breath, the hard edge in his posture softening. He forgot, just for a moment, the frustration of the case.

What hit him instead was the weight Maria had been carrying; the late nights and the endless hours.

She wasn't just his detective; she was human, battered by this case in ways he couldn't fully grasp. Empathy welled up despite himself, and he felt the quiet sting of guilt for pushing her so hard.

"You sure you're okay?" he asked, quietly.

Maria shook her head. "No. But I'm sure I didn't imagine any of this."

They stood in silence for a long moment, the hum of the fluorescent lights buzzing overhead like static between frequencies.

Finally, Bryans nodded once. "Alright," he said. "Then let's figure out what the hell we're dealing with."

He had decided to tumble down the rabbit hole with Maria.

Bryans frowned back toward the interrogation room. "How the hell does he know?"

"I don't know," she said, and meant it.

"You think he's our guy?"

She looked at the floor. "I don't know. I hate that I can't get a read on him. He's connected. I just can't figure how."

Bryans put a hand to the glass, watching Reed, who sat completely still now, head bowed.

"Maybe you should talk to him," he said.

Maria's chest tightened at the thought. She wanted to talk to him.

She needed to. But caution whispered at the edges of her eagerness.

Was he a suspect dangling bait, or a witness who'd stumbled too close to something impossible?

The way to approach him felt like walking a tightrope over open air. As if one wrong word, and she could lose whatever truth he held.

Maria nodded to her captain, pulled open the door, and stepped back inside.

Reed looked up the second she entered.

Reed's eyes locked on hers instantly, a flicker of relief and desperation crossing his face.

Maria felt the same pull, an unspoken urgency to hear him out, but unease coiled in her gut.

They both leaned toward the moment, eager yet wary. Two strangers recognizing each other in a dream they couldn't explain.

Maria sat across from him. No file. No pretense.

"Tell me about mirrors, Dr. Ashland."

Reed swallowed. His hands fidgeted in his lap.

"They're not just reflections," he said. "They're… passageways. Portals. They're alive." His words spilled too fast, like he feared they'd vanish if he held them back.

Maria's pulse quickened. She leaned back slowly, masking her unease behind a flat stare.

"I don't know how to explain it," Reed finished, voice fraying at the edges.

"Try." Maria pressed sternly.

"I've seen things. I go places in dreams, but they're not dreams. Not really. There's a place… I call it the Fold. The Elsewhere Fold."

"The… Elsewhere… Fold?" Maria queried. Reed ignored her and kept going.

Reed didn't even notice the moment he'd made the choice. His thoughts simply began spilling out, tumbling faster than he could control.

He was speaking faster now, anxious, fevered. "It's where realities intersect. The things behind the things. The mirrors don't reflect. They remember."

Maria leaned back slowly. A jolt ran through her chest at his words.

Her pulse quickened, every instinct screaming to press him harder, to finally pry loose the answers she'd been desperate for. But she forced her face into stillness, a mask of cold detachment. She couldn't let him see how much he had her. How deeply his story hooked into the private, impossible things she hadn't confessed to anyone.

"Mirrors… I don't know what's in them," Reed continued. "But it's something. Something that watches. Something that remembers. Like I said. They're alive."

He looked at her. "Reality is a mirror, broken into language."

Maria raised an eyebrow. "That supposed to mean something?"

"The mirror knows your shape better than you do," Reed paused catching his breath. The word-vomit was cathartic.

For the first time in a long while, Reed felt a flicker of hope. Maybe, just maybe, someone across the table was beginning to believe him, or at least wasn't ready to dismiss him as another lunatic ranting into the void.

He ranted on. "A man I met told me those things. He speaks in riddles. But the mirrors… they listen to him. I think. I call him Mr. Morrow and he wears a charcoal suit."

"Mr. Morrow? Is he our killer? Is he going to kill little Colin?" Maria asked, genuinely.

Reed looked down. Bloodshot eyes darting around. Thinking fast. "No. He's good. I think. He's helped me. He told me things to help stop Colin from being hurt," Reed said quietly.

Maria grew frustrated and pointed to the one-way glass behind her. "Is that our killer? Is that thing staring back at us going to hurt people?"

Inside, Reed bristled.

It was like shouting warnings through a locked door. Maria kept her distance, circling his words with suspicion instead of stepping inside them.

He wanted to scream, to shake her into seeing what he saw, but all he could do was sit there, suffocating in the space between her doubt and his certainty.

Reed shook his head slowly. "No. Not a mirror. Not exactly. Something from one, maybe. Something using them. Or… something pretending to be us. I don't know. I just know I'm not insane."

"You sound insane," Maria quipped.

"I know."

Maria rose carefully, every muscle taut with the pull of two opposing forces. Her gut was telling her Reed wasn't lying, her reason demanding she keep her distance. She hated how close she was to believing him, how badly she wanted his madness to make sense of her own fractured experiences.

Reed sat back, breathing hard. This had taken a lot out of him. He clung to the moment like a man on the edge of drowning, heart pounding with the fragile hope that she might be the first to believe him. That she might finally hear him, really hear him.

Maria went to leave before confusion swallowed her whole.

"Did any of the victims have a watch on?" he asked suddenly.

Maria had her hand on the door.

She didn't look back. "No. They didn't."

Behind the glass, Bryans leaned forward in his chair, elbows braced on his knees, eyes fixed on the exchange. He didn't give a damn about the riddles or mirrors anymore. He just wanted the universe to cough up one straight answer. For once.

Reed looked down at the table. Thinking.

Maria exited the room. She stepped into the hallway, joined Bryans, and started to speak.

Then: A voice from behind the glass.

Reed, yelling.

"What about the clocks?!"

Bryans and Maria froze, the words slamming into them. Clocks. It was the one detail sealed up tight, never spoken outside the case files, never whispered to the press.

Bryans's gut twisted. To him, it was the slip. The kind of too-perfect knowledge only a guilty man could have. His jaw clenched, eyes narrowing on Reed.

But Maria's stomach lurched in a different way.

Not guilt. Connection. Revelation. Reed knew.

He wasn't guessing, he wasn't bluffing. Somehow, impossibly, he was inside the puzzle with them. And if he knew about the clocks, maybe, just maybe he knew how to end this.

Reed was on his feet now. Staring at the mirror. Seeing them without seeing them.

"3:33?" he said, his voice shaking.

Maria and Bryans locked eyes, the silence between them sharper than words.

Both of them knew Reed held answers. But in Bryans's mind, those answers came from guilt, from being too close to the killings. In Maria's, they came from something else entirely.

It came from something stranger, darker, but not necessarily guilty.

Neither spoke.

There was nothing to say that wouldn't tear open the rift between them. So, they turned back in unison, their gazes fixed on Reed through the glass.

Whatever he was, killer or prophet, liar or witness, they knew one thing with certainty; that he was the key. And they were going to break him open.

"Three… thirty-three?" Reed repeated, somehow knowing they were looking right at him.

The silence answered for them.

26

CHAPTER TWENTY-SIX

The Shape of the Mind

Reed Ashland's apartment smelled like dust and long nights.

Maria stepped inside first, her eyes adjusting to the dark. Bryans followed close behind, flipping on the lights, which only half worked. One of the overhead bulbs buzzed, struggling to hold on. The entire place was flooded with flickering light.

"Jesus," Bryans muttered.

Papers littered the floor. Books were stacked on every surface, some open, some stuffed with napkins, Post-its, and torn-out notebook pages scrawled with handwriting that started neat but broke down into chicken scratch.

Visitors from the Void, The Conscious Universe, and *The Mirror and the Mind.*

Nearby, *Ancient Stargates* leaned crookedly against *Kant and the Shadow Self,* spines worn and frayed, survivors of too many readings.

It was like someone had crammed a metaphysics seminar, a UFO cult, and a philosophy conference into a single man's apartment, and none of them wanted to leave.

"Guy really knows how to throw a party," Bryans said.

Maria ignored him. She picked up a journal from the stack on the floor and flipped it open. Page after page of disjointed writing. Some entries written as academic notes, others, manic letters he never mailed. One passage circled in red caught her eye:

They come from the sky. They come from within. They come from everywhere. You cannot hide.

She turned the page:

Mirrors aren't reflections. They're thresholds to the unspeakable. The world is trying to remember how to be real.

"Alright…" Bryans picked up another book and whistled. "He's got a signed copy of Dark Matter and Dream Logic. This guy is my spirit animal," he joked. Maria smirked half-heartedly, then shot him a look, unimpressed as his humor grated against the weight of the room.

Maria scanned the shelf beside him. More books on astrophysics, ancient cultures, Mesopotamian tablets, and a surprising amount of material on linguistics and symbols. "He's pulling from everywhere. No clear line. He's just… reaching. Studying everything. As if he's researching the entirety of our existence."

Bryans pulled another book from the pile, flipped it open, and skimmed a few pages. His brow furrowed despite himself. "I'll give him this; guy wasn't dumb. Half this stuff goes right over my head. He's connecting dots across philosophy, physics, whatever the hell. It's… impressive, in a lunatic sort of way." He snapped the book shut and tossed it back onto the stack. "Genius tangled in madness. That's the worst kind."

Maria didn't answer. She was still staring at the shelves, at the sprawl of subjects Reed had devoured. Metaphysics, phenomenology, the nature of perception; it was the same current that once pulled her in, back when she was twenty years old and restless, sneaking books into her dorm and arguing about the soul with anyone who'd listen.

She hesitated, brushing a dusty spine with her fingertip. *Nietzsche and the Abyss.* "He was into philosophy. That's for sure."

Bryans glanced up. "Yeah. Got his PhD in it. University of Chicago. Specialized in epistemology and phenomenology."

Maria blinked. "Seriously?"

"Yep." Bryans shrugged. "I read his dissertation summary while you were checking with the DA. Dense stuff. Questions about how we know what we know. The nature of perception."

"All perception is a gamble," Maria said quietly. "Edmund Husserl."

Bryans looked up from what he was doing with a look that implied, "Excuse me?"

"Edmund Husserl. Austrian philosopher," Maria informed him as she squinted through the flickering light to read the names of books she had never heard of.

"Let me guess," Bryans said. "You and this guy share library cards to the loony bin?"

Maria let that one go.

"You and Felix should have dinner with this guy and trade quotes."

Maria ignored her boss's jests, mildly annoyed at his jabs at her younger self.

Maria closed the journal in her hands and looked around thoughtfully. The old her, the nineteen-year-old who got high in the quad and argued about Foucault and the soul, would probably have liked Reed Ashland. Before he broke. Before whatever happened to him happened.

"Tragic," she murmured.

Maria's hand hovered over a thick paperback jutting crookedly from the pile. A dozen faded Post-its stuck out from its edges. The title on the spine read: UFOs and the Nature of Reality.

She slid it free, feeling the brittle glue of years-old tape against her fingers. Opening to one of the bookmarked sections, her eyes fell on a scrawled passage circled twice in red ink:

UFOs have a realm. The entities have a realm. Every other mysterious being encountered on Earth has a realm. The mistake of human perception is thinking there is one answer for all questions. Maybe there are thousands of questions with millions of answers.

Maria's pulse slowed as she read it again. She wasn't sure if it was madness, genius, or both, but the words hooked her. Her mind slipped into their gravity, chasing the thought like it had been waiting for her all along. A realm for everything. Not one answer. An infinite fracture of them.

Bryans's voice carried from somewhere nearby, still talking, still flipping through Reed's scattered obsessions. But his words blurred to background static.

"Voss," he snapped finally. "You listening, or you planning to write a book report?"

Maria didn't look up. She let the corner of the page slip between her fingers, anchoring her.

Maria turned another page, the words pulling her deeper. She didn't care what Bryans thought. Something in Reed's chaos made sense. If not to him, then to her.

She panned the room slowly and paused for one moment on a framed picture of a little girl. She didn't know the girl, but her smile hit something in Maria's chest, a life interrupted. She subtly touched the silver ring on a chain under her shirt. A flash of sentimentality.

She bent down and picked up a loose page off the floor. "You think he really believes all this?"

"I don't think he pretends to believe it," Bryans said. "Whatever's going on in his head, it's real to him."

They stood quietly for a moment, letting the chaos settle around them. Then, Bryans exhaled and rubbed the back of his neck.

"Alright. I gotta piss. Don't make a mess," Bryans said.

Maria cackled sarcastically at his quip.

He disappeared down the hallway. Maria knelt again and examined another notebook. This one a hybrid of sketchbook and manifesto. Symbols drawn over and over. That mirror shape again and again. Half-finished explanations of what it meant.

From down the hall came Bryans's voice.

"Voss?!"

"Yeah?!"

"You need to come look at this."

She stood, wary of what she might find.

"Please don't tell me it's his porn stash."

"No," he said. "Worse."

She followed his voice down the narrow hallway and into the bathroom.

Maria entered with trepidation, every step pulled forward by a weight she didn't want to name. Her anxiety was not fruitless.

The bathroom was a ruin of light and shadow, the overhead bulb flickering weakly. Shards of mirror clung to the frame above the sink, while others scattered across the tiles, a frozen spray of glass rain.

Bryans stood motionless in the middle of it, his shoulders squared, jaw tight. He didn't speak, and didn't need to. His silence was a verdict. Each jagged shard another nail in Reed Ashland's coffin.

Maria took another step. Glass crunched beneath her heel, sharp enough to make her flinch.

She already knew why Bryans had called her in. She had known before she even saw it.

Beside the sink, an old alarm clock lay on its side. Cracked. Stopped.

Maria leaned down to look closer.

The minute hand was caught between ticks. Frozen at 3:33.

She looked up. So did Bryans.

They didn't speak. They didn't have to.

27

CHAPTER TWENTY-SEVEN

The Glass That Breathes

Reed lay on the narrow cot and stared at the ceiling until the hairline crack above him became a river. The cell's hum was an old refrigerator's death rattle: lights buzzing, distant keys, a cough two doors down rippling through the air.

His thoughts came jagged and too fast. Maria's face, Colin's laughter, Emily's silence, Bryans' scowl. All flashing in a sequence only the Fold might understand.

Maria—did she believe him?

Bryans, was he sharpening a case that would stick?

Colin, how do I stop what hasn't happened yet?

He swung his legs over the side. The metal frame ticked under his weight. The air felt... off.

The mirror above the sink caught him in its rectangle. Drab light. Gaunt face. Eyes stained with insomnia. He'd thought quitting drinking would make the glass kinder. It hadn't. The mirror didn't forgive; it *kept score*.

All mirrors did now.

He stood, drawn closer the way a tide is drawn to a silver coin. The surface looked ordinary enough. It was smudged and scratched by a decade of hands and boredom. Still, it troubled him like a word on the tip of the tongue that isn't yours to speak.

A sour metallic taste rose in his mouth. The air thickened, humming against his skin, the way a room does when something unseen leans in close.

He lifted his hand.

He reached out slowly, anxiety pouring from him.

He touched.

The surface moved.

A circle of ripples ran outward, wobbling the world inside the frame. Reed jerked back, heart pounding, then leaned in again despite himself and pressed. His finger slid through cool resistance. Then the knuckle. Then his wrist.

His forearm vanished into the mirror up to the elbow.

The sensation was wrong in several directions at once: cold and warm, weightless and heavy. He swallowed. Panic scratched the back of his throat.

He pulled, and the mirror pulled back.

He braced, boots squeaking on concrete. The glass had him. The surface belled around his arm like a clear membrane, and something inside it stirred, tasting him. He yanked harder and came free, stumbling.

For a heartbeat he simply stared, panting.

His forearm shimmered.

Not wet. Shimmering.

Light broke along it in angles. When he flexed his fingers, a fine crackle traveled his veins, the way frost takes a window.

The mirror answered. A rope of liquid glass seeped down the inside of the frame and reached for him with the mindless yearning of spilled mercury seeking itself. He stepped back; it found him anyway, climbing his skin in a thin bright band. The tug deepened. His elbow bent against his will.

"No…"

It pulled. He fought. The cot screeched across the floor as his heel caught it. The tug became a decision that wasn't his. Reed felt the room tip, felt his body choose the wrong gravity, and then the mirror unzipped and swallowed him whole.

He fell into water.

Cold darkness pressed from every side, the kind that turns sound into bones. He hung there, neither sinking nor rising, suspended in a vast black throat. Shadows moved in the medium like patient fish that had learned a new alphabet.

One shape kept pace with him at an unnerving distance. Something that was not quite octopus, all wrong in the angles, its arms drawing slow cursive through the dark. Where a head should be was a blur of glass. From that blur came a sound: a single, wet click.

Then another.

Then ringing.

It began small, like an alarm clock in a far room behind three doors.

Then louder. Closer. The tone fattened, becoming a telephone's old bell, the kind that lived on a desk, the kind you answered because someone always needed you.

Louder. The water vibrated with it, drumming Reed's ribs, shaking his teeth. He winced and clapped his palms to his ears. The ring rose into a swarm. His skull became the bell.

"Stop," he mouthed into the dark. Bubbles tore the word to ribbons.

It did.

Silence fell with the weight of a dropped sheet.

He was no longer underwater.

He was standing in a room so black it made darkness an understatement. Edges that went out and out and then kept going, a horizon that refused to curve back. The floor existed only because his soles said so.

Footsteps.

Sharp, clean. Dress shoes on a hard surface. They were not his.

A figure advanced along a line that wasn't there. The body was only a shadow, less a person than the thought of one.

The shadow stopped before a frame that grew out of the black. A rectangle, a window, a mirror, acting as a door. The figure stepped through.

On the other side, there were two.

They walked together to another frame, and when they passed through, three emerged.

Then four.

The clack of shoes multiplied, echoes breeding echoes until the room was a nest of footfalls.

Five became six became twelve.

Reed's breath broke into pieces. The sound layered and layered, an army marching without bodies, a hundred verdicts being delivered.

"Enough," he said, or thought he did. The noise pressed a hand over his mouth from the inside.

He shut his eyes because that was the last thing left to try. Pain needled behind them, white and insect-fast. It spiked, crested.

And then it was gone.

He opened his eyes to find the frames and their brood erased. Only the black remained, smooth as an unasked question.

Something spoke.

At first it was only pressure, like a fingertip against the glass of his mind.

Then a whisper threaded itself into that pressure, present but without a source. He turned, but turning didn't help; it came from every direction and none.

The whisper thickened into almost-words. Almost, almost. And then it moved in.

It wasn't in the room anymore. It was in him.

The whisper seeped through him, silent and unstoppable, filling cracks he hadn't known were there.

It crept along his nerves, curling into every recess, feeding on the quiet places he'd kept for himself.

His thoughts weren't his anymore. They pulsed with an alien rhythm, as if the voice had laid its eggs inside the marrow of his soul and was waiting for them to hatch.

A little girl's voice, near and intimate, placed just behind his left ear, inside his skull.

"This is why you're here," it said. "Your fiction breeds. It breathes. There's only one way out."

Light cracked through the world.

Reed sat bolt upright on the cot, breath hauling, the taste of metal in his mouth.

The cell's hum returned. Fluorescents, keys, someone snoring two doors down.

The mirror above the sink waited in its cheap frame like nothing had ever happened.

He stood.

His legs held. Barely.

He crossed to the mirror slowly.

The glass showed him debris from a life he recognized: the sallow skin, the days without sleep, the hair that refused to remember the shape it was taught.

He lifted his hand.

The fingertip met hardness.

Dry. Cold. Ordinary.

Just a mirror.

He didn't realize he'd been holding his breath until he let it go. It left him rough.

Somewhere in the long hallway beyond the block, a cart squeaked past and a radio murmured about nothing.

In the space that noise didn't fill, her voice returned, gentler now, the echo of a dream that wasn't done with him.

This is why you're here.

28

CHAPTER TWENTY-EIGHT

Not Enough Yet

The station buzzed with its usual static: phones ringing, boots scuffing across linoleum. The low murmur of cops and criminals alike moving through the current of another gray Chicago day.

Maria and Bryans walked beside each other, flanking the district attorney, Leonard Shaw.

Shaw was one of those men who always looked slightly annoyed, and now the rest of the world was paying for it. Shaw's tie was crooked in that way that suggested either a long day or a short fuse. He tugged at it once and rubbed at his temple.

His eyes swept the station like a judge surveying a courtroom, quick to find fault, slower to give credit. Even here, surrounded by cops who'd seen it all, Shaw carried himself as someone with the final word in every argument.

"Look, the guy's a headcase," Bryans was saying, his voice rising with every step. "Fanatical interests, journals stacked to the ceiling, a damn mirror smashed and a clock stopped dead at 3:33 in his apartment. And let's not forget him verbally accosting a family in a diner."

"Rocket Roll," Maria said quickly.

Bryans shot her a sidelong look that all but said Seriously?

Shaw didn't get it and didn't care. He waved a dismissive hand as though the details were gnats in the air.

"You've got nothing that sticks," Shaw said, eyes fixed ahead. "No murder weapon. No DNA. No witness placing him at either scene. That restaurant incident? Misdemeanor at best if the parents press charges. He's strange, sure, but strange doesn't equal guilty."

"He knew details he shouldn't know," Bryans insisted.

"But nothing admissible," Shaw snapped back."He can recant that in court. Claim his attorney wasn't present."

"Look, Captain," Shaw leaned toward the investigators for emphasis. "Unless he confesses, or one of your mirrors testifies in court, we're not holding him."

Bryans swallowed his frustration. Veteran of the force that he was, he was used to it. Maria didn't bother.

"This is bullshit," Bryans muttered under his breath.

Ahead, a uniformed officer opened a door, and Reed Ashland stepped through. Somehow, a little bit of jail time had done him good. He might be the one person who came out looking better than when he went in.

He was calm. Still. That same quiet gravity that seemed to follow him everywhere.

They locked eyes, Maria and Reed. The silence stretched between them, thin and tense. Something in Maria's chest tightened, a low ache she couldn't name, like déjà vu clawing at the edges of her memory.

What was it about this guy, about this case? Maria wondered, her senses flaring in his presence.

Somewhere in the darkness of her subconscious she could feel answers lingering. Answers to questions she hadn't even figured out how to ask yet. And somehow, impossibly, she knew Reed could help her find them.

Reed glanced briefly at Bryans, then settled on Maria.

His eyes lingered on her, searching for a safe harbor in a storm.

"You know I didn't do it, right?" he asked, his voice steady but carrying the faint tremor of someone desperate to be believed.

Maria held his gaze, unflinching. She wasn't about to let him know she was even considering believing him. Tough cop to the end, especially with a potential suspect.

"All I know," she said, her voice clipped and professional, "is we don't have enough to charge you. Yet."

A twitch of a smile ghosted across Reed's face. Not smug, not amused. Just… knowing.

Bryans stepped forward. "Don't leave town, Ashland—we're not done."

Reed nodded, almost gracious. He looked back at Maria, his voice dropping to just above a whisper. "You're asking the wrong questions," he said.

The words lingered in the air, impossible to catch, impossible to ignore.

Maria and Reed hung in the moment, their eyes locked.

Something inside her twitched. It was a spark of intuition flaring at the edge of consciousness.

A pressure built in her chest, part fear, part recognition. She hated the thought, but some corner of her knew he wasn't wrong.

Then Reed broke the moment.

He walked past them and down the hall toward the exit, his footsteps barely making a sound.

Maria and Bryans stood side by side, watching Reed's back as he drifted down the corridor.

To Maria, there was something uncanny in the way he moved. A man both tethered and untethered, carrying answers he couldn't yet give. She felt that strange pull again, equal parts dread and fascination.

Bryans' eyes, though, saw none of that.

To him, Ashland was a suspect walking free on a technicality, a man guilty in spirit, yet not in evidence. All he needed was one slip, one trace of proof, and he'd have him nailed.

As Reed stepped toward the door, Bryans called out, "Hey, Ashland, just one more thing."

Reed paused, turning slowly, eyes flickering with anxious curiosity.

"There were reports last night," Bryans continued, "about half a liquor store being thrown out a window and landing on a car down by your apartment building. You wouldn't happen to know anything about that, would you?"

Reed froze, quintessential deer in headlights. His face twisting into an awkward grimace that said nothing clear. His breath caught, shoulders hunching.

Without a word, he shuffled away.

Bryans smirked, glancing over at Maria. She was chuckling softly, the tension breaking just enough to let a little levity slip through the cracks.

Maria and Bryans stood there for a beat, watching him go.

"You believe him?" Bryans asked.

Maria shook her head slowly. "I don't know what I believe."

Bryans tilted his head. "But?"

She exhaled. "But I think he's the answer. I just don't know what the question is yet."

They watched the front doors swing shut behind Reed.

Somewhere in the distance, a clock ticked. Then it stopped, as if the sound itself had been cut with scissors.

29

CHAPTER TWENTY-NINE

Waiting in the Quiet

The late afternoon sun poured golden light over the quiet street, painting the leaves in fiery reds and amber hues. A soft breeze stirred the crisp scent of early autumn, carrying the distant laughter of children and wind chimes in a gentle dance.

It was the kind of afternoon Chicago's suburbs seemed built for: lawns clipped neat, porches dressed in pumpkins and cornstalk bundles, the first paper skeletons taped to windows in eager anticipation of Halloween.

The air carried the faint smoke of a backyard grill, mingling with the sharp sweetness of fallen leaves. Somewhere a dog barked, answered by another down the block, while a sprinkler ticked and sighed, reluctant to give up summer.

Families were winding down into their routines, cars easing into driveways, garage doors yawning shut.

It was the picture of ordinary. Almost painfully so, the kind of scene that convinced you the world was safe. The word 'picturesque' didn't do the scene justice.

And yet, something foreign seeped into the frame. A shadow, stretched long and strange, bled across the golden lawns. It moved without hurry, without sound.

A dark car sliced through the scenery like a blade, driving calmly.

Indecipherable sounds bled from within until the occupant's window slid down with eerie calm. Inside, *Sewer Blues* by Timber Timbre bled into the afternoon, low and crawling. Foreboding, skin-crawling, and wrong.

The killer's fingers clenched tightly around the steering wheel, pale against the warmth flooding the windshield. His eyes were cold and sharp, scanning the peaceful scene with a hunter's focus, a dark shadow amid the sunlit calm.

Plans and fragments swirled behind his eyes, anchored by a cold steadiness that belonged only to the truly unhinged. Another target, another waiting moment, another step closer.

Houses stood, silent and unaware. The engine hummed beneath him, a low pulse syncing with the rhythmic beat of his thoughts. He slowed as he neared the house at the end of the block.

A small figure darted across a neatly trimmed yard.

Colin, the boy Reed had tried to warn, chased a loose ball, his laughter ringing clear and bright. Pure joy spilled from every breath, every carefree smile.

The world around him shimmered in the warm glow of the afternoon.

He tumbled after the ball with all the reckless energy of childhood, sneakers slapping the grass, arms windmilling as he caught his balance and let out another peal of laughter.

His father jogged after him, half serious, half playing along, pretending to be outpaced by the smaller legs. Their laughter overlapped; high and light from the boy, deeper and rolling from the man, blending into something simple, timeless.

Near the porch, Colin's mother knelt in a small garden bed, dirt on her gloves, trimming back tired summer flowers to make room for autumn mums.

She looked up at the sound of their laughter, her face softening into a smile that seemed to belong to another age.

For a heartbeat, she simply watched her husband and son tumbling through the yard, the ball bouncing wild. Before returning to her work with a shake of her head, still smiling.

It was ordinary life, almost painfully so.

And yet, something unseen lingered at the edges, watching.

The scene might have belonged to a Norman Rockwell canvas, but in the periphery there was a smudge, a smear of shadow that didn't belong.

An eye without a face, a hunger without a name. It hovered just beyond sight, patient and deliberate, like the devil leaning close to admire a painting of innocence before deciding where to press his thumbprint.

The killer's eyes darkened, drinking in the scene. Why a child? The question circled in his mind, sharp and relentless. Innocence twisted the hunger deeper, made the game feel more… pure.

But the why didn't matter. Not really. It never did.

He had a role to play: a dark ritual carved into his bones. There was no room for mercy, no space for second thoughts. The child was a piece on a board larger than himself, an unwelcome move he had to make.

So, he crushed the question beneath a mask of indifferent steel. A sociopathic pride radiated from him: quiet, poisonous, certain. A smile tugged at the corner of his mouth. It was not tenderness, but something colder.

Calculated. Satisfied.

A low, haunting voice seeped from the speakers. The words were slow and unsettling, wrapping the car's interior in a funeral dirge disguised as a love song.

The killer mouthed the words, his lips curling into a wicked mimicry, a look of possession etched across his face.

He lingered, savoring the scene, drinking in the melody's rot. Still as a shadow carved from silence, the killer imprinted the innocence of the boy's laughter deep into the hollow corners of his mind. Then, without a word or sound, he eased the engine to life.

The low growl unsettled the quiet, bending the peaceful rhythm of the street out of shape.

A curtain shifted in a nearby window; a pale hand parting the fabric just enough for someone to glance outside. But whatever they saw, or thought they saw, didn't hold. The fabric fell back into place, and the house swallowed its witness whole.

The car rolled forward, slow and deliberate, its darkness sliding unnaturally across the lawns as it slipped away. An unwelcome silhouette fading from a perfect day.

He would return. He always did.

30

CHAPTER THIRTY

The Dance of the Absurd

Reed unlocked the door to his apartment with a hesitation that felt older than the key in his hand.

The lock clicked, the knob turned. However, something in the air shifted as he stepped inside.

Reed stood in the doorway, staring as if the walls might breathe; the lamps and furniture looked posed, frozen mid-performance, waiting for him to blink so they could move again.

The place was the usual wreck: books piled high, a trail of coffee cups, half a pizza box on the couch. But still, he could feel it. Someone had been here.

He stood in the center of the living room, eyes scanning slowly.

He asked himself when was the last time he took a shower. No idea. That wasn't good.

He went to the bathroom, peeling off the day like a wet coat.

Stripped to his skin, he stood before the cracked bathroom mirror.

It showed him in fragments. The left side of his face looked older than the right.

Remembering his dream, every pane of glass represented a trapdoor, every reflection a waiting mouth.

He touched the surface tentatively, half expecting it to ripple and swallow him whole.

Nothing happened. Just cold glass.

Reed let out a breath, relief washing through him in a fragile wave.

He turned on the shower and let the bathroom start to steam up, before he opened the door to his hot watery therapy.

Inside was not tile and steam, but a place that bent away from all sense itself.

Light twisted into colors that he could taste, reflections without sources fluttering across the walls. It was less a room than a hallucination wearing the shape of one.

Reed staggered forward, caught in a frenzy of shifting images: faces blooming and dissolving, echoes colliding with their own shadows.

His pulse raced, breath ragged, until the chaos folded in on itself. In an instant it was still, and he found his footing.

He found himself inside a room of mirrors, infinite reflections repeating like a song stuck in time.

The room shifted constantly, its surfaces alive.

Patterns crawled across the glass in slow, insectile waves, alive but unwilling to admit what kind of life they belonged to.

And in the center of this, waiting, stood a figure wearing an oversized tuxedo with one sleeve too long and a red rubber nose. His legs were made of broken clocks.

His smile was permanent and unnaturally wide. Mocking. Knowing.

His eyes blinked separately, one lid lagging behind the other like mismatched shutters in a storm, giving the impression his face was caught between two reels of film out of sync.

"Welcome," the Absurd figure said, "to the in-between where the sense you make is the lie you tell."

The words weren't spoken so much as absorbed.

Reed turned, catching movement in the glass.

A figure approached. It was tall. Cloaked in a shadow stitched to cloth.

The face couldn't be seen.

Then the Absurdity leaned over his right shoulder and taunted him with a riddle:

"Two selves dance within the glass

One born to live, the other to pass.

One tells truth with fractured breath,

The other whispers echoes of death.

Which is the mirror, which the soul?"

The message didn't come from a mouth. Its movements carried it, every twitch of an arm and tilt of the head sending the words straight into Reed's skull.

It was like watching someone dance a song you couldn't hear, except the lyrics were already inside you.

Through it all, the figure's giant, impossible smile never faltered, stretched too wide to belong to a human face.

When Reed turned to look over his shoulder, the figure was a mime in red.

They locked eyes and this Absurd mime suddenly screamed loudly and smiled. Then he was gone.

The liquid room of mirrors shifted suddenly and became one shapeless blob.

The nebulous form lunged at Reed. It absorbed him and he became a mirror that reflected images within himself.

It felt cold and suffocating, like wearing another man's skin turned inside out.

Shapes began to flicker across Reed's surface, memories trying to become flesh.

Three shapes manifested.

They faded into existence for mere seconds and then sank back into the abyss surrounding the mirrors.

The vagrant. Mary Johnson. And Colin.

Colin, the boy with the starlight laugh.

Reed wondered about the question he most likely didn't want the answer to.

"Why is he here?" Reed asked, his voice reverberating into nonsense.

The Father's voice came from behind him now. Popping into place. A grotesque jack-in-the-box, sudden and too close:

"The mirror devours a face in two,

One trapped in a fold none can view.

The soul laughs unseen,

In between what has been,

While the shadow forgets what is true."

The Absurd appeared before Reed once again.

He didn't walk or step; he seemed to fold through himself, limbs bending the wrong way, torso collapsing into angles before blooming outward in front of Reed.

For a heartbeat his head lagged behind his body, sliding into place a full second late, the grin already waiting where the face would be.

Now he was a decrepit old man dancing a deranged tap dance, all the while pointing finger guns at Reed with an unmovable smile.

The eyes were alternating accelerating blinks.

Reed tried to speak, but his throat produced nothing. Only a dry click.

In places of actual words, his thoughts rose, unbidden, whispering inside his skull: He's not just a jester. He's the Father of Absurdity. The one who walks backward through language, laughing at the order of things.

The name clung to his mind the way smoke clings to curtains, impossible to wash out.

When he opened his mouth to try to speak again, words died in his throat like flies in black syrup.

Language was gone. And so was Reed.

He spun and then the ground vanished, and he plunged into heat that wrapped around him instantaneously.

Bubbles clung to his skin in slow, sticky patches, bursting against his ears with muffled pops.

The air was thick with the cloying scent of artificial sweetness, a pink chemical perfume.

His eyes shot open. He was in his bathtub. Naked. Surrounded by suds.

He never took baths.

He sat up, heart racing.

On the counter near the mirror, which was no longer cracked, sat a bottle of *Mr. Bubbles* he had never purchased.

And a single gingerbread cookie with one bite missing.

Reed dried off quickly, dressed, and made for the front door.

He exited his apartment and glanced around the hallway.

The hallway was empty in the way only something carefully erased could be. Suspiciously unsuspicious.

He ducked back inside, rummaged through a drawer, and came out again with a piece of string.

He went back to his hallway quickly and tied a wisdom knot around the doorknob, pulling it tight. Then closed the door behind him.

Reed stretched out on the bed, willing himself toward sleep. The harder he chased it, the farther it slipped, leaving him wired and restless despite the weight in his bones.

After a few minutes he opened his eyes again, staring at the ceiling in raw frustration. It was mocking him, with its blank patience.

He looked to his left and in the space next to him in bed was something. A corpse.

Reed leapt from the bed, sheets flapping off him like startled birds.

His chest seized with a jolt of panic, breath caught halfway between a gasp and a shout. The floor felt too cold under his bare feet, his legs weak.

Confusion pressed against his temples, hot and dizzying, while his eyes darted wildly, searching for sense in the impossible shape beside him.

The body didn't move. He backed across the room, breath ragged. Staring. Panting in horror.

"What in the holy fuck?!"

Then it sat up. Or rather, began to rise in a way that didn't belong to muscle or bone.

The body seemed to float at first. Shoulders lifting, pulled by invisible strings, a slow and weightless ascent that gave it an almost angelic grace.

Light from the window caught its edges strangely, haloing the figure in pale shimmer, as though the air itself were trying to sanctify the moment.

Reed's stomach dropped, a cold rush flooding his veins, his ears filled with the hollow roar of his own pulse. Terror rooted him in place, every nerve screaming to run, but curiosity held him captive.

As the figure's face turned toward him, clarity struck through the haze of fear; he knew this presence. Slowly, impossibly, recognition cut through the confusion.

Mr. Morrow.

He had a message.

No cards this time.

Just monotone words.

The voice stretched thin and metallic, doubling back on itself:

"Find the child where lies are built into brick and the moon forgets its shape.

A court without justice. A chapel without faith. A height without stars."

The words did not leave his mouth, but oozed from the space around him. They echoed with no air, vibrating the walls, the floor, the marrow in Reed's bones.

Reed blinked. He was gone.

A chill washed through Reed's body, leaving his skin prickled and hollow.

Shaken and disturbed, Reed stood for a moment, gathering himself. He anxiously moved his eyes to the clock by his bed.

4:44 a.m.

The sight sent a shiver down his spine, a strange mix of dread and comfort.

The numbers glowed with an eerie calm, steady and unwavering. It made him feel almost safe and the contradiction unsettled him most of all.

The fleeting sense of safety evaporated, replaced by a rising dread that clenched at his gut.

An urgency welled up inside him. It was irrational and undeniable. Telling him he had to turn around, that something waited for him whether he wanted to face it or not.

Inch by inch he rotated.

And when his eyes finally landed on what waited behind him, a shock like

ice water surged through every nerve, leaving him hollowed, trembling.
On the wall, scrawled in blood, were the words:
PAY ATTENTION TO THE CURTAINS.

31

CHAPTER THIRTY-ONE

A Height Without Stars

"Find the child where lies are built into brick and the moon forgets its shape. A court without justice. A chapel without faith. A height without stars."

The words still echoed in his skull. Nonsense at first, but now they burned with meaning.

Reed slammed the door behind him and bolted down the stairs, breath burning in his lungs. He was running like something was after him, but in truth he was after someone.

He didn't know how he knew what he knew. He just... did.

It throbbed in his chest, an extra heartbeat that didn't belong to him, a rhythm tapping out directions in code.

His skin prickled, the air whispering secrets through the pores.

The certainty wasn't thought but sensation, as if déjà vu stretched over his bones, a memory of something that hadn't happened yet.

Colin's gap-toothed grin flickered in Reed's mind. The Rocket Roll's neon bleeding too bright around him, laughter stretched and warped.

Reed felt a pressure bloom behind his eyes; the memory itself was trying to claw its way out of him.

The thought didn't rise; it burst through him.

155

Colin was in danger. And Reed had to find him.

Heat prickled the back of his neck, sweat breaking without cause, every nerve screaming move now, move faster.

His pulse thundered so loud it blurred the edges of the world, as though his own body were turning into a siren.

Reed had to find him.

But how?

He didn't know the boy's last name, let alone where he lived. He hadn't been told. Not directly. Yet he was moving, possessed. Toward some known unknown destination.

It was as if a ghost whispered to him in Morse code.

His hands trembled as he started the car, eyes flicking to the clock on the dash.

2:33 a.m.

An hour. Somehow, he knew it would take exactly an hour.

Where? That part was still unraveling.

The image of Mr. Morrow animating from a corpse in his bed flashed into his mind.

He turned west. His intuition told him to.

The pull wasn't thought; it was lines of a prophecy etched straight into his nerves.

Every turn shimmered in his skull before the road even appeared, directions blooming behind his eyes.

The steering wheel was guiding him, a current flowing through his arms, pulling him toward a destination he couldn't name but already knew.

The streets were empty, just Reed and the dark.

The city at night unfolded around him. Streetlights blinking too slow. Too deliberate—eyes deciding whether to stay awake. Storefronts dozed behind their glass, neon signs buzzing with the patience of insects.

He drove with the headlights off for a moment. Then back on. He didn't need more attention. Definitely not from cops, not from anyone.

More images of Mr. Morrow popped into his head. Jump-starting his instincts.

Turn left.

Go straight.

Now right.

No GPS. No map. Just a sentence that shouldn't mean anything, yet now meant everything.

As he sped north on I-355, something flashed across his vision. A sign for an exit. He caught it out of the corner of his eye:

Glendale Heights.

For a split second the letters on the sign seemed too bright, glowing unnaturally, burning into his skull; a secret he'd always known but could never place.

Reed sat up straighter. "A height without stars," he whispered.

It was absurd, and perfect all at the same time.

He turned off and slowly, carefully navigated the streets of the quaint suburb.

Quiet residential streets unspooled before him, streetlights flickering.

He passed a few blocks, heart pounding in time with the engine. Then another sign.

The name didn't just appear; it announced itself. Rising out of the dark like a lighthouse beam cutting through fog. Except this light wasn't guiding him home; it was pulling him toward something inevitable, something waiting. An omen masquerading as an address:

Chapel Court.

Reed's breath caught.

Mr. Morrow's face flashed in his mind. His voice reverberating into his eardrums.

"A court without justice. A chapel without faith."

He turned.

Fate pressed its hand over his own, guiding him through the streets. The asphalt stretched before him, indifferent to whether it ended in revelation or ruin.

Nice homes. Silent homes. Too clean, too still.

One under construction.

Another crowded with cars outside.

A massive two-car garage, covered with a tarp.

Another with lawn chairs scattered in the front yard from an abandoned party.

"Wait…" he said aloud.

Something snagged at the corner of his vision. Not intuition but sight, real and undeniable.

It wasn't fate whispering now. It was his own eyes, finally catching up to what his nerves already screamed.

He slowed.

That big garage. Reed looked closer at the tarp where garage doors should be.

His heart jumped into his throat. All at once, scraps of his dreams began knitting themselves together.

Not a tarp.

Curtains.

Thick, oversized, hanging awkwardly, like theater drapes caught in a windless night.

Who puts *curtains* on a garage?

Suddenly, the riddles and visions weren't fragments; they were coordinates. Every dream, every whisper, every impossible sign had been pointing here, to this street, this house.

The image of blood on drywall surged into Reed's mind.

"PAY ATTENTION TO THE CURTAINS."

He didn't think.

He slammed the car into park, leaving it skewed in the middle of the road, headlights bleeding across quiet houses. He flung the door open and bolted.

His legs carried him before his mind could catch up; running, heart pounding, lungs burning. Anxiety clawed at him, fear gnawed at him, determination drove him harder with every step.

Was the boy still safe? Or already gone?

The questions slashed through him in flashes. *Was he too late? What would he do if he confronted the killer face-to-face?*

His body didn't care about answers. His body only knew NOW.

Feet hammering pavement, breath ragged, Reed hurled himself toward the house.

Somewhere behind the house, down an alley choked with shadows, a dark, ominous car sat idling. It was completely empty.

Its driver was already inside the house.

32

CHAPTER THIRTY-TWO

Behind the Curtains

Reed crouched low beside the house, breath shallow, heart pounding. He was running off half-remembered movie scenes and sheer adrenaline. He felt ridiculous, but he had to get into this house and save a little boy.

Colin.

The cold air stung his lungs. Every inhale felt too loud, like the night itself could hear him. His palms were slick, fingers trembling as they brushed against the siding.

The bricks pressed against his shoulder were damp and sharp, and for a surreal moment, he thought of prison walls. How he might belong behind them after this.

What the hell am I doing? He thought. He wasn't a cop. He wasn't trained. Yet here he was, crouched in the dark, trying to play the part of a savior.

The yard smelled faintly of wet leaves and gasoline, and the wind through the trees had the cadence of whispers. The shadows stretched long across the lawn, twisting into shapes. Every second dragged.

Still, he pressed forward. Because for all his failures, for all the wreckage he'd made of his life, he knew one thing: if he didn't try to save this child, then what was left of Reed Ashland would vanish completely.

He paused in his awkward creep to peek inside one of the windows.

Something shifted just beyond the window frame. At first it was only the still image of a hallway with family photos lining the wall, a toy truck overturned near the baseboard, the kind of ordinary clutter that made the intrusion feel even more obscene.

Then a shadow flickered past the far end of the corridor, fast and soundless.

Panic surged. His adrenaline spiked, a torrent of heat flooding his chest. His throat went dry, his heart thudded so hard it rattled his teeth.

He darted to the back door, hands shaking as he reached for the handle: locked. The next one: locked. He cursed under his breath, scrambling to think.

Then he reached the final door.

"Good God, how many doors does one house need?" he muttered, trying to break the anxiety. It didn't work.

It creaked open beneath his fingers. It was already unlocked.

"Shit..." he whispered. That wasn't a good sign.

The dread hit him like cold water. If the door was open, it meant he was already too late, that whatever horror had unfolded inside had been waiting for him all along. A sick certainty tightened in his stomach: he wasn't breaking in. He was walking into the aftermath.

He eased inside, every muscle coiled tight, arms out awkwardly at his sides.

His shoes scuffed the tile with tiny betrayals, his exaggerated tiptoe caught between pathetic and desperate. If anyone had been watching, it would've looked ridiculous. Except for the fact that his fear was real enough to choke on.

The house was too quiet.

Not asleep. Waiting.

The stillness pressed against his ears like a held breath, thick and unnatural.

No hum of a refrigerator, no distant creak of settling wood. Just silence, deliberate and heavy.

The air carried a faint scent of dust and something sour underneath, the residue of lives interrupted. Each shadow felt positioned, actors frozen in place until the cue arrived to move.

Reed moved cautiously, eyes darting around every corner, peeking into rooms with no idea where anything was. His whole body was buzzing, guided by something more primal than logic.

He crept toward the stairs.

Bedrooms are usually upstairs, he told himself, clinging to the logic. That's where little Colin would be.

Each step carried the weight of the world. He placed his foot down slowly, carefully, his whole body tensed. A thief in a nightmare.

But on the fourth step, the wood betrayed him. A sharp groan splitting the silence like a scream.

Reed froze, breath caught in his throat. He mouthed a curse, his stomach twisting with regret.

From above, a new sound answered back: footsteps. Slow at first, then quicker. Heavy. Purposeful. They carried the weight of a man who had been startled awake and was now stomping toward the unknown intruder in his home.

Reed's chest tightened.

His pulse hammered in his ears so loudly he thought the man would hear it before he saw him. Each footfall from the hallway above was a countdown, and Reed didn't know what it was counting down to.

Then the figure appeared at the top of the stairs, disheveled, confused, eyes narrowed as he struggled to see.

Reed froze in place, caught between fight and flight, his body unwilling to commit to either. He was paralyzed, a man trying to improvise survival in a situation he had no business being in.

It was Colin's father.

"What the hell?" the man demanded, voice sharp with panic and anger.

Recognition flickered across his face, and Reed's stomach dropped.

Reed opened his mouth, wanting to explain. I'm not here to hurt your son; I'm trying to save him. But the words jammed in his throat.

Anything he said would sound ridiculous, suspicious, or insane. For all his philosophies and theories, he had no earthly idea how to handle this moment.

"Sheila! Call the cops!" the father barked, his voice booming down the hallway with the weight of instinct.

He spun toward the bedrooms, every movement raw and protective, the kind of urgency that only came from a parent rushing toward their child. His shoulders squared, his steps quickened, and there was no mistaking where he was headed.

To Colin's room.

Reed stood frozen for a heartbeat, torn between retreat and action. His mind scrambled: *Should I run? Explain? Disappear?*

But the thought of Colin—small, helpless, terrified—burned hotter than reason. If Colin's father was running that way, then that's where Reed needed to be.

He lunged forward, legs pumping, chasing the man down the hall.

Halfway there, the realization struck him. To anyone watching, it would appear he was hunting the father, chasing him into his own son's room. Every step he took made him appear to be the intruder. The absurdity and horror of it twisted inside Reed, but he couldn't stop now.

Just then, the door across the hall swung open: a blur of black moved, a silver flash.

The knife sank deep into Colin's father's chest. He gasped, staggered back, and collapsed with a sickening thud.

"NO!" Reed didn't even realize he was screaming as he lunged, shoulder first, crashing into the killer. The impact sent the figure sprawling backward into the room, hitting the floor with a heavy thud.

The would-be murderer gasped as he hit, the sound sharp and ugly.

Reed scrambled upright, heart hammering, eyes darting wildly as he searched for the crib.

For one sickening instant, he couldn't see it, couldn't find it, panic clawing up his throat. Then, there it was. Against the far wall.

He rushed to it, nearly tripping over his own feet, hands fumbling as he leaned over.

Colin was there. Small, trembling, tear-streaked, wide-eyed with terror. His little arms reached out, not knowing who to trust, confusion flickering across his face.

Reed scanned him in a frenzy: tiny body, clothes intact, no blood. Alive. Safe. Thank God.

"Hey, hey, it's okay," Reed stammered, voice breaking under the weight of relief and fear. "I've got you. You're safe."

Colin sobbed, hiccupping, "Mmm… Mommy?!" His gaze was glassy, pleading, desperate.

Reed opened his mouth, but the answer never came. The knife entered his back. Once. Twice. Again. And again.

The pain was indescribable—searing, white-hot, exploding through his body with each plunge.

It felt like fire and ice colliding inside his spine, every nerve lit up in agony.

He tried to gasp, to cry out, but the sound strangled in his throat. The world shrank to nothing but the wet shock of steel tearing through flesh.

He went down hard, choking on his own breath. A wet gurgle spilled from his lips.

The killer crawled on top of him. Not fast, not frantic, but with a slow, deliberate glide, the way a snake coils itself around prey. His body seemed to flow rather than move, shoulders rolling, spine bending in a fluid, unnatural rhythm.

For a moment, he didn't stab. He just stared. Breathing harshly, teeth clenched, taking inventory of the damage he'd already done.

The rage on his face wasn't only murderous. It was offended, insulted. Reed's intrusion was an abomination, a stranger crashing into a family dinner and demanding a seat at the table.

The killer raised the blade again, intent on finishing the job, when he froze. From the hall, rapid footsteps. Closer. Sharp. Urgent.

He turned his head, squinting into the dark, trying to pinpoint the sound. The approaching presence was a blur, impossible to make out. But the next thing he registered wasn't sight at all. It was impact.

A devastating boot connected with his jaw and cheek, snapping his head sideways with a violent crack. His body flew off Reed and smashed against the far wall before crumpling to the floor.

Detective Maria Voss stood over Reed Ashland's bleeding body, pistol steady, her gaze cold and unflinching.

"Get up!" she growled.

The killer sprang at her, impossibly fast. They both tumbled to the ground. The gun went flying, clattering across the floor.

They rose quickly, both knowing what was at stake.

The killer threw a wild punch.

Maria ducked and countered: one to the ribs, another to the jaw. She hit him hard, then harder. Her fists a storm of fury and training and raw, maternal rage.

He crumbled to the ground a few feet from her. She pounced, pinning him, driving a fist into his throat, another to the temple. She was a mother. She knew what was at stake.

"*You fucker!*" she screamed in protective rage, matching his psychotic fury.

Every blow carried the weight of everybody she'd ever unzipped from a crime scene bag. Every nightmare her sons had woken her from.

She wasn't just trying to stop him—she wanted to erase him. To shatter his skull and drive her fists straight through to the hardwood beneath.

But then two deafening cracks rang out.

Maria's stomach and chest exploded with pain.

The gun had landed tragically close to where Maria had the killer pinned.

The killer had found it.

Maria flew backward, collapsing in a heap.

Colin screamed.

The killer slowly pushed himself upright, every motion jagged with pain.

His breath rattled, shallow and furious, each exhale spitting blood onto the floor.

He took in the room: Maria sprawled and unmoving, Reed broken in a spreading pool of crimson, Colin wailing in the crib and Sheila's voice cracking in terror from somewhere down the hall.

For a moment, his white eyes flared with the thought of finishing it—of lunging for the child and silencing the cries.

But the distant wail of sirens closing brought a grim reminder: his time was gone.

Worse, Maria's fists had left him ruined inside. His ribs felt shattered, every breath a stab of glass. Rage swelled in him, thick and hot, but survival forced his hand. He would have to flee.

He staggered toward the stairs, clumsy and unbalanced.

His feet missed, caught, slipped. Then he pitched forward, crashing down the staircase with a sickening tumble. Each step ripped a new sound from him—inhuman grunts, guttural curses.

At the bottom, he landed in a heap, blood dribbling from his lips, coughing out chunks onto the floorboards.

Still, impossibly, he rose.

He lurched, hunched and wheezing, leaving a grotesque breadcrumb trail of drops and spatters. A map of failure written in gore.

Above it all, Sheila's cries poured out again and again. "Raymond… Raymond… Raymond…" Her husband unmoving.

Maria unmoving.

Reed barely clinging to life.

Her voice was a funeral hymn screamed into the silence.

The killer burst out into the night, disappearing through the back door.

The silence outside was eerie and oppressive. Then it broke. A car engine roared, tires shrieked, and the vehicle tore down the alley in a grotesque, hasty getaway.

Inside, the house was a tomb of sorrow. Colin's sobs had softened into a tired, desperate whimper, "Mommy, Mommy," until even that began to fade, his small cries swallowed by the approaching thunder of sirens.

The sound swelled, filling the night with flashing inevitability, drowning the house in red and blue as the survivors bled into silence.

33

CHAPTER THIRTY-THREE

Fragments in Glass

Maria moved first. Barely.

A twitch. Then a breath as if she was surfacing from deep underwater. Her hand moved to her ribs: tender, already swelling.

Fingers trembling, pain flared white behind her eyes.

Her hands clawed at her vest, fumbling under the shirt, searching for proof she was still intact.

She pressed along her ribs, across her stomach, feeling for the wet warmth of blood, for the tear of skin. Nothing but bruises blooming beneath her fingertips. The Kevlar had caught the rounds, barely.

She was going to hurt for a while, but she wasn't really hurt. Not like Reed.

She looked over. Reed Ashland was lying on the floor, unmoving, soaked with blood.

His body was twisted at an angle no living man should rest in, shirt torn and clinging wet to his skin. The floor beneath him had turned black with spreading blood.

His face was pale, lips parted, eyes half-lidded in the way of someone hovering on the brink—too still, too fragile.

"Ash... land," Maria choked, her voice ragged, breaking against the pain

167

in her chest. It came out as a gasp, strangled by the knot of terror rising in her throat.

She tried to crawl toward him, each inch a war against the ache in her ribs.

He wasn't moving. His body looked slack, hollowed out, already claimed. She knew that look. She'd seen it too many times at crime scenes, and the dread hit her: he was gone. He had to be.

But she couldn't accept it. She forced his name out again, louder this time, pouring what was left of her strength into the syllables.

"Ashland!"

For a heartbeat, silence.

Then a wet, horrible gurgle spilled from his lips, blood bubbling against the floor as his chest twitched. The small, pitiful movement hit her harder than any scream could have.

He wasn't gone yet.

Something inside her cracked open.

She tried to yell but it snagged in her ribs, breaking into half-breaths, half-sobs.

"Help!" she finally managed, her voice ripping free at last—loud, raw, and desperate, cutting through the night.

Sirens howled in every direction, bouncing off the houses. The quiet suburban street was swallowed in red and blue.

Boots thundered on the porch. Radios buzzed sharp static.

The door crashed, swinging open hard and fast.

Maria passed out.

Cops poured inside, moving with a strange mix of precision and panic, training straining against the shock of what they'd walked into.

Orders were barked, flashlights cut across the walls, weapons drawn, then hastily lowered as the nightmare resolved itself into bodies. One officer pressed himself against the wall, gagging at the smell of blood.

Inside, the scene was chaos wrapped in silence: broken glass, blood, bodies.

The floor was slick and treacherous, crimson footprints marking every desperate step.

Radios squawked with clipped, overlapping reports, none of them making sense.

The living and the dying were tangled together, and the cops were left trying to separate one from the other, stitching order onto carnage by sheer will.

***

Medics swarmed him, working fast. His white shirt was now soaked dark. Stab wounds across his back, side, chest. Blood pooled beneath him.

"Multiple stab wounds; puncture trauma. He's crashing!" one of the EMTs shouted.

"Get the stretcher. We're losing him!"

A cop in the hallway muttered into his radio. "I think Detective Voss called this in? Some kind of stakeout, I guess?"

Another voice responded: "What stakeout? What the hell happened here?"

***

A door slammed open. Somewhere else.

The killer burst into his apartment, panting hard, every breath a ragged snarl.

Blood streaked down his cheek, dripping from his chin in ropes, spattering the floor. His eye was already swelling shut, the flesh around it purple and raw, vision reduced to a predator's tunnel.

He slammed the door with a violent kick, the frame shuddering, and staggered inside with the clumsy rage of a beast refusing to fall.

His bloody hand clawed at the wall for balance, smearing long streaks as he pushed forward.

Boots squealed against the tile, tracking crimson prints across his den. He shouldered past a chair, sent it toppling, then crashed into a lamp and hurled it to the floor.

The crash wasn't an accident; it was punishment. The apartment shook with his fury.

"Fuck, fuck…"

He yanked open drawers, tossing clothes, grabbing things: passport, a knife, some folded cash, a burner phone. His fingers slipped in blood. He growled in frustration.

He ripped off his shirt and glared at the fractured reflection staring back. His face looked like a Picasso sketch in red.

He wiped at the blood. It smeared. He wiped again. Useless. A breathless growl turned into a scream.

"Bitch!" he roared, slamming a fist into the mirror.

Cracks spidered across the glass, carving him into fragments.

A demented wail rang out in psychotic frustration.

***

Detective Voss wasn't sure how she'd gotten there; blinding lights, shouts, hands lifting her.

The world moved in jagged fragments, faces too close, voices overlapping in a storm she couldn't make sense of. Her body felt both weightless and impossibly heavy, every breath catching in her ribs.

Anxiety gnawed at her. Where was Colin?

Where was Reed?

The dad?

The thought of him bleeding out somewhere close by made her chest seize harder than the pain of her bruises.

Fear threaded through her confusion, a quiet, icy voice whispering everything was slipping away from her.

She blinked against the flood of lights, eyes burning, but the shapes around her stayed blurred, shadows shifting underwater. All she could do was let herself be carried, dread mounting with every step that pulled her further from the fight.

One moment she was being hauled out of the house, voices and lights crashing around her, and the next she was here. Perched on the edge of the ambulance with no memory of the distance in between. A blanket had been draped over her shoulders, an oxygen tube pressed beneath her nose. Her hands wouldn't stop trembling.

A medic's penlight flashed in her eyes, checking her pupils.

Behind her, a cop with clean boots and too much authority was speaking into a walkie.

"We've got a suspect in custody. Name's Reed Ashland. Looks like he snapped."

Maria's eyes snapped open. She wasn't even sure of where she was, but she knew what she had heard was wrong and reacted.

"No…" she breathed.

She tried to stand. Couldn't.

"Ashland? Colin?" She looked around, bleary. "The father?"

The medic tried to calm her. She swatted his hand away.

"No," louder, more awake, more certain.

***

Back in the killer's bathroom. He was wrapping his ribs with duct tape, shaking. The tape wouldn't stick. Blood oozed beneath it.

He kept glancing at the front door, half expecting sirens. None yet. That made it worse.

He looked at himself.

Not a man.

Something else.

His face was still dented with Maria's fists, his features warped and swelling.

His eyes blazed back at him from the cracked glass; wild, unhinged, trembling with equal parts rage and dread. They jittered in their sockets, pupils darting, the whites streaked red. Crazed. Psychotic.

The stare of a man who wanted to kill the whole world before it could get to him first.

He picked up the bloody rag again, wiped harder.

The cracks in the mirror stared back, carving him into fragments. The cracks didn't just distort his face.

They beckoned.

The face staring back wasn't one; it was many. None of them human.

One eye blinked when the others did not. One face had completely blackened eyes.

The images were all deranged and determined.

Lunatics. All hellbent on revenge.

****

Maria stumbled off the ambulance step. Her boots hit pavement. Her knees buckled, vision tunneling.

She heard the radio again.

"Ashland's being transferred now. Probably DOA. He's our guy."

Another voice came from somewhere else. "Tie it up in a bow," said a flat, bureaucratic voice. "Kid's safe, suspect down. Nice work, boys."

"No!" she hollered for the third time. It cracked something open inside her, a dam breaking.

Nobody was listening. Nobody asked what had happened. They were too eager to wrap it up neat, to make Reed the monster and close the case.

The anger roared through her ribs, mixing with the terror that he might already be dying somewhere without anyone fighting for him. Every second they wasted talking was another second closer to his death.

Some random uniform grabbed her arm and tried to stop her. "Hold on there, sweetheart!"

Her fist shot forward before she even thought about it.

Bone met cartilage with a wet crack. Satisfaction flared—brief, electric—at shutting up the condescension, but it was followed instantly by a spike of pain through her bruised ribs and the sting in her knuckles.

She didn't care. She pulled in a breath that scraped through her throat and pushed on, stumbling but refusing to stop.

"No!" she screamed, spinning toward the cop in charge. Her voice was raw, furious. "That's not right! That's NOT RIGHT!"

The cop turned, startled. "Detective, you need to sit down!"

"Fuck you!" Maria spat. "Ashland saved Colin! He SAVED that little boy!"

"Get her stabilized," the cop muttered. Someone moved toward her.

Maria staggered, eyes swimming.

The world pitched and rolled.

Her knees buckled once, twice, her body refusing to obey. She tried to raise a finger, to point at anyone who would listen, but her arm felt weighted, dragging through water.

"Call… Captain… Solomon Bryans…" she muttered, the words slurred, broken by the jagged rhythm of her breathing.

Then the world tilted for good. She let it.

The pavement rose to meet her, hard and cold, the grit biting into her cheek. The chill of it spread into her skin, almost welcome after the heat of pain searing her ribs.

Her eyelids fluttered, heavy, and the chaos above her blurred into streaks of red and blue.

Voices became echoes, hollow and far away.

She stopped fighting.

***

Somewhere down the road, Reed's ambulance howled toward the hospital.

His eyes fluttered.

Pain dissolved into static.

And somewhere inside that static, something whispered: 3:33.

Somewhere in the dark, Colin cried for his mother.

And somewhere else, a killer packed a bag.

The night wasn't over.

It was only shifting.

34

CHAPTER THIRTY-FOUR

The Space Between Things

Maria sat on an examination table in the hospital. She was anxious, visibly frustrated; the checkup felt like a waste of time after everything that had just happened.

Maria hated hospitals.

A nurse had just finished checking her vitals, but she barely registered the touch. Her ears were tuned elsewhere: outside the room, just down the hallway.

Two voices.

One belonged to Captain Bryans. The other was a younger, worked-up uniform.

She couldn't make out the words, only the rhythm: anger, disbelief, blame volleying back and forth. She knew her boss well and he was getting hot under the collar by the sound of it.

Then silence.

The door opened.

Captain Bryans stepped in, jaw tight, eyes already assessing.

"You okay?" he asked.

Maria ignored the question. "Is Ashland going to be charged?"

Bryans sighed, rubbing the back of his neck, his eyes lingering on the

174

bruises peeking above her collar. "Let's talk about you first. You just got shot."

"It grazed the vest. I'm sore, but I've been worse." Her words came fast and clipped.

"Is Ashland going to be charged?" she pressed quickly, not giving him space to pivot away.

Bryans's brow furrowed. He was studying her, the tightness in her jaw, the restless fire in her eyes. He wanted to tell her to slow down, to care about herself for once.

But she was already leaning forward, shoulders tense. The question about Ashland was the only thing on her mind.

She was still simmering over how the uniforms had been so ready to paint Reed as the monster.

The pause stretched, heavy.

She looked at him.

He looked back.

A silent standoff.

His concern versus her fury. Neither willing to blink first.

After a beat, he gave in. "With your statement, probably not." Bryans didn't bother hiding his disappointment. He didn't like Ashland. Never had. He was hoping to pin the case on him.

Not just to close the case. He wanted the killings to stop, and everything seemed to fit Ashland to a tee.

"What the hell happened?" he asked impatiently.

Maria sat up straighter, eager to tell her story.

"I was staking out Ashland, as we discussed. I followed him to Glendale Heights. Watched him go inside. I went in too. Upstairs, he was being attacked. The suspect had a knife. Stabbed the father, stabbed Reed. I stepped in. Fought him. He got my gun, shot me, and ran."

"And Ashland?" Bryans probed.

"Saved the kid. He didn't do anything wrong," Maria explained.

"From what I could tell, he interrupted the killer. I think he must've woken up the father, who was spooked and ran to the boy's room. The killer was there and stabbed the dad. Then stabbed Ashland. That's when I stepped in. Used all the damn excessive force I could on the bastard."

She leaned forward, eyes sharp, unable to hold back. "How's Colin? The father? Ashland?"

Bryans didn't answer right away.

He leaned back slightly, running the pieces together, reshaping the theory he'd been working off of all night. For the first time, the picture of Ashland as the suspect cracked, leaving something messier in its place.

"Captain!" Maria snapped, her voice rising with impatience.

His gaze snapped to her; his tone curt. "Colin was unharmed. The father's hurt, but he's going to be okay. And Reed…" He paused, jaw tight. "No one knows. He's in bad shape. Everyone was surprised he was still alive when they brought him in."

Silence settled between them.

Maria looked down at her hands, twisting the blanket in her lap, her chest aching with more than just bruises. Worry pressed into every part of her: Colin's cries still echoing in her ears, Reed's blood still hot in her memory.

Sadness clung heavy and suffocating.

Bryans leaned back in his chair, rubbing his temple, staring at nothing in particular.

For a moment, he wasn't the impatient captain. He was just a man trying to make sense of a puzzle that refused to fit. Ashland wasn't the monster he thought he had in custody. Which meant the monster was still out there.

He exhaled slow, the sound rough, and forced his thoughts back to where they should've been all along: the victims.

The little boy who'd nearly lost everything.

The father stabbed in his own home.

Reed bleeding out because he got in the way of a knife.

Still… a question gnawed at him: If Ashland was innocent, then how the hell did he know so much about this case?

He broke the silence first.

Bryans crossed his arms. "What the hell was he doing there?" he asked.

"I don't know," she said, more quietly.

She wanted to believe it didn't matter. That it was enough he had tried to help. But even she couldn't explain it.

"But I saw it. Reed wasn't the attacker. He was trying to stop him. He was checking the little kid to see if he was okay when the guy put a knife in his back."

Maria turned her head, pleadingly, toward Bryans.

"Sol," she said. She rarely used his first name. "He was trying to help."

Bryans closed his eyes tiredly and sighed. They both paused for a moment and Maria looked at her captain sympathetically. She knew the worlds he lived in and the responsibilities he juggled. It wore on him.

"What's Ashland's condition?" she asked earnestly.

Bryans shook his head slightly. "Critical. Surgery."

He didn't say it with malice, but he didn't say it with warmth either. Maria felt her jaw tighten.

A knock at the door. Another officer entered, clipboard in hand, face too eager for the weight of the moment.

"Captain, Detective, we got a lot from the scene. Prints, blood, and the knife the suspect dropped. A kitchen knife, not the same type used for the carvings."

Bryans frowned. "So he's got more than one."

"Yeah. We're running the prints now. Also, footage. Street cams. South alley behind the house. Vehicle enters just before the attack. Leaves from the north side right after. Black Hyundai Sonata. We're enhancing the stills, trying to pull plates now."

Bryans nodded. "Good work, officer. Thanks."

The officer left.

Maria swung her legs off the bed.

"Where the hell are you going?" Bryans snapped.

"The station," she said, already putting her jacket on.

"You need rest," Bryans advised.

"I need a composite sketch drawn. While the memory's fresh."

Bryans sighed, long enough to make a point. "You're going to fall over in ten minutes."

"I'll fall over after the sketch," Maria said, walking out.

Bryans stared at the door after it closed.

"Why do I bother?" he muttered to himself.

***

Fluorescent lights hummed above the surgical table. Gloved hands moved fast: scalpel, suction, clamp. Blood pooled, wiped away, pooled again. Gauze. Cauterize. Stitch. A heart monitor dipped. A nurse adjusted the IV. Time melted into breathless urgency. Machines hummed; life and whatever waited beyond waged their quiet war.

Reed Ashland lay still, his chest sliced open, a team of doctors and nurses working in efficient silence.

Death and hope played their own brand of chess.

No one was watching from the gallery above.

Except for a reflection in the window of the observation deck. Just for a second, there he was.

A Man in a Charcoal Suit.

Expression unreadable.

Hands behind his back.

A whisper that didn't belong to the room curled against the glass. "Not yet."

And then he was gone.

The monitor beeped on.

35

CHAPTER THIRTY-FIVE

The Perfect Table

It was a hallway. Or a tunnel. Or maybe a throat.

A long, dark, pulsating cavern alive with dread.

Reed moved through it without walking, dragged by a current that didn't exist. The walls, if they were walls, breathed softly. A sleeping animal dreaming in red. They undulated. Whispered. A flicker of fluorescent light buzzed overhead, followed by a smear of static that bent space.

At the end of the corridor, mirrors floated in midair. Some shattered; others smooth and rippling like water. Reed saw his reflection in each.

Wounded. Lost. Drunk. Younger. Older. Terrified.

In one, he was holding Emily. In another, he watched her vanish in a hospital bed. In another still, Maria stood beside him, gun raised, eyes burning.

No words fit the storm inside him. Each image split him open in a different place.

The sight of Emily was a knife twisting in his ribs, a reminder of love he could never hold again. The hospital vision gutted him, dragging up helplessness so raw, it threatened to peel the skin from his soul.

Reed felt himself fragment alongside the mirrors, his heart scattering into a dozen selves he could no longer gather.

Was he the drunk, the coward, the grieving father, the desperate man reaching for answers in shadows? Or was he all of them, condemned to flicker between reflections forever?

He reached out desperately, as if the reflections were a life raft in a vast, treacherous sea of sorrow. The mirror shattered at his touch.

The shards didn't fall. They drifted upward, rearranging into something new. A window. A window looking into a room he didn't recognize.

Reed pressed closer, and the glass or whatever it was grew warm, then cold, then clammy.

His eyes tried to focus, but the room inside refused to hold still; walls stretched and shrank, colors bled together and then drained to black and white.

A smell leaked through the seam: burnt hair mixed with lavender, sweet and foul at once. His ears rang with a low electrical hum, yet beneath it he swore he heard the clink of silverware and the static buzz of a detuned radio overlapping in grotesque harmony.

The window was no window at all, he realized; it was a wound, a place where meaning itself had bled out. His body recoiled, but something deeper pulled him forward, whispering that this was the only direction left.

He crawled through.

Both feet down carefully. Now he stood on a lake.

Or above it.

The water reflected nothing: no moon, no stars, no Reed. Just a blank surface, polished obsidian.

In the distance, a child laughed. Then cried. Then laughed again. The sounds echoed wrong, dragged across metal.

The sound hooked something deep in him, tugging at nerves older than memory.

It wasn't just laughter or crying. It was both at once, a twisted chorus that bent joy into grief until the difference no longer mattered.

Reed felt it scrape against his soul, leaving him hollowed, vibrating with a terror he couldn't name.

"Dr. Ashland."

The voice came from behind him, soft and musical.

He didn't so much hear it as feel it. The syllables drifted in the air, seeping through his skin, threading into his pores. Each word bypassed his ears and lodged directly inside him, blooming in the hollow spaces of his chest, something living inside his blood.

He turned and saw her.

She was faceless but feminine. Her dress flowed, embroidered with shifting symbols that flickered between language and madness. She spoke, but not verbally. The words appeared in Reed's head as images.

"You are somewhere between stitch and seam," she said. "A thought not yet spoken."

Reed tried to speak but no sound came. He felt a dry heave in his throat.

She tilted her head, but not in any human way.

Her neck bent, resembling a hinge that didn't belong to bone or muscle. The motion was slow, deliberate, grotesquely graceful, time stuttering around the gesture.

Reed's lips finally moved. "What... what do you want from me?"

The words didn't leave his mouth so much as rip their way through him. Speaking felt like his brain was being pulled apart. Every thought latched to a different invisible fish, each darting in a different direction through black water. His skull throbbed with the tug-of-war.

The sound of his own voice came out broken, refracted, a choir of himself screaming underwater.

The lake shuddered in answer. Its black surface rippled without wind, waves convulsing, mirroring his panic. Each tremor spread outward into the void until the horizon itself bent.

Above, the sky flickered. Blue for an instant, then static gray, then a bruised violet that bled across. The mirrored fragments overhead began to chime against one another, a brittle, hollow music that scraped along Reed's teeth.

With every word that left him, the world fractured more: symbols bled out of the faceless woman's dress, twisting into shapes that almost resembled letters before crumbling into ash midair.

His emotions weren't his alone anymore. They were environmental. Fear became weather, pain became architecture.

She leaned in, her breath cold as mirrors. Sharp, metallic, with the faint scent of dust and wet stone. An exhale through a mausoleum.

"You know who. The one with many faces carved into one. The boy in the black coat. The butcher of memory. He watches."

Flashes detonated in Reed's skull.

Colin's scream stabbed his ears.

Maria's blood tasted like copper on his tongue.

Mr. Morrow at the foot of his bed was a weight on his chest, suffocating. The man in the charcoal suit flickered inside a void that pressed against his skin, prickling every nerve.

And the clock stopping at 3:33; its silence rang louder than any explosion, vibrating in his bones until he felt hollow.

"Why is this happening to me?" he felt more than said. His mouth wouldn't open properly, language no longer belonged to his throat. The words dripping from memory into the air where they hung.

"Because you're awake," she whispered.

The phrase struck him hard. His spirit blazed with a realization so immense it burned beyond comprehension. An awareness both terrifying and sublime, radiant with meaning he couldn't decipher.

She floated backward, eyes dimming. "You must follow the thread."

Reed wanted to scream questions, but none came. His language wasn't just absent, it had been stolen. The alphabet of his mind scattered, vowels dissolving into mist, consonants curdled into static.

The lake beneath him split with a shriek, glass dragging across bone. Black water fissured in jagged lines that glowed white for an instant, and then the surface itself howled. It was a guttural, inhuman cry that reverberated through Reed's ribs.

Then, he fell.

The scream cut off, and the air itself yanked into silence.

And instantly, silence. A restaurant. Warmth. Jazz music curling through the air, low and dreamt.

Velvet booths, candlelight, clinking glasses: the patrons had no faces. Just soft gray ovals. They chewed without mouths. Forks rose and fell with mechanical rhythm.

The host stood at the front. Ominous.

The killer. Clean-shaven. Smiling wide. Apron tied like a noose.

His hands rested on the podium, fingers tapping out a rhythm too mechanical to be human.

"Would you like a seat, sir?" the host asked, his voice smooth yet hollow.

Reed nodded slowly, unsure why. His head moved before the thought formed. The motion wasn't his. It belonged to the room, to the will of something watching.

"I have the perfect table for you… it's in the basement. You'll love it." He smiled in a way that made Reed's skin crawl.

He gestured to the back hallway.

Two black cellar doors groaned as they swung open on their own, the hinges shrieking. The sound didn't echo. It bled, seeping into the velvet hush of the restaurant until every faceless patron paused mid-chew, forks frozen in the air.

Beyond them, a void darker than night. Not absence, not shadow, something thicker. The darkness had substance, an essence that breathed outward in slow, sticky pulses.

It was beckoning, not with words but with gravity itself, tugging at him the way a grave tugs at a body.

Whispers floated up from that throat of black.

They didn't just enter his ears. They seeped straight into his brain, burrowing behind his eyes, vibrating against the fragile seams of his skull. Each murmur twisted a different nerve: fear, longing, grief.

The more they came, the more the restaurant twitched around him. Light bulbs buzzing too bright, shadows thickening and collapsing, the faceless patrons glitching mid-motion.

At first the whispers blurred together, static-filled, like someone trying to reach him through a phone with bad reception. A garbled voice, broken syllables. He didn't even recognize his own name. But the signal sharpened, word by word, the static thinning into clarity.

"Ree…"

"Ree…d…"

And then—clean, undeniable:

"Reed."

The sound struck him. His name. His identity, anchored. For the first time in forever, he knew who he was.

"All will be well," said the host with the killer's smile. His voice carried the theatrical lilt of a ringmaster but twisted. The introduction to a circus no sane soul would ever enter, a show where the performers bled and the audience never left. "Just go inside."

Reed hesitated. A creeping sensation filled him. The whispers grew louder. They spoke in riddles. Some begged. Some hissed.

"Go inside!" the host snapped. His smile faded into a grimace.

Reed stepped back.

"Go inside, Dr. Ashland," the killer growled, voice now deep and inhuman. Robotic and beastly all at once.

His ears popped, sudden and sharp, and he felt hot breath brush the back of his neck.

"Dr. Ashland, we're waiting for you," he heard behind him.

And then, another voice. Quiet, intimate, threading through the chaos. Mr. Morrow. Whispering his name in the calmest tone Reed had ever known. Reed.

The word steadied him. He opened his mouth and whispered back, "Reed." His voice low, deliberate, each syllable crisp.

The effect was instant. The entire room convulsed; walls warping, chandeliers swaying, faceless patrons jittering in spastic loops of motion, their cutlery clattering in distorted rhythm.

The demented host froze, staring at him with venom. "You son of a bitch!" he spat. The words sharp enough to splinter the air. He didn't seem to be talking to Reed.

Everything began to twitch and crack—ceilings buckling, the cellar doors snapping open wider with a groan.

CHAPTER THIRTY-FIVE

Reed turned and ran.

***

In the real world, monitors beeped steadily. Tubes hissed and clicked. Reed lay unconscious on the hospital bed, a tube down his throat, chest bandaged and pale.

Reed Ashland was clinging to life in ways most people would never understand.

36

CHAPTER THIRTY-SIX

The Gray of Morning

Captain Solomon Bryans pushed through the front doors of the 18th Precinct just after 6 a.m. The sky outside was still more gray than blue. The kind of early that made everything feel like it hadn't quite decided what kind of day it wanted to be.

The streets were damp from a night rain, steam curling out of the grates, and the city moved in slow motion: delivery trucks idling and a few tired faces clutching coffee cups.

He hadn't slept much. A few hours on the couch in his office, maybe. He'd gone home, poured a drink, stared at the wall, and then driven back. Habit. Guilt. Duty. He wasn't sure anymore.

The weariness clung to him, every step heavier than the last—a man edging closer to the cliff of burnout without quite falling. He was halfway down the main corridor when Officer Nolan flagged him.

"Captain. Morning."

Bryans grunted in reply, not slowing. This early bird didn't want a worm.

"Voss just left."

That stopped him. He turned. "What?"

"She came in around four. Wanted a composite sketch drawn up."

"Of the suspect?" Bryans said, immediately realizing the stupidity of his question.

"Yeah. Not much to go on. Detective Voss said it was dark and everything happened fast. Sketch artist did what he could," the officer replied, eager to please the captain.

Bryans pinched the bridge of his nose. "When does that woman sleep?"

Nolan shrugged with a sympathetic smile. "Not this week, apparently."

Bryans sighed and waved for the folder Nolan was holding. He flipped it open as they walked. It was just a rough pencil drawing: vague facial structure, short dark hair, angry eyes. It could be anyone.

"This won't get us far," Bryans muttered.

"We're still working on the street cam footage," Nolan said. "Footage from the alley behind the kid's house is promising. Should have a plate soon."

"And the blood?" Bryans asked.

"Already sent to the lab. Rush order. Could be later today for something surface-level. Anything deeper or more precise could take weeks."

Bryans desperately wanted something, anything, from this latest crime scene. A lead, a scrap, the smallest thread to pull. He was sick of chasing a ghost who had already proven he was willing to take the life of a toddler.

Bryans sighed and nodded, then closed the folder. "Prints?"

Nolan hesitated. "Nothing."

Bryans stopped walking again. His stomach dropped. "Come again?"

"The prints we got, we ruled out the family. And we ruled out Ashland's prints already. He's in the system from a DUI years back."

Bryans shook his head, jaw set. "Of course he is."

"The unknown set—we ran them and nothing came back. Looks like the killer has never been arrested for anything," Nolan added.

"Great." Bryans clapped the folder shut and handed it back.

For a moment, his eyes drifted into a thousand-yard stare. He usually didn't let things get to him on the clock. He saved that for a beer at home late at night, but this case earned an exception, if only for a few seconds.

"Thanks, Nolan. Keep me posted."

As Nolan turned to leave, he paused. "One more thing. Voss said she's going to talk to Ashland's ex-wife. Claire."

Bryans did not respond immediately, just looked past Nolan toward the front doors where Voss must have exited not long ago. She didn't stop. Not even to breathe.

She was stubborn as hell and too good to lose.

"Of course she is," Bryans muttered. "She ever consider taking a damn nap?"

"Dunno," the officer replied nonchalantly. "Didn't want to make the suggestion honestly," he said. A very small smirk formed at the corners of his lips.

Bryans bowed his head and gave a subtle chuckle. "Yeah, I don't blame you."

Nolan raised his eyebrows in something close to agreement and moved on.

Bryans stood in the hallway for a few moments longer, thinking.

He agreed with her. Ashland was the key. Maybe not the killer, but close to whatever this whole goddamn thing was. If Voss was chasing the personal angle, maybe he could pull on something more professional.

Bryans turned and started walking again. He pulled out his phone and started searching for something.

It was time to visit the University of Chicago.

Time to see what kind of man Dr. Reed Ashland used to be.

Before the bottle. Before the bodies. Before the mirrors.

37

CHAPTER THIRTY-SEVEN

What We Carry

The coffee shop was quiet, too quiet for a weekday afternoon in Chicago. Maria didn't mind. The lull in the air matched the heaviness in her chest. It was equal parts residual pain and anxiety. The lights hummed faintly above, and through the wide front windows the gray sky pressed down on the city, turning the passing cars into shadows sliding through a muted aquarium.

Claire Ashland sat across from her, hands wrapped around a ceramic mug. She was younger than Maria expected, or maybe just softer. She had the look of someone who'd once been full of light, and had learned, carefully, how to survive after it flickered out.

For a fleeting moment, Maria saw Emily's features in her. The same delicate jawline, the same searching eyes.

"You wanted to talk about Reed," Claire said, not unkindly.

The name left Claire's lips, sending ripples of memory through her: nights of laughter, days of confusion, arguments that bled into embraces. Each recollection carried its own sting or sweetness until she felt she was drowning in the whole spectrum of what it meant to love someone flawed and brilliant.

Maria nodded. "I want to understand him better."

Maria had no doubt Reed was innocent, but she was still trying to figure out what was going on. And for her, that started with Dr. Reed Ashland and his story.

Claire sighed and glanced out the window.

Maria's question made her chest ache with the weight of sorrow and old disappointments. Yet beneath it, so faint it shamed her, was the ache of a warmth she thought she had buried. An echo she wished she could silence.

"We met in college. I was pre-law. He was, well, he was everything. Philosophy major, but he took physics, psychology, anthropology… you name it. He was brilliant, exhausting, electric. Always five steps ahead of a conversation and completely lost in his own head at the same time."

Maria didn't interrupt. She listened intently, every word filing itself away. Not just because she needed answers to stop a killer, but because she wanted to understand Reed himself.

Something in her own past made her gravitate toward him. It was unvoiced but undeniable, a tenderness not of romance but of recognition. A mother's reverence for a man who had stood in front of the knife meant for a child.

"We got married right after graduation. It felt right. Chaotic but right. He had this… energy. To him, the world was made of puzzles waiting to be solved. It was fun. Even beautiful sometimes."

She paused, stirring her coffee, though it didn't need stirring.

"When Emily was born, things got harder. He loved her. God, he loved her. But he struggled. Parenthood is a kind of tethering, you know?"

Maria nodded and gave a sympathetic smile. She knew.

"Reed didn't want to be tethered. Not in a selfish way, but in a cosmic one. He wanted to know what was out there more than what was right here. And Emily… she grounded him. That both saved him and broke him."

Maria finally spoke. "Cancer?" She already knew. She subtly touched the silver ring beneath her shirt.

Claire nodded, eyes going glossy. "Leukemia. She was ten. It was fast. Ugly. Reed tried to be strong, but… he unraveled. He drank more. Talked about signs, messages, symbols. Started reading these obscure books. UFOs, interdimensional theories, ancient civilizations. It wasn't a hobby anymore.

It was a religion."

"Was he ever violent?" Maria asked gently.

Claire shook her head, firm. "Good lord, no. Never. Not once. Not with me. Not with Emily. He was… fractured, not dangerous." Her voice was starting to quiver slightly.

"He started seeing patterns in everything. Dreamed of Emily. Said she was trying to tell him something from the other side. I begged him to get help, but …"

"But?" Maria prompted.

"I couldn't do it anymore," Claire said softly. "I loved him. Still do, in some strange, faded way. But I had to leave. For my own sanity."

Detective Voss had encountered plenty of darkness in her time on the force, but it hadn't deadened her empathy. She took pride in that, always determined to hold onto it.

"You know," Maria began, "he saved a little boy's life. Took a knife in the back to do it."

Claire covered her mouth as emotion hit her. Her eyes squeezed shut, and she nodded, shoulders trembling.

The thought of Reed, broken but still capable of such selfless courage, cracked something open inside her.

The silence that followed was gentle, but heavy. Maria felt it too.

Claire's grief was raw and honest, and it pulled at something deep within her. She thought of Emily: gone too soon, a marriage in ruins, and for the first time, Maria felt the ache of that loss. She thought of her own boys, Eli and Tommy, and a sudden chill crept over her at the mere thought of losing either of them.

She blinked back her own tears, stood, placing a hand briefly on Claire's shoulder.

The gesture carried no words, only an understanding. Two women bound by the impossible weight of family and loss, even if their stories were different.

"Thank you," she said.

Claire managed a faint smile, the kind that was genuine yet trembling, already losing its battle against the tears gathering in her eyes.

"Is he going to be okay?" Claire managed to get out over the heavy thump in her throat.

Maria bowed her head and closed her eyes briefly. Trying to be honest yet sensitive was always the toughest part of her job. She sighed with dejection and said, "I don't know. He's in bad shape."

Claire broke down briefly and caught herself. She wiped a tear away. Maria felt herself start to cry again and fought it off by looking away.

"Tell him…" She paused and looked away, trying to gather her composure.

"I'm proud of him. For saving that boy," she finally said. She lowered her face away from Maria, not wanting her to see the breakdown about to happen.

Maria nodded, squeezed Claire's shoulder once more, and turned to leave. Her face was set in the practiced mask of a tough cop, but the shimmer in her eyes glowed with compassion.

She didn't look back, not because she didn't care, but because she cared too much.

As she pushed the door open, a stiff, brisk fall wind barreled in. It was one of those Chicago gusts that cut through coats and rattled the glass in its frame.

The sharp air pressed against her as she stepped through the door.

She didn't flinch.

Some pain was colder than weather.

38

CHAPTER THIRTY-EIGHT

Fractures and Folds

Reed lay still beneath the thin hospital blanket, wires sprouting from his chest. Monitors blinked with clinical indifference. The ventilator's hiss was steady, mechanical, breathing for him, but hollow.

His face was pale, lips parted slightly, eyes sunken but peaceful. Without the muted pulse on the monitor, he might have been mistaken for dead.

The door opened without a sound, but the air shifted as if the room itself had inhaled. Space bent for a moment, then let her through.

A nurse entered. Or at least, she wore the shape of one.

Her scrubs were soft blue, perfectly pressed. Hair pinned in an old-fashioned style that felt decades out of place. She carried no clipboard, no chart. Just a presence that unsettled and comforted all at once. It wasn't merely out of place in the hospital; it felt out of place in reality, her edges not quite matching the frame.

She approached his bedside without hesitation.

She stood for a long while, looking down at him.

Not scrutinizing, not analyzing, but watching. Waiting.

There was no clinical detachment in her face.

She sat; the motion was slow, ritualistic.

Her gaze never left Reed, steady and protective.

And she never said a word.

***

Maria waited outside the school gates, rubbing the weariness out of her eyes. All the coffee in the world hadn't helped. She'd been up for nearly forty-eight hours. No real sleep, just restless, endless vigilance.

But this moment was hers. The rare times she picked her kids up were treasures, and today was one of those days.

She made a point to do it today, because she knew what she was in the middle of.

Eli and Tommy burst from the doors, their faces lighting up the moment they saw her. They didn't expect her; most days, someone else was there. But they loved the surprise.

There was nothing that matched childhood enthusiasm.

Eli, always quiet but sharp, closed the gap first. His eyes held something older than his thirteen years: a knowing, a weight. He smiled softly, but Maria could tell he was reading her, sensing the exhaustion beneath her smile.

Tommy followed, a whirlwind of words and energy, oblivious to the heaviness in the air. He jabbered about his day: about a new game, a funny teacher, a lost shoe. His voice a stream that didn't stop, even as no one really caught the details.

Maria smiled at her sons' different energies and asked Eli how his day was.

"Oh, you know. Not as bad as yours." His remark carried a strange weight for a child, tinged with the perceptiveness and maturity of an adult who had already learned too much.

Maria blinked, caught off guard. He smirked at her, and she felt both sadness and pride at once.

She hugged him tightly. "There's a bad man out there," she whispered. "And I'm going to find him."

Eli met her gaze, steady and wise. "I know, Mom. You'll get him."

She smiled, even as tears began to press behind her eyes. "You're so damn smart, you know that?"

Eli shrugged, playing it cool, but the pride in his eyes gave him away.

Tommy finally noticed the quiet between them and stopped mid-sentence. Both Maria and Eli turned to get his attention. Tommy grinned and threw his arms around Maria.

The hug was warm and sudden, pressing against the ache in her chest.

"Go get him, Mom. He's bad. I love you."

How the hell did he know what was going on? Maria thought, laughing quietly to herself.

Her heart cracked wide open. She blinked back tears and whispered goodbye, hating this part but knowing she had no choice.

As she released them both from her sentimental hug, Tommy added with unshakable enthusiasm, "And when you get home, we'll have some… Chicken nuggets!"

Eli smirked and let out a small chuckle, glancing at Tommy, trying hard not to break into a full laugh. Only Tommy could pull that from him so easily, and irritate him just as quickly, a constant reminder of how bound together they really were.

Maria laughed and cried all at once, and her heart was about to explode.

✳✳✳

Captain Bryans stood in the echoing hallway of the University of Chicago's philosophy building, surrounded by oak-paneled walls and dusty academic reverence. The place smelled of old paper, worn tweed, and just a hint of smugness. Tall arched windows let in slanted bars of pale light.

He hated it.

He respected education, admired intellect, but he despised the pretense, the condescension of men who thought a little bit of knowledge made them better than everyone else.

Dr. Desmond Edwards emerged from his office with the kind of smile that had been polished in faculty lounges and tenure meetings: polite, hollow, sharpened with intellect but dulled by ego.

"Captain Bryans, yes? I appreciate your coming by. Always happy to help law enforcement, though I admit this is a little… unexpected."

"That's right," Bryans said, already annoyed. The surroundings reeked of self-importance. So did Edwards.

Edwards gestured into his office, filled with shelves of thick-spined books and carefully curated degrees. They sat. The doctor crossed one leg over the other with practiced ease. Bryans followed and sat.

"What can I do for you, Captain?" Edwards asked, his smugness just barely hidden behind civility. Bryans' disdain was buried just as deep.

"Just trying to get a better sense of Reed Ashland," Bryans said. "Thought someone who worked closely with him might help fill in the picture."

Edwards looked down and let out a long, careful sigh. The kind that carried the weight of old irritation.

It was clear he'd tried to file Ashland away, to bury the memory under coursework and committees. He didn't like talking about him, but professionalism demanded he play the part, and the act itself seemed to sour his expression even further.

"Oh, Reed was, well, brilliant, of course. A gifted mind. He had a way of pulling ideas from thin air and spinning them into something fascinating. Very … Socratic, in that way."

Bryans raised an eyebrow. "That sounds like a compliment."

"It is," Edwards said, though his smile wavered. A man forcing medicine down his own throat.

"But brilliance and professionalism are not always the same thing. Reed was… erratic. He couldn't focus. He'd get obsessed with fringe ideas: metaphysics, consciousness theory, what he called 'dimensional bleed.' Interesting coffee shop talk, but hardly academic rigor."

Bryans nodded slowly. "And that was a problem for you, I take it?" For once, he felt a strange flicker of himself standing in Reed's corner.

Edwards sniffed lightly, the idea offended him.

"It became one. He started turning lectures into improvisational theater. Bringing in students to talk about dreams, synchronicities. He'd quote esoteric mystics instead of Kant. Not to mention the drinking."

Bryans leaned forward slightly. "On the job?"

"Yes," Edwards replied quickly, almost relieved to have a more concrete failing to point to.

"During lectures, he'd slur. Even the hungover students began whispering about it."

Bryans wasn't surprised. He'd already seen enough of Reed to know alcohol clung to him like a second skin, but he kept his expression flat, unwilling to give Edwards the satisfaction of agreement.

"And you fired him?" Bryans asked sharply.

Edwards hesitated. "He took a leave. At first voluntary. Eventually… it was for the best."

Something shifted behind Bryans's eyes, a flicker of sympathy for Reed he wanted to choke down but didn't. His dislike for Edwards was strong enough that, just this once, he allowed himself to side with Ashland.

"Funny," he said. "Everyone else I've talked to described him as troubled but kind. Empathetic. Sounded like someone dealing with pain, not someone causing it."

Bryans held Edwards with an unblinking stare, the kind of look that could strip a man of his excuses. For all his degrees and cultivated superiority, Edwards was visibly unsettled.

Dr. Edwards shifted in his seat. "Look, I'm sure he meant well. But academia isn't a therapy session. And frankly, Reed often mistook being unconventional for being right. That's a dangerous line in our field."

Bryans continued his tough cop stare.

He stood, rising with a quiet indignation that came less from the words exchanged and more from Edwards' very presence. "Well, thank you for your time, doctor."

Bryans had had enough of the man's smug air to last a lifetime. Across the desk, Edwards straightened as well, relief flickering across his polished features as the ordeal of this visit was finally nearing its end.

Edwards offered a handshake. "Of course. I hope you find what you're looking for."

Bryans didn't take the hand. He just stared at Edwards a little longer than necessary, letting the silence stretch until it grew awkward. Something he did on purpose, and enjoyed more than he'd admit.

Edwards shifted under the weight of it, his polished composure cracking just slightly.

"Yeah," Bryans finally muttered. "Me too."

He walked out of the office with the growing sense that if Reed Ashland had enemies, they wore elbow patches and called it intellectual integrity.

***

The hospital smelled of antiseptic and sorrow.

Maria would never get used to hospitals.

She moved down the corridor with the cautious tension of someone who'd seen too much and still didn't trust what was around the corner. Every door looked the same. Every hallway hummed with the same light and quiet dread.

Her ribs ached with every step, bruises beneath Kevlar and memory.

Room 413. This was supposed to be it.

She stood outside it for a moment, hand hovering over the handle.

She'd come here for answers, or at least the promise of them.

The city was full of whispers, mirrors that seemed to lie, clocks that broke in unison, people saying things they shouldn't know. It was all too much, too strange, and she wasn't sure anymore what she believed. Certainly not everything Reed Ashland claimed, but dismissing him outright felt dangerous too.

He had something. She couldn't name it, couldn't trust it, but she knew it was a piece of the lock they were trying to crack.

After all that had happened, she needed to be here.

To see for herself that he was alive. To check on him. To look at him with her own eyes and know that when he finally woke up, he might have the words to pull this case into focus. Until then, she had to wait. And she hated waiting.

She pushed the door open.

Reed Ashland lay still beneath white sheets, pale against the cold blue light of machines. Tubes ran from his arms. His chest rose and fell, mechanical, but real. Barely real. A body caught between worlds.

Maria stepped closer.

For a long time, she didn't say anything. Just stood there, arms crossed, eyes locked on him like she was trying to pass a test she hadn't studied for.

This man.

This mess of a man.

This strange, broken genius who believed in conspiracy theories, UFOs, alternate realities—bled for a boy he barely knew.

He was the case personified, every contradiction made flesh. An enigma wrapped in a riddle, cliché as it sounded.

She exhaled. She backed up and leaned against the sink behind her.

Above the sink was a mirror.

"I don't know what the hell you are," she said quietly. "Victim. Suspect. Prophet. All of the above?"

No answer. Just the soft beep of monitors and the quiet, almost imperceptible whisper of breath.

Maria stared at him, caught in the clash of images she'd pieced together: Reed the loving, doting father and husband from the fragments she'd heard from Claire.

Reed the respected academic with a restless yet brilliant mind.

Reed the paranoid drunk drowning in bottles and theories.

All of them were true. All of them were him. And none of them told her which version of the man lay before her now.

"You said you saw things," she murmured. "Things in mirrors. Things in dreams. And I wanted to laugh... or punch you." The thought made her pause and laugh internally for a brief moment.

"But then you took a knife for that kid. And I started thinking... maybe you weren't so full of shit after all."

Behind her, the mirror shifted slightly.

She leaned forward off the sink. A weird feeling crept up in her, barely perceptible, but growing.

She stepped closer, moving to the foot of the bed, and leaned over slightly, focusing her words on the unconscious Reed. Some part of her believed he might still hear her through the fog.

"You'd better wake up, Ashland. Because I need answers. And I think you're the only one left who's even asking the right questions."

She hated saying it, even silently, but she might actually believe him.

She stayed there for a long while. Watching. Waiting. Thinking.

The mirror behind her was watching too.

***

Captain Bryans yanked open the door of his car with more force than necessary, still grinding his molars from the meeting with Dr. Desmond Edwards. That smug son of a bitch had smiled his way through twenty minutes of academic doublespeak.

He slid behind the wheel, then paused.

Something was tucked beneath his wiper.

A ticket.

"Aw, come on," he muttered.

He stepped back out, snatched it up. It wasn't city-issued. Wrong color. No emblem.

Just a thick white piece of paper, folded into thirds. On it was a room number: B172-P. And a winding, overly wordy description of how to find it in the lower levels of the psychology building.

At the bottom, scribbled in ink that looked like it had nearly torn through the page:

Come alone.

Bryans sighed and rubbed his temples. "Oh, for the love of…"

He wanted to crumple the note, toss it in the nearest trash can, and forget it ever touched his windshield. But instincts sharpened over decades told him better. He couldn't just walk away, not when Reed Ashland's name was already circling in too many dark corners.

He let the irritation burn off, shoved the paper into his pocket, and forced himself past the annoyance, following the winding directions toward the room.

The office was half-forgotten, wedged between a disused research lab and a storage closet. The hallway lights flickered overhead. Bryans opened the door slowly, hand near his hip, just in case.

The room smelled faintly of dry-erase markers and Red Bull.

Inside stood a woman, late twenties or early thirties, Vietnamese-American, maybe five-foot-nothing, drowning in a blazer too big for her frame, trying to avoid being mistaken for a student. Round glasses slid down her nose, and underneath the blazer she wore jeans, Converse, and a faded T-shirt with some obscure band logo.

She froze when he entered, eyes wide behind round glasses.

"You're Bryans," she said, a question and an accusation. "Detective. No, Captain. Sorry. Captain. I read the title in the faculty alert. Sorry."

Bryans shut the door behind him. "You wanna tell me what this is?"

"Oh! Yes. Okay. So… hi. I'm Erin Tran. I'm an assistant professor in the psych department here and I… I used to work with Dr. Ashland. Well, not with him, not in the same department, but we talked. He was one of the only ones who didn't think my work was ridiculous. Well, maybe he did, but he didn't say so, which is kind of the same thing."

Bryans preferred Dr. Edwards to this. The thought surprised even him; he hadn't imagined anyone could make that smug bastard seem like better company, but somehow Erin's jittery rambling managed it.

"Professor," he cut in, raising a hand. "Start from the beginning. And breathe."

She blinked. "Right. Okay. Sorry. I tend to… ramble."

"No shit?" Bryans deadpanned.

She nodded rapidly, then gestured to the folding chair across from her. "Please. Sit. Or stand. Whichever. Just… listen."

Bryans stayed on his feet, arms crossed. Statuesque in his demeanor.

"I've heard the rumors," she began. "About what happened to Reed. About the murder. The kid. The attacker. And now all this weird energy on campus, people whispering, saying Reed snapped, or went underground, or got possessed, which is… okay, stupid… but something happened. Something happened."

He tilted his head. "You called me here for gossip?"

"No, no, no. God, sorry, okay, look." She took a breath, steadying herself.

"A few months ago, I went to Reed's apartment. He'd been working on these… ideas. About mirrors. About time distortion. He said he was studying alternate planes of existence. Other realities. He thought he'd found one."

She hesitated, then finally gave it a name. "He called it the Elsewhere Fold."

The word Fold flickered through his memory. Reed had muttered it once in interrogation, and he'd dismissed it then. Now, the echo unsettled him in a way he couldn't quite shake.

Bryans winced. She kept talking.

"He told me," she went on, "that at exactly 3:33 a.m., there's this… he called it a perceptual seam in consciousness. A tear in the map between waking and dreaming. He said mirrors could reflect more than light at that moment. They reflect memory. Or possibility. Something layered behind reality."

She was picking up speed again, words tripping over each other.

"He had this old analog clock. He held it up to the mirror in his bathroom, and when it hit 3:33…" she snapped her fingers. "Both cracked. The clock and the mirror."

For a split second, he could almost hear Maria's voice in his head. Her sharp whisper about Mary Johnson's body vanishing in the glass, there one moment and gone the next.

Bryans looked away, lips tightening. "Mirrors?" he muttered.

She heard him, even though he hadn't meant her to. He didn't want to get sucked into this, but he couldn't deny the pull.

He sighed. "Then what happened, Professor?"

Erin smirked awkwardly, held up a finger. "Assistant professor," she corrected, before continuing.

"And then… he was gone."

Bryans narrowed his eyes. "Gone."

More disappearing people. More mirrors. Bryans masked his intrigue with dry skepticism.

"Yeah," she whispered. "He disappeared. I don't remember how long. Seconds? Minutes? I dunno… my brain got scrambled. I swear, Captain, I felt something in the room. Not a person. A presence. Something aware. Then I heard Reed calling from the bathroom. He was curled up in the tub. Covered in sweat. Looked awful, honestly. He said he had no idea where he was."

"Let me guess," Bryans said. "You didn't get any of this on video."

"No," she admitted.

"And honestly, part of me wonders if I ever really saw it. It's like… something hacked my brain. Something got in and corrupted the memory. Or—okay, I know this sounds ridiculous, but maybe reality itself didn't want me to remember."

He didn't respond. Just stared out the small, dusty window, jaw clenched.

The silence stretched, thick and uncomfortable, as Bryans tried to sift through the insane and the ridiculous this case kept throwing at him. Alternate realities. Mirrors swallowing people. Every fiber of his cop's brain told him it was nonsense, but the images wouldn't leave him alone.

Across from him, Erin stood twitching slightly, eyes darting, anxious as ever, wondering how her words had landed. If they had landed at all.

"I know how it sounds," she eventually said quietly.

"Batshit insane is how it sounds," Bryans said, nearly interrupting her.

A nervous beat passed before she finally admitted, softly, "I know."

"But," Bryans muttered, "you're not the first person to mention mirrors. Or 3:33 a.m."

Erin's head snapped up. "I'm not?"

Bryans hated that he was in this flickering room talking to a paranoid academic. But what he hated more was that some part of him believed her.

He mentally kicked himself. Reality was starting to corner him.

"Forget I said that."

She squinted at him. "You came alone. That means you believe something.

Even if you don't want to."

He turned sharply. Locked eyes with her.

"I believe in evidence," he said, pacing now. "And right now, I've got a toddler that was nearly butchered, a detective losing sleep and possibly her mind, and a suspect who got stabbed trying to save the kid. And then—" he waved a hand at Erin, half-exhausted, half-mocking, "there's all this."

He stopped. Looked at her hard.

"So, you tell me, Professor Tran:

What the hell is going on?

Who is Reed Ashland?

Why is my detective acting like she saw a ghost in a mirror?

Where's the goddamn killer?

Why do clocks keep stopping at 3:33?

And… and I hate that I'm even asking this.

What the hell is the Elsewhere Fold?"

***

Maria stood at the foot of Reed Ashland's bed, staring down at him. Sympathy in her chest, questions in her throat, and wonder curling behind her eyes.

Even unconscious, this man stirred something in her.

But was it him… or something else entirely?

Behind her, the mirror shifted again. Just a tremor in the glass, almost too slight to catch. But the longer Maria stood there, the more it seemed to lean toward her.

The reflection didn't just echo her movements; it hinted at her feelings, the faintest ripple of unease tracing across the surface when her stomach tightened.

It was as if the mirror weren't reflecting her at all but mimicking the pulse of whatever lived inside her.

The captain was probably right. What she needed was one solid night of real sleep. But doubt pressed in harder than the fatigue.

What was she even doing here? She had boys at home. She'd picked them up at school just to chase this?

To stand beside a man who might never wake up?

Was Reed Ashland's unconscious body really going to hand her the answers to the universe?

She was trying too hard, stretching herself too thin. Rose was with the boys, thank God, but how long could she keep leaning on her?

The thought needled at her. She should just go home. Chicken nuggets sounded good, she quipped to herself.

What time was it anyway?

She reached into her coat pocket and pulled out her phone.

Tapped the screen. Looked down.

3:33 a.m.

"What the…?"

That couldn't be right. It was just past dinner. She had to be seeing it wrong.

She tapped the screen again. Held it up to her face.

Unbeknownst to her, the phone's display reflected in the mirror behind her.

Still: 3:33 a.m.

Something shifted inside her.

Then a crack. A jagged line right down the center of her phone screen.

She froze.

Cracking noises behind her.

Slowly, she turned. She didn't want to see what she already knew was there.

Her eyes went wide.

The mirror was starting to splinter.

The phone shattered in her hand. She flinched.

The mirror followed.

And then—everything around Detective Maria Voss folded.

39

CHAPTER THIRTY-NINE

Whispers Between the Pages

Maria Voss drifted through a place that defied dimension; no ground beneath her feet, no ceiling above her head. Lit from nowhere and everywhere, the space seemed to inhale.

Then: the paper.

A single sheet, floating and fluttering. She reached for it, slowly.

The page carried a dreamlike curiosity. An answer dangling just out of reach. But the closer her fingers came, the more fragile it seemed, trembling.

She strained against the heaviness in her limbs, and just as she brushed its edge, the sheet dissolved into smoke, vanishing through her grasp.

Maria took in her surroundings: a bizarre library, ancient and absurd.

The walls stretched impossibly high, vanishing into shadow. The ceiling, if there even was one, was lost beyond miles of spiraling staircases that went nowhere and then forgot they existed.

It felt buried, as though she stood in a vault carved from the bowels of the earth, yet the geometry around her hinted at something impossibly advanced; metal gleams that caught no light, shifting seams that suggested construction far beyond human hands.

The place breathed paradox: arches curved in ways that looked stolen from futures not yet imagined.

This place was alive. Not pulsing or breathing, but aware. Watching.

Maria's thoughts scattered. *Where am I? What is this? What is happening?*

Maria turned slowly. Her boots didn't make a sound.

Books drifted, some flipping lazily, others vanishing when she reached out. The shelves weren't shelves at all. Not anymore. One blink and they were spires. Another, and they bent inward, folding into impossible geometry.

Every time she tried to approach a book, the floor shifted.

Angles pivoted. Shapes, colossal and unreadable, slid between her and understanding. Like guardians made of thought and math.

She managed to graze the spine of one floating book. It recoiled. Then hovered, trembling, just within reach. It opened. Pages fluttered and then stopped. Open to a page of words that were all shifting and moving so fast that Maria couldn't tell what they were.

The books were skittish and untamed, jerking back from her touch.

This library was a deranged petting zoo, and every creature in it refused to be petted.

Then all the words vanished and the book dissolved.

A presence moved near her. Smooth. Unseen. Felt in the skin and gums.

Not a being. Not exactly. More like the whisper between pages that had never been written. A ripple of unreality across the nothing.

And then it was gone.

From the ether came a figure, drifting slowly toward her. Cloaked in shadow and gleaming thread, its mouth stitched with gold wire. Until it opened and the wires parted like spider legs curling back.

"You wear your name loosely," it said. None of the words were heard. They were being dragged across her brain. Felt. Imprinted. Not spoken.

Maria tried to speak. Nothing. Her lips didn't work. Her name wouldn't come. Even her breath felt borrowed.

The very idea of speech slipped away from her. A skill she might have once had in another life but no longer remembered how to use.

A name rose toward the surface and then collapsed, not just forgotten but emptied of definition. She couldn't remember what a name was. Why anyone would need one, what purpose it served.

The concept unraveled in her mind, leaving her adrift in silence, less a person than an outline without a label.

"You are too full," the shadowy figure hissed. "So much memory behind your eyes."

A mirror blinked into existence beside her. Then another. And another. Dozens. Floating. Orbiting.

Each showed her. Versions of her.

Maria in her childhood backyard. Laughing, barefoot, bruised knees and Kool-Aid lips.

Maria at graduation, clutching her diploma. The world hadn't gone sour yet.

Maria in a patrol car, face lit by red-blue strobe, staring down a blood-soaked alley with a dead girl in it.

And then—

Her sister.

Not the crime scene. Not the autopsy table.

Alive.

Smiling.

Turning to say something that never formed.

Emotion struck like a collapsing cathedral.

The sight of her knocked the air from Maria's lungs, her chest seizing.

Her vision blurred with tears she couldn't summon fast enough, and her hands trembled, reaching instinctively toward the impossible.

The Fold absorbed it. Her anguish rippled outward, bending the world around her. Shelves buckled inward, shadows cracking before reassembling wrong.

The whole place pulsed with her grief. Reality itself was trying to recoil from what she felt.

She collapsed to her knees. Or maybe she had no knees here. She just folded.

***

Reed was running through pitch darkness. Blind. Windless. It was not panic, but purpose. Chasing or being chased, it made no difference.

The abyss swallowed everything. There were no stars, no horizon, no ground he could trust beneath his feet. Only the thud of each step echoing into nowhere in slow motion.

The air was thick and soundless. The world had been muted. Still, something inside him drove him forward, a pull without logic. It wasn't courage or fear. It was the certainty that he had to keep moving, that somewhere in this endless black was the thing he was meant to find… or the thing already waiting for him.

Then the floor vanished.

He fell.

The plunge was endless. He braced for the crash, for bones to shatter and lungs to empty on impact. But it never came.

Instead, he landed.

No sound, no pain, no jolt.

One instant he was plummeting; the next he was simply there, lying in a bed. His hospital bed. Sheets cool against his skin, monitors beeping steadily.

He glanced suspiciously around. The room looked normal. Too normal.

At his side sat a nurse. She looked oddly out of place. She was clearly a nurse, but her hair looked out of date and her clothes didn't fit right.

She looked at Reed.

He relaxed instantly. Oddly comforted. There was something impossible in it, the look itself carried a frequency only he could hear, soothing a wound he didn't know he still bled from.

Her eyes weren't just watching him; they were inside him, quieting the static in his head. It was unnatural, unsettling even, but the calm it delivered was undeniable. Like being wrapped in a lullaby sung from the other side of a mirror.

"He knows," she said, her voice soft, subterranean.

Reed stared.

"He knows Maria," she went on. "He knows her in ways only he can know."

She turned her head slowly toward the mirror above the sink.

It wasn't broken.

Inside it: a flicker of Maria. Holding her boys. Laughing in her kitchen. Sitting cross-legged on a rooftop. Crying over her deceased sister.

For a moment, Reed felt that strange calm deepen, curiosity warming his chest. Then the warmth cooled, replaced by dread crawling up his spine.

The image wavered. Maria dissolved into shadows, her outline bleeding away.

In her place, something else started to take form.

A shape, ominous and deliberate, emerged from the shifting silver of the glass. The figure thickened, sharpened, until Reed knew, without needing to see the face, who it was.

The killer.

Smiling. A smile that stretched too wide, teeth bared with delight.

Then laughing. Laughing so hard his eyes squeezed shut, his whole body quaking with some private joke Reed would never want to understand.

And then, stillness.

His eyes opened. Bottomless black.

"Now," he said. "It has to happen."

Reed tried to shout, but all that came out was the sound of bees. Swarming. Buzzing from his chest, his throat, his ears. The room vibrated.

He looked back to the nurse.

He blinked, and she was gone.

In her place was Maria.

Sitting upright. Perfectly still. Vacant.

A wax doll in human shape. Her eyes empty. Her breath imperceptible.

Reed stood, uncertain how, and leaned toward her. Maria didn't move an inch. She didn't turn her head or avert her eyes in any way. A catatonic robot.

Her skin was warm, real. But her spirit felt elsewhere.

Then—she blinked.

Her head snapped to look at him and her eyes were black.

The motion was so sudden, so sharp, Reed flinched.

A chill clamped his chest, his stomach dropping, every muscle wired tight with fear.

Those eyes: bottomless, predatory, erased the comfort she'd given him moments before, leaving only the raw jolt of terror.

And the world around Reed shattered.

The crack ripped outward with a soundless violence, and before he could even catch his breath, everything was breaking, collapsing in perfect time with the panic thrumming through him.

He fell.

***

Maria was spinning out of control. Lost in a vortex of emotion and uncertainty. Nothing around her stood still or made sense.

The floor tilted and flexed under her feet. Images flared and vanished in the corners of her vision: faces, places, fragments of memory that dissolved before she could grasp them.

Every sound bent and warped: whispers dragging, the beat of her own heart echoing.

Then everything stopped, and Maria was on all fours.

Disoriented would have been a welcome sensation. She stood slowly and cautiously.

And then she was back in the room from before. Surrounded by mirrors. Each one reflected her, but not quite. She was brushing her hair with a snake. Speaking backward to her sons, who now had mirrors for faces.

In one, she was maniacally tap-dancing on a ceiling made of her own teeth.

Maria heard distant laughter and then the screams of a woman. A girl. Young. She could tell instinctively that it was her sister.

She wanted to scream. Instead, she vomited.

The bile rose and hung in the air. Reshaping. Congealing. Becoming something impossible to name, but unmistakably deliberate.

A rectangle manifested. Small. A card. With an odd geometric shape that

Maria couldn't identify.

Then a full deck of cards. Tarot-like. Made from her sickness, spinning and shuffling with impossible precision.

The mysterious figure from before appeared and caught them midair.

It fanned them out resembling a magician at the end of the world.

"This is not prophecy," it said. "This is exposure. The soul flipped inside out, not to see. But to be seen."

Maria tried to speak again. Still nothing.

The enigma before her leaned in. All around Maria, the mirrors began shifting. Moving together. Becoming one. They became luminous, then a blob. Finally, it became a figure. Then the mirror was gone. Engulfed by shadows.

"Long gone will be the lines," it whispered. "They're blurred, and now you must unlearn the alphabet."

Letters swirled around her, none she recognized. They melted, slithered, reshaping into symbols beyond comprehension. Language was dying.

"Pick," it said, gesturing toward the cards. "And we shall know the road and the occupant. Only the vehicle leaves behind the stench."

Maria stared. She didn't move. She didn't want to pick a card.

"Okay," the shadowy entity whispered, slinking closer. "Maybe your friend should pick."

What friend? she thought. Eeriness entered her and slithered up her spine.

A whisper of breath against her neck.

She turned.

The killer stood behind her.

Black eyes. Grinning.

The library turned inside out and she was gone.

The mirror figure blinked into existence briefly once more and then folded into itself, holding only a dark reflection with no face.

40

CHAPTER FORTY

Déjà Vu and Dust

Nurses scrambled; urgent footsteps, shouted orders, the harsh beeping of heart monitors spiraling into a crescendo. The steady rhythm fractured, then vanished. Flatline.

Maria's eyes fluttered open, confusion folding over her. She hadn't meant to nap. She hadn't even realized she'd closed her eyes.

Her head throbbed, she was disoriented.

For a moment she didn't know where she was at all. The tiled walls and dull fluorescent glow were foreign, unreal. Then it hit her. The shower. What the hell? She'd napped in the shower?

Her body told the same story.

She felt damp, soaked through, as if she'd just stepped out from under the spray. But there had been no water. Only sweat, slick against her skin, heavy in her clothes. Her chest heaved with the afterburn of exertion.

Every muscle hummed with fatigue.

Somewhere in the distance, the chaos seeped through the cracked door: alarms, hurried voices, footsteps pounding.

Reed. Flatlined.

Her stomach tightened. The pieces clicked into place.

A deep breath, then another. Dragging her scattered thoughts back into

213

something resembling order. Her pulse was still racing, her body shaky, and she braced herself, gathering the loose ends of her mind the way she would gather case files off her desk: not neat, not perfect, but enough to move forward.

She pushed herself up and stumbled toward the sink, desperate for an anchor in the storm. Splashing cold water on her face, she caught sight of the mirror above the basin. She immediately shook her head.

No. Not now. Not that.

Her skin prickled at the sight of the mirror. She swallowed the nausea rising in her throat and forced her eyes away.

The events crept back to her like the slow dawn.

Her fingers fumbled for her phone. The screen was shattered, spiderweb cracks spread across the glass. The shattered glass echoed the splintered pieces of her mind.

She remembered the phone cracking. Mirror cracking. Falling. Folding.

Where Reed had been, the room stood empty. Sterile and silent, a hollow shell after the storm.

The sight hit her harder than she expected.

He was gone, wheeled off in a rush of hands and urgency, and the echo of it pressed into her chest. The sterile quiet wasn't relief; it was dread. The truth settled cold in her stomach: Reed might be dying.

Under the bright lights of an operating room, his fate now hinged on steady hands and luck she wasn't sure he had left.

Then Maria's feet moved of their own accord, drawn to the mirror mounted sideways on the far wall. She refused to meet its gaze but could see the jagged crack cutting through its center.

Her eyes drifted downward.

On the white tile floor where she'd stood, just before everything fell apart, someone had drawn a strange geometric shape in what looked like black chalk. The black chalk lines twisted beneath her gaze, sharp angles merging into curves that defied logic. A cipher from a forgotten language.

A deep chill slid down her spine. She whispered, barely audible, "What the hell?"

For a moment, Maria was lost in thought.

The memory slammed into her with brutal clarity; the first Mary Johnson crime scene.

The bedroom.

The faint, dark outline pressed into the carpet, the imprint next to the bed where Mary's body had been found.

Her instincts flared, that familiar prickle at the base of her skull she'd learned never to ignore.

The shape on the floor of the hospital room matched it. Exactly. Not similar. It was identical.

Her breath hitched.

For one vertiginous second, she felt caught between recognition and revelation, suspended in the certainty that she'd stepped into something far bigger than the moment in front of her.

Without knowing why, she spoke: "Why does déjà vu feel like homesickness?"

41

CHAPTER FORTY-ONE

Captain Bryans sat in his office, eyes glued to his phone, while a Northwestern football game played. The room was dim, cluttered with case files, coffee cups, and a faint scent of stale cigars. He wanted to take his mind off his job.

A knock. The door opened abruptly. An officer stepped in, holding a folder.

"We got some lab results for you, Captain."

Bryans snapped upright, the football game forgotten. "Great. Let's see 'em."

He followed the deputy down the hall, stepping into the lab just as Maria Voss walked in. Bryans caught her eye.

"Voss! We've got something," he said, gesturing for her to join.

Maria rushed over as they entered the lab.

"What've we got?" she asked, quick but measured.

Bryans looked toward the officer who'd first come into his office. The younger man gave a clipped reply: "Blood and video."

Bryans let out a breath he hadn't realized he was holding, a flicker of optimism breaking through his exhaustion. "Maybe we finally got something solid," he said, the words edged with relief.

Maria nodded, though a trace of doubt lingered in her expression.

"Let's hope so," she said, her voice quieter, tempered. Hopeful, yes, but not nearly as certain as her captain.

Dr. Maxwell Blake, forensic evidence technician, stood near a bank of monitors, already tapping away on a keyboard. Next to him lounged his counterpart, Marcia Roosevelt, digital forensic analyst.

The group traded brief nods and murmured greetings, perfunctory, almost automatic. No one lingered on pleasantries; the urgency in the room pressed them past small talk.

"Alright," Blake began, adjusting his glasses. "No match on the fingerprints. The blood samples so far are inconclusive. No database hits. This guy's clean, as far as arrests go."

Marcia leaned forward, cutting in with a sly grin. "That's because you didn't need the blood or prints in the first place."

Blake's eyes flicked to her, awkward and a bit off-balance. Maria and Bryans exchanged amused glances.

They knew Blake and Marcia well enough by now to recognize the rhythm. This was their usual back-and-forth, equal parts rivalry and camaraderie. A kind of forensic banter that played like clockwork whenever they were in the same room.

Bryans sighed. "Okay, okay. Come on, Marcia. Spill it."

Marcia grinned wider. "License plate. Street cameras caught his car entering and leaving the alley behind the house right when the attacks happened."

Blake looked momentarily upstaged. Maria and Bryans were impatient now.

"We already knew that, Marcia," Bryans remarked.

"Alright, alright," Marcia said. "His name's Daniel Avery. We have an address."

They started toward the door, but Marcia held up a hand. "Hold on there, chief."

Bryans hated being called chief for whatever reason. Marcia knew that.

"Before you go guns blazing. One more thing. His current employer had him do fingerprinting five years ago as part of a background check. They actually gave us the prints; no warrant, just a request. They want their name off the record, so they've been very helpful."

Bryans raised an eyebrow but said nothing. Maria was blank-faced. She had been since arriving except for a little smirk every now and then about Blake and Marcia. Beneath it all, though, both she and Bryans carried the same restless wish; to skip the analysis, the waiting, all of it, and just fast-forward to putting the cuffs on this guy.

Marcia continued, "Those prints from five years ago don't match the ones lifted at the crime scene."

The air seemed to drop out of the room. Maria and Bryans both felt it. The wind had been knocked clean out of them.

Come on. Of course. It always had to be something with this case.

Bryans frowned. "Maybe the car was stolen. Is that Sonata hot?"

Marcia shook her head steadily in the negative.

"Okay then. Accomplice?" Bryans responded.

"Whatever he is, he's definitely a person of interest." Marcia volleyed back.

Maria, quiet until now, stopped the group with a firm hand. Everyone turned to look at her. Bryans shot her a look of exaggerated, sarcastic shock that said: *oh, now you've got something to say?*

"Finally decide to join us, Voss?" Bryans quipped. He was chalking up her conspicuous silence to exhaustion.

"Blake," Maria said, "pull up those prints from his employer. Not the crime scene ones."

Blake complied, and the image appeared on the monitor.

Maria squinted at the monitor and leaned in slowly. She was studying and pondering.

Maria asked Bryans for his phone. Bryans furrowed his brow and shot her a look that said, 'Excuse me?'

"My phone's broken. Don't worry about it. Just give it here," Maria ordered her boss.

She was in command of the room now, no question. There was an edge in her tone that made even Bryans comply. She clearly had some kind of point, though no one yet knew where she was going with it. Still, every set of eyes in the lab followed, eager to see what she'd reveal.

Bryans gave her the phone, watching curiously.

Maria hastily flipped it into selfie mode and took a picture of the fingerprint image on the screen. She handed it back.

"Email that to Blake," she said, pointing to the image on Bryans' phone.

Bryans shrugged and did as instructed, looking more confused than ever.

Maria immediately pointed to Blake's computer. "Pull it up as soon as you get it," she directed, her voice sharp with urgency.

Blake received it. "Okay… and now what?" he said, confused.

Maria pointed. "Compare this picture to the crime scene prints."

Marcia threw her hands up. "We already tried. They don't match."

Bryans sighed and shook his head as he watched with agitated bewilderment.

Blake added, trying to stop Maria's momentum, "Also, you took the picture in selfie mode. So, the impressions will be reversed, Detective Voss."

Maria shot Blake and Marcia a sly look, a flicker of confidence breaking through her otherwise guarded expression. She nodded. "I know."

Maria leaned in to drive her point home to Blake.

She spoke slowly with emphasis. "So, I want you to take the picture Bryans just sent. The reversed print. And then compare it to the crime scene ones."

Silence. Everyone stared at the monitors.

"Okay," Blake said, turning back to the keyboard.

His fingers pounded the keys in quick, irritated bursts, the clatter carrying his skepticism louder than words. He pulled up the two sets of prints, already bracing himself for the inevitable mismatch.

The machine processed. Then a sharp, electronic chime cut through the room; half alert, half alarm. The screen flashed.

Maria had been right.

Blake slunk back into his chair, dumbfounded in his silence.

"They match," Blake finally said.

Bryans rubbed his temples. "How the fuck did you know to do *that?*"

There was a flicker behind her eyes, like a memory she hadn't lived yet.

She said nothing.

Bryans' frustration boiled over. "I want answers. How the hell does this happen?"

He swung a hard glare at Maria, who only met his stare with a calm, almost coy tilt of her head. The lack of apology in her eyes only made his jaw tighten.

When he turned the glare on Blake, the technician shrank a little in his chair, suddenly all too aware of the captain's fury pressing down on him.

Blake finally offered a possibility. "Maybe the prints were planted or transferred. But given the circumstances and the crime scene, I—uh—really doubt that. So, I don't know." Blake drifted off, not wanting to complete his sentence.

Bryans shook his head and threw his Cubs coffee mug.

The mug shattered against the wall. Coffee splattered across the drywall. Everyone flinched, except Marcia.

"I'll buy you a White Sox one," she quipped.

Normally, Bryans would enjoy her banter but not right now. He'd had enough of this investigation and his detective's weird insights that made no sense and would never hold up in court. Nothing was ever normal with this case.

Maria, unbothered by all of this, squared her shoulders. "Let's go get this guy."

Bryans glanced back at the smoldering mug on the floor. He hoped the rest of this might be easy. But deep down, he already knew better.

$$42$$

CHAPTER FORTY-TWO

Through the Glass

The SWAT team moved efficiently, silent, precise, weapons drawn, down the fourth-floor hallway of the Kenwood apartment building. Captain Bryans and Maria Voss trailed close behind, guns holstered, eyes sharp. At the door to Unit 4C, a gloved hand knocked once.

"Daniel Avery! Chicago PD. Open up."

No response.

The battering ram hit hard. The door folded inward with a splintering crack, and the team swept in with mechanical fluidity. Shouts filled the space.

"Clear!" "Back hallway, clear!" "Kitchen clear!"

Voss and Bryans moved through in tandem, eyes sharp, ears tuned for the smallest sound. Every corner, every shadowed nook, every closet door was given its due. Each came up empty.

With every unchecked space, their anticipation ebbed, the disappointment settling heavier on their shoulders. The house felt less like a scene about to break open and more like a hollow stage where the actor had already fled.

The man they came for, Daniel Avery, was gone.

Bryans exhaled through his nose and holstered his weapon. Maria didn't move. She stood in the middle of the living room, taking in the space. She was enigmatically disappointed when it didn't.

The apartment was clean, too clean. Minimal furniture. Sparse decoration. A modern sofa, a single bookshelf, a desk with no computer. The only thing that stood out was what was broken.

Mirrors. Several of them were cracked or shattered, some covered hastily with sheets. And clocks. Two in the living room, one in the hallway, another on the kitchen wall. All of them stopped.

"All stopped at 3:33," an officer muttered behind them.

Bryans turned and raised an eyebrow. "You serious?"

"Yeah. We checked three times. There's also blood in the bathroom and hallway. We can run that."

"Good," Bryans uttered not really caring, because it would probably just come back as unicorn or fairy blood, knowing this case.

He looked down in dejection and sighed.

Then, muttering "Jesus Christ," he turned to Maria. "So this guy, Daniel Avery. Thirty-three years old. Manages a grocery store off Pershing.

No priors. No flags. Lives alone. No pets. No social media. Parents live out in Rockford, both retired teachers. Guy barely exists on paper."

Maria nodded but said nothing. Pondering.

"He doesn't fit the profile," Bryans went on. "He's the opposite of what Felix said to look for."

"He does live alone. Never been married. No kids," Maria said, giving him a contrarian grimace.

"So, what? Felix was wrong. Hell, his prints were wrong. Mirrors. Clocks…" Bryans trailed off. He wanted to direct his anger at everyone and everything in this case.

"The prints weren't wrong," she said, voice low. "It's the guy. And it's not the guy."

Bryans closed his eyes for a beat. Counted to three. "You know I'm getting real sick of the riddles, Voss."

"You wanna punch a pillow a few times? Maybe a mirror?" Maria's sarcasm hit a nerve.

He turned to leave, snapping open his radio. "This is Captain Solomon

Bryans. I want an APB put out on Daniel Avery. All city units. Suspect is possibly armed and dangerous. Repeat, armed and dangerous."

His voice faded down the hallway.

Maria remained.

She stood in the doorway of Avery's bedroom, staring inward. It was sparse; neatly made bed, empty nightstand, a floor lamp flickering near the window. A long crack ran down the mirror on the closet door, akin to a scar carved into the reflection.

The ticking of his alarm clock had stopped long ago, but Maria could still feel it.

She stepped into the room.

Something in the air here felt… wrong. Not in a physical sense. It was a tone just slightly off-key. Or walking into a room after a dream, realizing the colors were a shade too soft, the shadows a little too long.

True, a killer lived here, but it was more than that.

She turned toward the window.

It was nothing special, just a simple pane of glass, framed by tan curtains. But it called to her. It didn't call with urgency, but with familiarity.

Something had shifted in her ever since the hospital, and now the world whispered differently.

Rooms didn't hold objects; they held echoes, impressions. The evidence wasn't evidence anymore. It was suggestion, vibration, the faint outline of meaning brushing against her senses.

The air here was thick with it. She felt herself closer to grasping some larger truth, though the edges kept slipping away. A dream she almost remembered but could never quite name.

She stepped closer to the bedroom window, slowly, and looked out.

Half-bare trees clung to rust-and-fire leaves, swirling in gusts that bruised the pavement with autumn.

But she didn't see any of that. She was searching. For what she couldn't say.

The answers were out there, hovering on the tip of her tongue.

Across the street. Five floors up.

A man sat alone in a dark room, curtains pulled halfway open. In his hands, a pair of black binoculars. He lifted them slowly.

Maria's form came into view. Her outline framed in the light of Daniel Avery's bedroom window. Still. Unmoving. Beautiful, in a tragic sort of way.

The man watched her watching nothing.

And then he smiled.

He lowered the binoculars and whispered, "Now you know, don't you?"

A pause.

"Now you see," he whispered.

He leaned forward into the dark, as if sharing a secret with the shadows.

"You don't belong in this world... *AiraM ssoV.*"

43

CHAPTER FORTY-THREE

Which Eye to Open

Reed Ashland lay on an invisible bed in a room of infinity. White. Endless. Without depth or dimension.

The silence wasn't silence at all. It was layered. Distant hums, the pulse of machinery that seemed to keep time with his own faltering heartbeat. The sterile scent of antiseptic filled his nose, sharp and bitter, but underneath it lingered something sweet, almost floral.

The white walls glowed too bright, colors bleeding at their edges, and for a fleeting moment Reed understood everything. The contradictions of his life had folded into a single, fragile clarity.

He floated, slowly, gently. Suspended in liquid light.

His eyes were closed.

His hands folded neatly over his chest. His body laid out for a funeral no one would attend.

Then—

His eyes opened.

The light fractured, and the whiteness shattered into shadow.

Everything flipped.

Reed found himself upside down, suspended in darkness.

Weightless.

225

Alone.

The black went on forever in every direction, thick and formless, except for one thing: footsteps.

Measured. Distant. Steady.

One after another, echoing through the void.

Like a grandfather clock…

Slowly walking toward him.

It was impossible to tell how long it took.

Could've been seconds. Could've been centuries. Time was irrelevant here.

But the sound drew nearer. Louder.

Until finally—

A shape began to form in the dark.

At first, it was just motion.

A ripple in the void. A smear of suggestion.

Then it clarified. Took shape.

And then it manifested out of the darkness.

A Man in a Charcoal Suit.

Clean. Crisp. Timeless.

Mr. Morrow.

He stopped in front of Reed, whose body still hung upside down, face in front of the figure before him. Completely immobile.

Their faces were inches apart. Reed's expression bewildered, Morrow's unreadable.

Then Morrow spoke softly. A whisper that didn't come from his mouth.

"The air smells of burnt wires and regret, doesn't it?"

Reed blinked. Didn't answer.

There was nothing between them. No floor. No sky. Only the endless dark and the thrum of something wrong in the air.

Morrow went on.

"You can wake up now. If you can remember which eye to open first, that is."

A faint ticking began somewhere far off.

"Time's curling, Reed. A noose… around her neck. And she doesn't even know she's choking."

A pause. Morrow's eyes glinted.

"The Fold is holding its breath with her inside."

Reed's heart started to beat faster. Or maybe it was the sound around him, growing louder. The ticking? A pulse? A warning? Whatever it was started faintly, grew louder, and now it was all around him.

Morrow stepped back into the dark.

His voice echoed one last time as he turned to leave, fading with every syllable.

"Tick, tick, tick…

That sound you hear isn't time.

It's a choice."

The throbbing wasn't around him anymore. It was inside. Crawling through his veins. His body felt on the verge of detonation.

The darkness buckled. The sound became unbearable.

Reed gasped.

He was awake.

The hospital room came back into focus like a painting being reassembled from ash.

Ceiling tiles. IV drip. The faint hum of machines.

He tried to sit up but failed. Pain held him in place.

Beside him sat a nurse.

She smelled of lavender and dust.

Something was off.

Her scrubs were ill-fitting, the nametag missing. Her hair tied up in an outdated bun. Something out of another decade. Or century.

She looked at him and smiled. A sad smile. Too still, painted on.

"Where am I?" Reed asked, his voice dry and cracked.

The nurse leaned in, close enough for him to see the faint shimmer in her eyes.

"You are now," she said, her voice echoing the rustle of wind through trees.

Reed blinked.

His eyelids drifted closed from exhaustion.

When he opened them again, she was gone.

A real nurse burst into the room, calling over her shoulder.

"He's awake! Somebody get Dr. Ilan in here!"

The machines beeped faster. Hands moved around him. Lights blurred.

Reed closed his eyes once more.

Sleep took him again.

But something stayed with him. Curling in the corner of his mind. Somewhere, far off, the ticking had not stopped.

44

CHAPTER FORTY-FOUR

They All Came From the Same Place

Maria pushed through the glass doors of the station with her shoulders tight and her mind in knots. Her thoughts circled, waiting to strike. She knew Bryans was somewhere in the building, and she wasn't ready to face him yet.

He was in a mood. The kind of temper that came when a case had spun too far out of control. He'd get through it, she told herself. He always did. But not now. Not this afternoon.

The smell of burnt coffee hung in the air. She poured herself a paper cup of it anyway, black and bitter, and snagged a powdered donut from the box left half-open on the counter.

She chewed quickly, standing near a cracked-open window, letting the autumn breeze drift through.

For a moment, it carried her away. She wondered how Eli and Tommy were doing at school, if they were paying attention in math, if Tommy had remembered his lunch. The thought grounded her. Then she snapped back to detective mode.

She tossed the empty cup in the bin and cut across the bullpen with clipped strides. Every step armoring her back up for the hunt: sharp, fast, relentless.

Maria found Officer Darnell leaning against his desk, flipping through paperwork. The young officer straightened when he saw her.

"Hey there, Voss," he said. "I heard Avery wasn't there, huh? Find anything good at his place?"

"Not really," Maria answered curtly. She wasn't in the mood for chatter. "I need some things done. Can you write them down and get on it?"

Darnell blinked at her sudden intensity, caught off guard. The easy grin he'd worn a second ago faltered as he scrambled upright. His hands fumbled across the desk, knocking aside a half-empty coffee cup before finally landing on a notepad.

Maria got right to it. "Every address Avery ever lived at. All former employers. Known associates. Immediate family, locations. Ex-partners, friends. All of it."

His pen scratched furiously. "Wow. Leave no stone unturned, huh?"

"Absolutely," Maria said, her eyes sharp. "He tried to kill a small child. We need him in custody yesterday."

Darnell swallowed, nodded quickly, and hustled off to do the work.

Maria dropped into her chair with a sigh. The station noise swelled around her; phones ringing, keyboards clattering, the hum of a world still moving even as hers narrowed to the killer. She hesitated, then pulled out her phone and dialed a number she knew by heart.

"Agent Harlan," came Felix's voice. Smooth and even, a welcome anchor in the middle of all the bizarre uncertainty that had wrapped itself around recent days.

Maria leaned back and smiled coyly to herself. She began, "Self-knowledge is no guarantee of happiness, but it is on the side of happiness and can supply the courage to fight for it."

Felix laughed softly. "Simone de Beauvoir? Nice try."

She couldn't help but smile. "Caught me."

"What can I do for you, Detective Voss?" Felix asked.

"Did you get the bio on Daniel Avery I sent you?" Maria asked. "We're pretty sure he's the guy."

Felix sighed deeply. "Yeah. And I know what you and Bryans are thinking. He doesn't match my profile?"

"That's right. What's your take?"

"Well," Felix said carefully, "I'm not arrogant enough to claim infallibility. But it surprises me how little in my profile matches Avery. Except that he lives alone. And that's hardly conclusive."

Maria let out a dry laugh. "Last time I ask for your help then."

Felix chuckled back. "Let me know where to submit my badge and weapon."

"I'll settle for a coffee on you. Throw in a shot of whiskey for Bryans. He needs it," Maria joked. Felix chuckled again.

Maria grinned at the exchange, but pressed on. "Seriously though, what do you make of how far off you were?"

There was a pause before Felix answered. "My gut says he's framed. With the fingerprint anomaly and all."

Maria's eyes narrowed. "So, you noticed that too."

"Oh, yeah," Felix said quickly. "I looked at everything you sent over. Those prints… they looked planted. Backwards, reversed. Odd as hell."

Maria's jaw tightened. "Again, mirrors. That wasn't lost on me."

"Yeah, that matters. Like I said in my profile. He sees himself, and he's killing a part of himself." Felix explained.

She stared across the squad room at the mirror hanging on the far wall. The surface shimmered faintly in the overhead light. A chill pressed into her spine.

"And the symbols carved in the victims' heads?" she asked. "The fact they let it happen before being strangled?"

Felix hesitated. "I'd ask if you were certain, but I know you. And I know Rose. I'm willing to bet you've quadruple-checked it."

Maria didn't respond, but the silence was enough for Felix.

"If that's the case, I'd say the killer knew them. All of them. A ritual. Some kind of cult, maybe. Obscure, nothing I've ever heard of. Avery might be the leader and the victims his followers, and he's either punishing them or performing a ritual? A sacrifice?"

"None of the victims were in any kind of cult," Maria said flatly. "They didn't even go to church. And little Colin; he certainly wasn't in a cult."

She allowed the faintest edge of dry humor to creep in. "Although I am suspicious about the *Mickey Mouse Club*."

Felix let out a rueful laugh. "Yeah, no, I wouldn't think so. But if the victims allowed the carving to occur, then I stand by my assertion that they all knew each other, and it was some kind of ritual or even an execution maybe."

A shiver of recognition prickled in her gut. Felix was circling something real. They knew each other somehow, even if the evidence refused to give her a single thread. There was a bond between victim and killer, some common ground that tied them together. But what? The answer hovered just beyond reach, taunting her with its nearness.

Maria's eyes stayed on the mirror. Her voice dropped to almost a whisper. *"They all came from the same place."* The words slipped out before she knew why she'd said them.

"What was that?" Felix asked.

Maria blinked, tearing her gaze away. "Nothing. Forget it. I appreciate your help, Felix."

"You betcha," he said warmly.

Her phone buzzed. A text. From Bryans. So maybe he wasn't in the building after all.

The text read: YOUR BOY IS AWAKE AND STABLE.

Maria's chest tightened. Reed.

"I've gotta go," she told Felix.

"Alright, Maria. Don't be a stranger."

"We'll talk soon," she promised, then hung up.

She grabbed her coat and headed for the door.

Reed Ashland was waiting, and she needed answers.

45

CHAPTER FORTY-FIVE

Static in the Bones

The view from the driver's seat was a frame. The windshield a lens on the world he moved through.

To him, the city wasn't streets and buildings, but a living thing. Skin stretched over bone, pulsing with traffic and electricity. Perplexing, yes, but appetizing in a way he could never explain. Like staring at a creature you don't understand, yet knowing, in some marrow-deep certainty, that you could prey upon it.

A car idled at the curb, ordinary enough to blend into the city traffic, and yet wrong. Not a Sonata. Definitely not. The lines of this vehicle were softer, older, painted a dull shade that could be gray or green depending on how the light hit it.

Forgettable.

Perfect.

He sat low behind the wheel, hands moving with the kind of patience that unsettled. When he adjusted, it wasn't just driving; it was a ritual. The leather wheel creaked as he turned it. Slow. Deliberate. A serpent coiling. His hand shifted the gear stick with a grace too fluid to be human, an undulating motion that seemed borrowed from some darker anatomy.

Outside, people streamed in and out of the precinct.

Uniforms. Civilians.

Tired faces and hurried shoes. None of them mattered. Not really.

His gaze drifted lazily from one to the next until it settled. His stare snapped sharp as a trap onto her.

Maria.

The crowd dissolved around her like paint washed from a canvas, the world's edges smearing until only she remained. His pupils seemed to narrow, his focus tunneling, locking on her with a hunger that hummed low and electric in his skull.

Everything else was noise, static, background meat.

But this Maria, she vibrated in the frame, a signal breaking through the interference, and once his attention found her, it clamped down with the inevitability of teeth closing on bone.

This Maria.

She came out quick, moving with purpose. A folder tucked under her arm.

He could feel the hum of her alertness even from here. A cop's intuition, sharp enough to sense a tail if it wasn't careful. He let her take the lead, waited a beat longer than natural, then slipped the car into motion.

He reached forward and turned the volume up slowly.

From the stereo came a low, shivering throb. Nine Inch Nails. "I'm Not From This World." The bassline crawled through the cabin, a pulse, a reminder. The throb filled him. A soundtrack to hunger, the rhythm of a hunt older than memory. The song suited him.

He followed her through the streets, never too close, never too far. Lights rolled past the windshield in a stutter: green, then yellow, then red. Each change felt less like traffic control and more like omens.

Finally, Maria turned and disappeared into the parking deck of the hospital. He slid in after her, careful. Careful.

The place smelled of exhaust and damp concrete. He let his car prowl a few rows before he eased into a spot. A hunter's vantage. Just close enough, just far enough. Angled just so that her car remained in sight but his own sat in the blind space between overhead lights. Strategic. Predatory. Grotesquely patient.

Every sound carried: dripping pipes, a car door slamming somewhere above, folded back on itself until the garage felt alive, whispering secrets to the walls.

He watched her step out. The echo of her shoes on the cement carried longer than it should have.

She crossed toward the entrance. The doors took her. Swallowed her whole.

He felt a sudden, sour jealousy. Disgusted that the glass and metal had touched her before he could, that they had the privilege of devouring this Maria while he could only watch.

Inside that building was Reed. Colin's father too, broken but not gone.

Maybe the boy and the mother were tucked away somewhere behind those sterile walls. The whole lot of them, bundled in fate.

The thought curled hot in his gut. How easy it would be to erase them all, to silence their breathing, to Fold them into nothing.

The temptation was sharp, bright, almost sweet on his tongue.

But no. Not yet. That indulgence could wait.

This Maria could not.

His lips twitched at the thought, not quite a smile.

Always this Maria, set aside for the altar of his intent.

But just as she faded from view, the sensation struck.

That alarm in his marrow. A radar built into his skin, into his bones. Something wrong. Out of place.

He shifted, eyes flicking across the deck. Rows of steel and shadow.

Nothing moved. Nothing.

Then he saw it. A sliver of motion near her car. A figure, or the shadow of one, passing across the driver's side window.

Too quick to catch fully, too strange to dismiss. The figure's movement bent wrong, as if its limbs belonged to a dream: jointless, fluid, slipping through the air.

Someone? Or something?

This Maria?...

46

CHAPTER FORTY-SIX

Ash and Voss

Reed Ashland opened his eyes slowly, the sterile ceiling above him swimming into view, light humming faintly. Time itself felt broken, as though he might have been gone for hours or a century.

The steady rhythm of the EKG ticked beside him, uncertain, faltering in its own strange way.

For a moment, he couldn't tell if this was life or some slow drift into the other side. His body felt both impossibly heavy and untethered.

Then shapes sharpened, edges claimed their places, and he saw her.

Detective Maria Voss sat in the corner of the room, half-silhouetted by the pale light. Arms crossed. Coat still on. She looked tired, more than he remembered. Her eyes, fixed on him, seemed to hold back a storm. Not suspicion exactly, but caution.

"What are you doing here?" he asked. The words rasped out of him, each syllable dragging over a throat gone dry.

She shifted in the chair. "Keeping an eye on the killer."

Reed blinked. His pulse jumped once on the monitor. A sharp unease ran through him. Surprise twisting into something closer to fear.

"You still think it's me?" he asked, exasperated.

Maria gave a small, coy smirk and let the silence hang for a beat, deciding

236

how much to let him squirm. "Calm down. Nobody thinks that anymore. We got a good suspect. He's on the run, but we've got our guy." She stood slowly, joints cracking.

Then Reed's mind caught up to the rest of him.

Images bled back in: Colin's house swallowed in shadows, the scream of a boy down the hall, the glint of a knife catching dim light. Maria's voice shouting. The sudden crush of impact, heat blooming in his chest.

"Colin?" He shot up more than he should have and winced.

"He's fine," Maria said quickly.

Reed collapsed back into the bed. A long breath. Then he looked back at her. A jagged bolt of pain shot through his ribs when he tried to speak again, but he forced the words out anyway.

"Are you sure?" His voice cracked, threaded with panic.

Maria leaned forward, her tone steady. "Yes. He's fine."

Reed shut his eyes, but the urgency clawed its way back. "What about his parents? Are they okay?"

Maria hesitated only a second. "The dad was hurt, but he'll pull through. His mom's perfectly fine. Terrified as hell but physically unharmed." A pang of guilt struck him; another family scarred by a nightmare he couldn't seem to stop dragging people into.

Reed let out a shaky breath, tension draining from his shoulders. He tried to steady himself. Maria watched him, the corners of her mouth tightening. She felt a flicker of sympathy for how obvious his pain still was.

"How are you feeling?" she asked gently.

Reed gave a humorless laugh. "Like I should be dead."

Maria arched a brow. "Not quite," she said, then added dryly, "but don't piss me off."

Reed chuckled, the sound catching on pain, and Maria gave a small laugh herself. "Sorry for that," she muttered.

"Not exactly bedside manner," Reed said, still wincing.

Maria shrugged. "Hey, I brought flowers."

His eyes flicked toward the empty nightstand. "Where are they?"

"Metaphorical ones," she said smoothly. "Don't push your luck."

Despite himself, Reed laughed again, softer this time. The humor stung, but it grounded him. Reed's eyes lingered on Maria, steady, searching, weighing something he hadn't decided whether to say aloud.

She noticed. Her brow furrowed. "What?" she asked.

"You're in danger," he said quietly.

She didn't even blink. "Yeah. I know."

Reed tried to push himself up again, urgency flickering in him. "Maria, I'm serious. There are things, dreams. The Fold. The symbols. The mirrors. They're all—"

"Reed, calm down." She reached out with one hand, gently pressing him back against the pillow. The touch wasn't forceful, but it carried the weight of quiet authority.

His breath hitched, words rough. "Who is he? The guy you're after. What's his story?"

"I can't divulge that information, Dr. Ashland." Maria cut him off, turning away. Arms crossed.

She glanced at the shattered mirror above Reed's sink. Just briefly. Then she spoke. Her voice was calm.

"You must unlearn the alphabet."

He froze.

The words rippled through him, dredging up a memory: shadowed halls where a dozen strange beings whispered the phrase in unison.

"Where did you hear that?" he asked adamantly.

They stared at each other, each wondering what the other knew. How deep it went. Neither of them moved, the clock's hum the only sound.

Maria's jaw tightened, her expression unreadable. She could feel the edge of the cliff under her feet, Reed's words pulling her toward a drop she wasn't sure she wanted to make.

Finally, she broke the silence, her voice low and careful.

"I heard it in a dream," she said.

"It wasn't a dream, Detective," Reed snapped back.

"Then what was it?" she volleyed back.

He looked away, jaw tightening. "I don't know exactly. It's between the lines, so to speak. Something just outside the page."

He thought of it again: the crayon. *REED, BETWEEN THE LINES.*

Maria hooked a hand around the back of a chair and dragged it closer, turning it backwards before sliding into it. She rested her arms across the top rail, posture casual but eyes sharp.

"Go on," she said.

There was eagerness there. More than she wanted him to see, but she masked it behind a veneer of control, pretending she was merely humoring him.

He did. Slowly at first, then faster. Like a dam giving way.

"Rooms that bend. A library with books you can't open. Books that scream when you touch them. Moving geometry, ideas that can walk."

Reed's hands clenched at the sheets. He leaned forward slightly, then sagged back.

Maria said nothing. Her face was carved stone, but her eyes flickered. She was listening.

"There's someone else, too," he said. "A presence. Always changing. Sometimes human, sometimes not. Whatever it is, it speaks in riddles. I call it the Father of Absurdity."

She leaned forward slightly. Enough for Reed to notice. Whether she believed him or was building a case, he couldn't tell.

"I saw the victims there," he continued. "I saw you. And the killer."

That made her shift.

"What was I doing there?"

"I don't know," Reed replied.

"What about him? The killer?"

"I don't know that either."

She let out a long, frustrated sigh. It swelled in the room like a balloon about to pop. "What do you know?" she pressed. She kept the police-mask in place for appearances, authority covering belief.

Reed looked at her carefully. "That when you're there… you're not really you. There might be more than one version of a person in the Fold. Maybe that's what the two Mary Johnsons were. Maybe one got out. Or both. I don't know. But they crossed over somehow. Through the mirrors. That's why they were identical. I think at least one of them came from the Fold."

She went still. "The Fold?"

The word struck her. For an instant, the hospital room wavered. Her mind pulled back to a place where mirrors rippled and reshaped themselves, endless corridors bending. The memory flickered and was gone, but the chill of it clung to her skin.

"That's what I call it. The Elsewhere Fold. I told you and the captain that. Remember?"

Maria swallowed. *The Elsewhere Fold,* she thought. She wasn't sure if she was mocking it or trying to decode it.

"I see people in mirrors sometimes," he went on. "They're not just reflections. They're dangerous. Sometimes they watch. And sometimes… they become."

His voice shifted.

"Become what?" Maria asked.

"Us."

She stared. Silent. Waiting.

"Mirror souls," he said. "That's what I call them."

"Mirror souls? Like, evil twins?"

"No. Not always evil. They're… versions. Replicants. Echoes that get to decide who they want to be. Some good. Some bad. Just like people. But they're born from reflection. And they can come into our world."

Maria leaned back, arms crossing again. "Absurdity's the right word," she muttered.

Reed caught it. He leaned in.

"Why are you so interested all of a sudden?"

She didn't answer.

"You were there," he said, more firmly now, leaning into the words.

"I saw you," he pressed, confidence growing with each word. "I know you've seen it too. You weren't just humoring me. You were there."

Her eyes dropped.

That was all he needed.

"I know it's hard," Reed said. The fervor drained from his voice, leaving something quieter, steadier. His eyes softened as he looked at her. "It's disorienting. Even when you already believe it. I did. And it still felt insane."

He could see how much weight she was carrying, how much harder it must be to let go of logic and procedure.

Confusion, curiosity, and anger tangled in her chest. She understood how Bryans must have felt. Sitting across from Reed, listening to fragments of impossible stories.

She looked up, struggling. "What is it?"

Reed shook his head slowly. "The Fold knows you. It shows you what's happened. What's coming. That's how I found Colin."

"The Fold told you?"

He hesitated. "No. A man did. I call him Mr. Morrow. I told you about him."

"Yeah…" she rubbed her temples. "I remember."

"He helps… I think. He warned me you were in danger."

Her eyes softened, just barely. A lump crawled into her throat.

"The killer, he's after you next. Is there someone with your kids? You have boys, right? I saw them too," Reed said.

Maria stood suddenly, trying to escape the moment. She paced to the window, then turned back. Snapped into detective mode.

"Tell me about time, Doctor Ashland. Why 3:33? Why the clocks? The mirrors? Why are they all broken?"

Reed exhaled. Slower now.

"Time doesn't really exist there. But mirrors do. They see our world. And they show it to the Fold. 3:33 is… maybe when both realities glance at each other. Or collide."

Maria raised a brow.

"I don't know," Reed admitted. "Maybe the number matters more than the hour. 333. Spiritually, it means manifestation. Thought shaping reality. And in the Fold, emotion does shape reality. Things happen that match what you feel. What you believe."

Maria hummed.

Reed hesitated, then asked again, softer this time. "Your kids… they're okay?"

Maria's head snapped toward him. "They're fine!" she barked, sharper and louder than she meant to. The anger in her voice cracked through the room.

Reed didn't flinch. He just looked at her, steady. The silence stretched until Maria let the air drain out of her.

Another pause, heavier now. Reed broke it, his voice low. "Boys, right?"

Maria froze. Slowly, she shook her head. "How the hell do you know that?"

"I saw them," Reed answered quickly. "There."

Maria froze. There was no way he could have known that. The truth pressed in, and with it came the rising panic that her children weren't untouchable.

Maria shifted uneasily, sliding a hand into her coat pocket. She pulled out her phone under the cover of silence and tapped out a terse message to Bryans: SEND A UNIT TO ELI AND TOMMY'S SCHOOL. CHECK ON THEM AND ESCORT THEM HOME AFTER DISMISSAL.

The reply came almost instantly. DONE.

Reed noticed the glow of the phone. "What was that?" he asked.

Maria locked the screen and slid it away without meeting his eyes. "Nothing."

Maria swallowed hard and pushed the fear down, locking it away. When she spoke again, her voice was all business.

"Okay. Enough about numbers. Now, Mr. Morrow, tell me about him. What is he?" she demanded, pressing harder now, her tone clipped and commanding.

Reed felt a twinge of disappointment as he watched the walls slide back into place, her eyes sharpening.

"Mr. Morrow always shows up at 4:44," Reed added.

Maria arched a brow. "He's got a time slot too?"

"And a symbol. A knot. The wisdom knot. He left it for me once. When I left it for him… on my front door… he came."

CHAPTER FORTY-SIX

She snorted. "He's got his own bat signal. Impressive."

Reed forced a thin smile, trying not to let her sarcasm crawl under his skin. But that last jab stung more than he wanted to admit.

"You asked about time, okay? The Fold has a rhythm. So does Morrow. But like I said, I don't think it's the hour that matters. I think it's the number. 444 is what they call an angel number. A sign someone's watching over you. It means your guides are near. Supporting you. Helping you navigate."

He paused, looking at her. Maria's glare hid her eagerness to hear more.

"And that fits him. Morbid, cryptic, unnerving. But he helps. He warned me about Colin. And about you."

Maria didn't move.

"So, you don't believe me," Reed said at last. His eyes narrowed, studying her the way she'd been studying him.

He started pushing back, pressing against her defenses to see if they would crack. "But here you are. Asking these questions. You didn't come to babysit. You came for answers. If you didn't believe even a little, then why are we having this conversation, Voss?"

That name hit her harder than it should've.

Only cops called her that. And just the ones who knew her well enough to earn the right. For just a moment, she faltered. A flicker, then the wall she'd built around herself crumbled.

Reed pressed in gently.

"You've lost someone. Someone close. A friend or a sister, maybe?"

Her eyes widened, disbelief flooding her.

How the hell did he know that too? He couldn't have known. Her hand shot to her chest, clutching the silver ring beneath her shirt.

Reed didn't reach for her. He just noticed it.

"I saw it," he said. "I saw you watching her. I saw you lose her."

Maria's breath hitched. A tear welled and fell before she could stop it. Her grip on the ring tightened. She hated that he saw it.

"Who was it?" Reed asked softly. "Did they give that to you?" He nodded toward the necklace she wouldn't let go of.

Maria's head bowed. A sob escaped, brief and raw, and she swallowed hard, reining herself back in. She looked at him, eyes glassy.

"How…" she began. Anger rising; a defense.

"I told you," Reed said, voice calm. "I saw it."

They hung in the moment. Maria struggling to hold back the tears threatening to spill again. Her voice cracked, raw and shaking, each word forced through the barrier of controlled breaths.

The relief surprised her. She'd been carrying so much for so long with nowhere to set it down, and now, with him, the weight began to ease.

Rose was probably sick of the late-night calls and endless favors. Bryans, for all his loyalty, was worn thin by her hunches.

But Reed, he was already broken open, already living with his own ghosts. For once, she didn't have to pretend. For once, she could breathe.

"I barely tell my own children about her. About their aunt. I guess it's selfish. It's just too hard for me."

She paused again to gather herself. Reed listened, silent and steady.

"Our dad? We never knew him. Our mom was a drunk. We both left at eighteen and never looked back. She was my entire family until my boys were born."

Reed's thoughts drifted to Emily. A familiar ache settled in his throat.

"My sister was my only friend. Any problem, any heartbreak, any bad day—she was there. With advice. With guidance. She always knew how to get through to me, even when the rest of the world couldn't. I idolized her. Her wisdom. The perfect older sister."

Maria took a deep breath.

"And then she was gone. Murdered. They never found the guy." Her voice cracked on the last word.

"Her name was Lucia."

Tears came now, running freely as she turned away, jaw clenched.

Reed didn't speak at first. He just looked at her. Noticing the pain, the strength it took to share it. Then his eyes dropped to the necklace she wore. A simple silver chain.

Maria followed his gaze and touched the pendant instinctively.

"It was her ring. She always wore it," she said, her voice softer now. "I put it on a chain after… and I never take it off."

She looked down and gave a soft, wistful laugh.

"It was stupid, really. Some junior high boyfriend gave it to her. Broke her heart. She kept it anyway. Said it reminded her that 'this too shall pass.' That nothing is permanent. Everything changes. Everything heals. I carry that with me every day." Maria looked down at the ring, chin quivering. "I have to," she added.

With a crooked smile, she continued, "In reality, it's just a cheap ring from some middle school douchebag."

Reed let out a small laugh, genuine. So did she. Reed's eyes lingered on her with quiet sympathy.

"I lost my daughter," Reed said quietly.

Maria nodded. "I know."

He looked up, startled.

"Cancer," she added.

Reed stared at her. The moment cracked something open in him.

"How do you know that?"

"You were a suspect, remember?" she said. "I investigated you. I know a lot about you."

Reed leaned back, half amused. "I think I feel violated now."

She chuckled, just a little, and the weight in the room lifted. For a second.

"She was everything," Reed said. "But there were days… I hated being a dad. Not always, but sometimes it felt like drowning. And after she died, I hated myself for ever feeling that way. I drank to forget. I drank to avoid."

"I know," Maria said. "I talked to Claire."

Reed rolled his eyes and threw up his hands. "Great. So you really do know everything."

Maria smiled. "It's nice to hear it from you, though. Not just the file. Not just the gossip. It's honest. You're not just some conspiracy nut chasing saucers and dreaming of ghosts."

Reed smirked. "You're chasing broken clocks and mirrors."

She opened her mouth to push back. But didn't. She just gave him a look that said: *You're not wrong.*

Silence fell. Too heavy to be casual, too intimate to be professional. Reed broke it.

"I am confident that there truly is such a thing as living again… that the living spring from the dead… and that the souls of the dead are in existence."

Maria looked at him. Their eyes locked.

"Socrates," she said.

Reed blinked, surprised. She saw it in his face.

"I studied philosophy once upon a time," she said.

He smiled. "You paid attention in class. Most of my students just slept one off while I lectured." They both laughed slightly.

Maria looked away, hesitant. "I wanted to teach it. At one point."

Reed's eyebrows lifted. "Really?"

She nodded.

Reed adjusted his gaze. She wasn't just a skeptic in a trench coat. There was depth. He saw it now.

"You were young," he said, almost teasing. "I saw you."

She frowned. "What?"

"Sitting cross-legged on a rooftop. You looked like a hippie, actually."

Maria groaned. "Don't."

Reed laughed. "It was kind of charming."

She rolled her eyes, but it was true. At nineteen, that was her. She hated that he had nailed it.

"Lucia changed that?" Reed asked gently.

Maria dropped her gaze. Her voice small.

"Yeah… you could say that," she said, wistful.

They sat in it: pain, connection, bewilderment.

Finally, Maria looked up. Her voice low. Almost a whisper. She hesitated and then finally said, "Ash?"

He turned. No one had ever called him that before. But from her, it felt right.

She held his gaze.

"How do we catch this guy?"

Reed thought for a long moment. The warmth between them didn't vanish, it hung beneath the question, woven into the air.

He let out a breath. Then answered.

"Voss… I don't know."

$$47$$

CHAPTER FORTY-SEVEN

Ashland, Interrupted

The hospital room had settled into a rare stillness, the kind that felt earned after everything had been said. Maria leaned back in the chair by Reed's bedside, arms crossed, eyes soft but alert. Reed watched her from his pillow.

Then the door creaked open. The sound shattered the fragile cocoon they'd been in, breaking the quiet connection that had settled between them.

Captain Bryans stepped in, his expression somewhere between suspicious and tired.

He glanced from Maria to Reed and back again.

"Late to the party?" he quipped.

Maria straightened slightly. "What's up, Captain?"

Bryans raised an eyebrow. "Me? I was gonna ask you the same thing. I got a couple uniforms over to the school. What's that about?"

Maria shifted in her chair, folding her arms tighter. "Just being careful. After what went down in that house, I hurt him bad. If he's still out there, he might come for me."

Bryans tilted his head, brow furrowed. "How would he even know you're alive? And in what shape? Sounds to me like you kicked the shit out of him. How's he supposed to know anything about you, or Tommy and Eli?"

Maria hesitated. The words Reed had just whispered to her still clung to her, dark and heavy. If she repeated them, they'd sound insane, even to Bryans. She thought better of it. Shrugged instead.

"Call it a hunch from a careful mama."

Bryans studied her a moment, then let out a grunt that passed for acceptance. "Alright. Fair enough. But then what are you doing here?"

She gestured vaguely toward Reed. "Uncovering truths. About the case. About the killer. And reminding myself I'm done with philosophy."

Bryans rolled his eyes, sighed, and was ready to move on when Reed spoke up from the bed.

"Your killer is more than a person, Captain."

Bryans paused, turned slowly. His face was carved with fatigue, patience worn thin, and it showed plain he was in no mood for whatever Ashland had to say.

Reed's voice was low but steady, his eyes locked onto Bryans. "He's a soul. A soul on a journey from which he cannot ever escape. If you want to find him, you have to understand the next step in that journey. His intentions may not be clear to everyone, but... from what I've seen, what I felt, he's coming for Voss next."

A long silence.

Bryans stared at him. Then turned to Maria.

"So, did you deputize this guy or something?"

Maria snickered and looked away. "He's... got a lot to say."

Reed gave a clumsy salute. "Reporting for duty, sir."

Bryans gave him a look—not angry but parental—the kind of look that said 'don't make me pull this car over.'

Reed's hand dropped and he slumped against the bed with exaggerated regret. He hoped they forgot his attempt at a joke immediately.

Bryans folded his arms, fixing Maria with a look.

"So, let me get this straight... you had me send a couple guys to fetch your kids because he thinks the killer's after you?"

His tone wasn't sharp, but the edge was there. Bryans knew Maria could be in danger. He didn't doubt that, but the idea of her hitching her wagon to Ashland didn't sit right with him.

Maria just smirked subtly at Reed.

Bryans shook his head and moved closer. "I talked to Rose. Blood found at the apartment matches what we found in Glendale Heights. It's Avery. We've got uniforms out tracking his known contacts, old coworkers, girlfriends, even a cousin he once got drunk with in college. If they don't find him at any of those spots, we widen the net."

He paused. "The guy's barely left the city his whole life. No passport. No exotic retreat. A creature of habit."

"He'll go after Voss," Reed said again. "I'm sure of it."

Bryans studied him. Not with hostility now, just the weight of someone juggling too many possibilities and not enough certainty. He turned to Maria.

"You want us to keep a protective detail?"

Reed was impressed with himself that the captain listened to him.

Maria stood, stretching slightly. "Let's go back to the station and talk about it. I need some terrible police station coffee right now."

She offered Reed a crooked grin. "Give me a minute. I'll catch up."

Bryans gave a nod and turned toward the door.

"Bye, Captain," Reed said cheerfully.

Bryans didn't respond. He just walked out.

Reed watched the door close behind him. "I think he's starting to like me."

Maria turned back toward him, arms crossed again. "Sure, Ash. Keep telling yourself that."

She laughed, and for a moment, it was the kind of laugh that stitched the world back together, if only briefly.

Their eyes lingered on each other, something unspoken passing between them. Fragile, but real.

Maria uncrossed her arms, softening just enough. "I'll check in on you later."

Reed smiled faintly, the kind of smile that came harder these days but managed to surface anyway.

As she moved toward the door, he found his voice again.

CHAPTER FORTY-SEVEN

"Voss…"

She turned in the doorway, silhouetted by the hall light.

"Seriously… be careful."

$$48$$

CHAPTER FORTY-EIGHT

Whispers and Footsteps

Maria Voss stepped into the parking garage as if descending into a tomb.

The overhead bulbs hummed with a sickly drone, their glow uneven, casting more shadow than light. Some had burned out entirely, leaving long stretches of darkness that yawned between pale islands of illumination.

Parking garages were always unsettling. Echoes traveling too far, footsteps sounding closer than they were, the stale reek of exhaust clinging to the concrete. But this one carried something heavier.

The walls seemed to exhale cold, the still air pressing in. It didn't just linger; it loomed.

Maria walked with purpose. Clack, clack, clack. Each footstep sharp against the concrete. But the sound carried too far, bouncing back at her in a way that made her chest tighten. Each step sent out into the dark, received by something unseen, something waiting.

Then: another footstep. Not hers.

She stopped. So did the other steps.

If ever there was a moment where breath was held, where a chest tightened, this was it. The silence didn't just settle; it thickened.

She started again, slower now. All her senses were sharpened, pulled taut, every nerve standing on alert.

Rows of cars loomed, hulking silhouettes, their windows catching slivers of light and throwing them back as warped reflections. Each gap between bumpers felt ominous; every shadow a body poised to step out.

The air carried that faint, oily tang of rubber and gasoline, and it clung to her throat as she moved.

Then it came: a flick, a bump, or maybe nothing at all. Footsteps, one beat behind.

She stopped. The absence of sound pressed on her eardrums, daring her to breathe. She waited a moment. Prepared. Then she turned like a soldier on high alert.

Just rows of parked cars and creeping shadow.

She exhaled through her nose and resumed walking at a normal pace, head high, pretending not to be wound tight as a tripwire.

She heard them again: faint, trailing, just behind. This time she didn't stop.

She pressed forward, stride steady, refusing to give the sound the satisfaction of her hesitation. Maybe the steps were getting louder, maybe not. Hard to tell. Harder to ignore.

Then, just before passing a black sedan, she pivoted sharply and ducked behind it.

Footsteps scrambled in the darkness ahead. Too fast, too scattered. They didn't match the rhythm she expected. Too many of them. Or none at all.

Crouched low, she steadied herself, her breath shallow and quick in her chest.

Her pulse drummed in her ears, each beat reaching down into her fingertips. Eyes darted from shadow to shadow, trying to pin down the steps, the source, anything. But there was nothing certain, just the hollow groan of the garage and the suspicion that someone else was moving out there.

Maybe it was nothing. Maybe some poor soul wandering rows, looking for their car. But Maria wasn't taking chances.

With slow, deliberate care, she drew her weapon from her hip, the metal weight steadying her hands even as the rest of her trembled inside.

She was ready for whatever was waiting.

She retraced her steps, every movement measured, every angle covered.

Her eyes cut side to side, sweeping under the cars, between their frames, scanning mirrors and windshields for any twitch of movement or glint of eyes.

Each reflection was hiding a shape, every shadow a crouched figure waiting to spring. Her grip was locked tight, finger brushing the trigger—steady, ready. She wasn't about to lose her weapon this time, not here, not again. If something came out of that dark, she'd be the one in control.

A flicker of movement in the rearview of a nearby Jeep made her flinch. She turned quickly, gun drawn.

Her own reflection.

"No mirrors," she whispered. "Not here."

Something scattered off to the right, far down the row. She spun toward the sound.

Nothing.

Her breathing slowed: shallow, deliberate.

She froze, listening. A pattern began to take shape.

Whoever, or whatever, it was, they were tucked in the rows ahead, hidden among the metal hulks. She could feel it in her gut, that cop's instinct tightening into certainty. Fine. If they wanted to lurk, she'd bring the fight to them.

She slipped off her shoes and continued barefoot, moving quieter now, a shadow among shadows.

She cleared a row of SUVs. Passed a column. Checked every corner.

Then: voices.

Not loud. Whispers.

Words that weren't quite words: half-laughter, half-breath. Sliding over each other, threading into the hum of the garage. Sometimes they sounded close, brushing the back of her neck; sometimes far, echoing from nowhere at all.

She stopped. Closed her eyes.

The whispers converged into a single tone. She clenched her jaw against the vibration.

Then silence again.

Then—thump—far to her left.

She turned fast, gun raised.

Movement. Blurred.

Something low to the ground?

No. High. Where shadows touched the ceiling.

Maria crept forward, weapon ready, eyes sharp.

She didn't blink. She didn't hesitate.

Whatever it was that was following her. Harassing her. It wasn't going to get the drop.

Then, an explosion of motion.

Something slammed into her from the side, fast and surgical.

A blow to her wrist. Her gun skidded across the floor.

She didn't see the face. Just fists. Feet. A macabre pirouette of limbs.

She fought back. Elbows and knees. Her back hit a car. Then the floor.

Stillness. Darkness.

She coughed. Tasted blood.

Soft, meticulous footsteps receded.

A long pause.

She lay there blinking, vision stuttering.

Somehow, between blinks, she caught a glimpse. A silhouette. Slender. Wrong. Something about the way it moved bent against the rhythm of the world, angles where there shouldn't be. And yet… there was something about it she recognized, a flicker of familiarity woven into the wrongness, like seeing a face from a dream you can't fully place.

Maria was confused. Baffled. Her voice emerged groggy, half-lost in the quiet:

"What the hell are you?"

Somewhere in the distance, faint and wrong, she heard the ticking of a clock.

But it wasn't ticking.

It was whispering.

The word: "you."
Over and over, just slightly out of time.

49

CHAPTER FORTY-NINE

The Quiet Before the Scream

The clink of dishes. Running water. The soft rustle of pajamas on carpet. A cough from down the hall. The muffled blip of a cartoon still playing on low volume in the living room, forgotten by a boy who'd already surrendered to sleep.

The house carried the small chaos of family; shoes left by the door, homework spread open on the kitchen counter, a jacket draped over the back of a chair. It was the sound and clutter of life insisting on normalcy after a day that had been anything but.

Maria moved through it all methodically.

Dinner was long over. Eli had gone down without a word. He was old enough to brush his teeth, set out his clothes, and crawl into bed on his own. He still liked her to tuck him in though. To smooth the blanket and turn off the lamp. A quiet ritual he wasn't quite ready to give up.

Tommy, as always, had lingered at the edge of sleep with questions and bargaining.

"Just one story?"

"No, Tommy. Sleep."

He'd pouted, turned away. She said goodnight to no response from her temperamental youngest. That was routine. But as she pulled the door nearly shut, she caught the soft, pouty murmur of a "good night" drifting out after her.

Maria checked the lunches. PB&Js packed. Juice boxes tucked beside the freezer packs. Doritos for Eli and Pringles for Tommy. Pop-Tarts ready for the morning. Strawberry as always.

Now: toothbrushes, backpacks by the door, lights dimmed just right. All of it done with surgical precision. Her limbs felt heavy, but her hands moved without needing instruction.

Her eyes lingered on corners, counters, doorframes; checking, scanning. Maybe making sure no chore had slipped past her. Or maybe something else. The focus felt odd and out of place.

Later, she stood in the dark of the living room, watching through the front window, the glass cool against her fingertips. Streetlights bled their amber glow onto the pavement below, stretching long, crooked shadows across the sidewalk.

The sky above was a deep, bruised blue, pierced by the occasional flicker of a star trying to remember its own name. The world felt paused, holding its breath, waiting for something to stir in the darkness.

A breeze shifted the curtains. She blinked, sighed, turned away.

Face washed.

Teeth brushed.

Hair tied back.

Lotion on her hands.

Alarm set for 6:00. Phone placed face-down.

Pistol on the nightstand, magazine checked twice though she already knew it was full.

She moved through it step by step, each action following the next.

She climbed into bed, pulled the covers over her, and exhaled. It was less rest than procedure, her body clicked through the final motions of a day she hadn't quite lived in.

The house settled into silence. Nocturnal peace. The kind that carried its own weight; pipes ticking faintly as they cooled, the refrigerator humming, the occasional groan of wood as the frame adjusted to the night.

Outside, a car passed on the street, its headlights sweeping briefly across the curtains before vanishing. Then stillness again. Heavy, watchful.

A locked door.

A soft click. Not loud, barely there. The kind of sound that might've been nothing at all, except it carried a weight, a finality.

He slipped in through the back entrance: kitchen level, clean, quiet. No splintered wood. No forced marks. No broken glass.

Just the faint tremor of metal against metal, a polished tool coaxing the lock open.

Daniel Avery slipped inside, a glide of darkness across linoleum. The air barely noticed him. He smiled, not broad but tight-and-crooked. An expression that twitched at the corners, more shadow than joy.

Every step was calculated, every creak of the floorboards memorized and avoided.

He didn't need a map. The house unfolded for him like it had been waiting.

He slid forward in silence, a devilish serpent slithering through a garden, tongue tasting the air, relishing the nearness of prey.

His eyes flicked across the signs of life around him: crayons scattered on the counter, a jacket half-slid from a chair, a pair of sneakers left untied by the door. The wallpaper, the photographs, the smell of detergent clinging to the carpet. None of it mattered. What mattered was the pulse of the place, the rhythm of sleep, the fragile boundary between dreams and waking.

He followed it upstairs, down the hallway.

Third door on the left. He opened it without hesitation.

There she was: under the comforter, turned away. A body-shape beneath soft cotton and faint moonlight. Avery grinned.

This wasn't just the kill. This was the moment. The last breath of a doomed thing. The quiet before the scream.

He steadied himself, chest rising slow, absorbing the stretch of his lungs.

Anticipation was eating him alive, gnawing from the inside out. His fingers twitched once, then stilled. It was time.

He pulled the knife from his pocket with his right hand, smooth and silent. Reached out with his left, fingers poised to touch the sleeping detective.

Slow, deliberate, each joint flexing with predatory care.

His hand crept forward, trembling strands alive with tension, reaching for the trapped bug at its center. Every inch was control, patience, hunger wound tight in the curl of his fingers.

This Maria...

The covers exploded upward.

A blur. A roar. A figure rising fast.

"Peekaboo, motherfucker."

Captain Bryans.

The knife flashed—*schlick*—and blood spilled from his right arm. He cried out, stumbled. The killer kicked him hard, and Bryans went tumbling over the bed.

Avery spun and bolted for the hallway.

CRACK.

A sickening blow to the face.

The aluminum bat dropped him to one knee. Maria Voss stood looming over him in the hallway, eyes wide, face stone. Determined. She didn't say a word.

He looked up, dazed, blood dripping from his nose and lips.

Then he laughed.

"Oh really? Not just me, huh?"

Maria didn't respond.

He swung. She ducked, blocked, and drove into him as fists and feet collided.

He threw her against a wall. She returned the favor with a knee to the ribs and a vicious elbow to the throat.

He landed a punch on her jaw, the crack sharp in the air, yet Maria barely flinched. Her head snapped to the side, but she came right back at him, eyes blazing, pain had become fuel instead of weakness.

She hammered three right hooks into his face, each one heavier than the last, the wet impact leaving Avery reeling. Shocked at her sudden, brutal strength. Harder than before.

The reopened wounds on his face spilled fresh blood, and with each blow his grin faltered just a little more.

It was a dance of pain and rage: violent, clumsy, intimate.

They grappled, bodies colliding against walls and furniture, the struggle moving with a savage rhythm that felt choreographed. Each impact was another beat.

The house groaned around them, picture frames toppling, glass shattering underfoot. A toy truck cracked in two beneath Avery's heel. Domestic order collapsing into wreckage. Family life splintered beneath their violence.

Avery twisted and bucked, managing to break free for an instant. His grin flared as he scrambled to his feet, ready to lunge again. But Maria was faster. She slammed into him with a force that knocked the air from his lungs, driving him flat to the floor.

Her knees pinned his shoulders down, weight crushing him in place. The fury in her movements wasn't just survival. It was something deeper, sharper, a determination that threatened to outmatch even his murderous devotion.

His breath came hot against her wrists. His shirt was slick, staining her knees. The contact too close, too human. The pinning was an embrace now, the kind of intimacy only brutality could create.

Her hand trembled as she drew the gun, but the moment the barrel pressed to his forehead, the tremor vanished.

She locked in, steady, breathing hard through her nose, eyes locked on his.

Avery froze beneath her.

For once, he didn't resist. His bloody grin softened into something even more unsettling: stillness. He raised his hands slowly, palms up, offering surrender. Yet his eyes never left hers, drinking in her resolve, her brutal calculation.

The silence between them was heavy, thick with something unspeakable. Maria didn't blink. Didn't move the gun.

And then, with a dreadful indifference, Avery's lips curled into a sinister grin.

"Is it time?" he whispered, voice low, taunting.

She was going to do it. She wanted to do it.

The world had gone muffled. Everything slowed, distant. The only sound was Avery's pulse beneath her, steady as a drum.

Then...

"VOSS!!"

Bryans. From the bed. Bleeding. Hurt. His voice cut through the fog.

Maria turned. Met his eyes.

The look he gave her wasn't fear. It was something worse. He didn't recognize her.

She blinked.

Whatever switch had flipped, snapped back off again. She lowered the gun, tentative, reluctant.

A moment passed.

Then she reached back and grabbed her cuffs, glaring down into her would-be killer's eyes. He returned her gaze. It was as if they were sharing some dark universal secret, and both knew the other understood.

"Call it in," Bryans muttered, still holding his arm. *"Book this piece of shit."*

Click.

50

CHAPTER FIFTY

Something's Off

The familiar lights buzzed overhead. Cheap coffee, Lysol, and cold metal filled the air. A long hallway. Brick and concrete. Doors with thick locks. Welcome to the Cook County Jail.

The place carried the stale weight of confessions and lies, every sound swallowed by walls that never forgot.

Reed sat in a wheelchair near the booking desk, one arm in a sling, the other resting on the armrest. His face was pale but calm, an odd composure settling over him.

Maria stood near him, arms crossed, blank-faced. Bryans leaned beside the door, shoulder wrapped, arm stiff. He'd looked better but was content. He could put this case away finally.

Hopefully.

"I still can't believe you pulled this," Bryans muttered.

Maria didn't blink. "He was coming for me. Reed knew it. I knew it. It was a good opportunity to get him."

Bryans shook his head, still trying to make sense of it. "With your kids upstairs?" Bryans looked at her, hard. "That's not like you, Maria." He rarely used her first name. "You wanted a detail on them one minute and the next, you call them off."

She shrugged. "I was with them. It had to look real. Otherwise, he wouldn't bite."

She looked at him unyieldingly and added, "We got him, didn't we?" Bryans looked away.

He turned back and watched her a beat longer. Something wasn't right. There was a weight to her that hadn't been there before. Something in her eyes was off, distant, Elsewhere.

"You should take a few days," he said. "Rest. Nap a lot. You look like hell."

Maria's voice was flat. "Yeah. Maybe."

"No maybes. This is done. Just do it," Bryans ordered.

He turned away and looked at Reed.

Ashland looked up and smiled. Bryans didn't return it.

The captain walked over, slow, pride dragging at his boots. "Dr. Ashland," he began, the words tripping over themselves. "I really… I, uh… appreciate the help you've given us on this. I hope you heal up fast."

Reed blinked, caught off guard. For a second he thought he'd misheard, but no, the captain's tone had shifted. It startled him, and, though he'd never admit it out loud, it flattered him too. Some part of him, still raw, still aching, wanted Bryans to see he wasn't the villain in the story.

"Why, Captain Bryans…"

"Don't make this more than it needs to be," Bryans snapped.

Reed smirked. "Call me deputy?"

Bryans scowled. "I regret shaking your hand now."

He abruptly turned to walk away.

"And stop throwing shit out your damn apartment window in the middle of the night," he added over his shoulder. "You do that again, I'll put you in the cell right next to Avery."

"I appreciate you!" Reed hollered after him, laughing.

Maria didn't laugh. She hadn't moved.

The silence stretched between them, heavier than it should have been, and Reed found himself studying her back, curious, unsettled by how still she was.

"How are the kiddos?" he asked finally, trying to bridge the gap.

"Fine."

Reed watched her. Wanting to say something else, but unsure what. The connection of their talk the previous day was no longer there.

"You okay?" Reed asked genuinely.

"I'll live," she said.

He nodded slowly, though the longer he looked at her the more uneasy he felt. The silence pressed in, making him shift in his chair.

"This whole thing left a mark, didn't it?"

She paused. Then finally: "Yeah. Something like that."

***

Bryans walked into the cell area. Keys at his belt. Boots echoing against the tile.

The corridor stretched too long, each barred door a black mouth yawning open into shadow. The overhead lights buzzed, casting sickly halos on concrete that looked wet even when it was dry. Time felt wrong here; stretched thin.

Daniel Avery sat on his cot. Arms resting on his knees. Hands clasped. Head down. Still.

He might have been mistaken for a man at prayer, but there was nothing holy about the posture. The stillness wasn't peace, it was coiled, waiting. His body blended with the drab walls and shadows, a shape you could almost overlook if you didn't know to look closer.

Bryans stepped into the doorway. Said nothing. He just watched him.

There were things about this case that still didn't sit right. Holes. Questions. Not the kind you could file into a report, let alone present in court. But Bryans wasn't just a man of conviction, he was a man of truth.

He wanted to know what had happened in this case. What happened to Voss. What happened to Ashland. He came up empty every time he thought about it.

Somewhere in the silence he thought he heard it: the faint, muffled sound of a clock ticking. No clock in sight. No rhythm he could place.

Bryans shook his head, brushing the thought away. Jailhouse nerves, nothing more. He forced his focus back where it belonged, on the man in the cell, the one he couldn't afford to mistake for anything less than dangerous.

Avery didn't look up. Didn't acknowledge him. Just stared at the floor like it held answers no one else could see.

Then, finally, he spoke.

"You never asked me what I'm doing here, Captain," Avery said, voice tinged with mockery.

Bryans's brow furrowed. He didn't like how the words landed. It resembled everything else in this case: off. It returned, tapping somewhere deep inside his skull, then vanished.

"You're here," he said, the words slower than they should've been, "because you killed people, and we caught you."

For some reason he couldn't name, Bryans found himself measuring each word. The unease made him cautious, and he hated that.

Avery moved. Like a puppet being maneuvered. Limbs unfolding with an unnatural slowness, joints bending. He lifted his head, the motion stiff, mechanical, yet precise. Then he turned.

His eyes found Bryans and locked there, unblinking, a stare too steady to feel human. It was the kind of gaze that suggested someone behind the curtain, wearing a face that wasn't entirely his.

His face didn't change. His voice was low. Quiet. Final.

"That's not what I meant."

51

CHAPTER FIFTY-ONE

Someone Else's Smile

Claire's new place was a two-story brownstone off South Aberdeen, nestled between a dog grooming boutique and a pawn shop that used to be a florist. The front steps were chipped and weathered, a jagged welcome that made the building look older than it was.

Reed stared at them as he and Maria walked up in silence, the air around him thick with unease. Every step forward seemed heavier than the last, the closer he got, the more the past pressed in on him.

He hesitated at the door.

Maria didn't say anything. She just looked at him. When he finally turned toward her, eyes searching, she gave the faintest of nods.

"Why did you do this?" he asked.

Maria tilted her head, almost amused. "I had a plan."

That's what she'd said, anyway.

Reed blinked, waiting for more, but she only smirked. The look of someone who already knew the ending of a film you hadn't seen. It was a small smile. And kind. But it didn't quite reach her eyes.

Reed took a deep breath, facing Claire's front door. He turned toward it slowly, shoulders straightening, forcing himself into a posture that felt steadier than he really was. For a moment he just stood there, gathering the fragments of composure he had left. Then he knocked.

His pulse quickened with the sound, each rap echoing louder in his chest than in the quiet street. A part of him almost hoped she wouldn't answer. That the house would stay dark, and he could walk away pretending he'd tried.

Claire answered the door wearing a faded Northwestern sweatshirt and holding a coffee mug. Her eyes widened at the sight of Reed, then flicked to Maria, assessing the situation.

Reed felt a surprising wave of relief just seeing her, a flicker of something softer threading through the tension. A twinge of nostalgia for a time when the sight of her meant safety, not anxiety.

Claire stared at her ex-husband. The silence hung in the air, heavy and expectant, demanding that someone, anyone, be the first to break it.

"Claire…" Reed stammered.

"Come in," she said, her voice flat.

Maria gestured that she'd be in the car. This was a moment for just the two of them.

Claire's eyes lingered on the car for a second longer than necessary as Maria departed, then back to Reed.

Reed stepped inside, slowly. No one spoke. They moved to the living room and sat down, their movements awkward and mismatched.

"Would you like some coffee?" Claire asked after a moment, her voice calm but edged with formality.

The question caught Reed off guard, surprising him more than it should have. He blinked, nerves tightening in his chest, and stammered, "Y-yes, please."

"Still like French vanilla?" Claire asked.

Reed nodded. "Yeah." She still remembered how he took his coffee, and the familiarity of it settled over him like a blanket he hadn't known he wanted to be wrapped in.

She disappeared into the kitchen, and Reed looked around the room.

It seemed strange. The last time he saw her was in court and before that, his memories of her living space were just of their house together. It was kind of bizarre to see her living somewhere else with all her stuff. He remembered exactly where everything used to sit in their old living room.

Claire re-entered with two cups of coffee.

"Thanks," Reed said modestly.

"Welcome."

Silence. Darting eyes. Two people aching to talk but frozen. The elephant between them was silent, immovable.

"So," Reed started nervously. "This place is nice. Really. You always had great taste. Decorating, furnishing… it's really great. Seriously." Reed rambled.

"Strange, isn't it?" she said, her voice softer. "Right after the divorce, I remember thinking… you'd actually love this place." Claire gave the slightest of smirks, and for a fleeting moment she felt it too. The faint warmth of something familiar brushing past before it was gone.

Reed laughed, too loud, too forced. It only made things worse.

He realized it the moment the sound left his mouth and cut it short. The silence that followed felt even heavier. His mind scrambled for an escape hatch, some way to change the subject before the awkwardness cemented itself.

Reed looked in the corner of the room and spotted an upright piano he recognized. "Boyfriend help you get that thing in here?"

Claire gave him that look: equal parts amusement and *really, Reed?*

"I mean, uh—er—that's the only way you'd get that thing in here," he said, nodding toward the piano. Claire looked over at it curiously.

"I'm the only one who would ever move that thing for you. And that was when we were dating, not married. Once I put a ring on it, I was done scoring brownie points. No more moving that clunky music box." He smiled and laughed.

Claire looked down and laughed too.

Reed had broken the tension and then fumbled it by pushing too far.

Getting up and moving toward the piano, he joked, "What shall I play?"

"Reed?" Claire blurted out.

He turned and looked. Trying to hide his anxiety and failing miserably.

"How are you? You were almost killed." Claire asked with a sympathetic look on her face.

"Good enough to show up to my ex-wife's house and ask to play her piano." Reed quipped.

Claire laughed and snorted a little. They shared a laugh and looked at each other. Reed remembered how she used to do that: snort at the tail end of a laugh. The small, ridiculous sound touched him more than it should have. For a moment, the humor between them felt familiar, fragile but real.

They had always made each other laugh. It was easy to forget, after everything they'd endured.

"Seriously," Claire implored. "How are you?"

Reed sat back down. "Getting better. Still sore, but the doctors say I'll heal up in a few months. Can't lift more than 10–15 pounds until then." Reed nodded toward the piano. "So, don't even ask."

Another shared laugh.

Reed returned to the seriousness of the question. "I'm going to be fine. I have to watch what I eat though. Be nice to my system for a while, you know?"

"Are you still…" Claire asked nervously.

"Drinking like a fish?" Reed interrupted, finishing the question for her.

She looked at him with something softer, sympathy, maybe. Something close to sorrow.

Reed laughed insincerely. A defense mechanism against the shame he felt for what he put her through, and for himself, for the wreck he had become.

"Yeah," Claire answered even though she didn't need to.

"No. I uh… I quit that. It's only been a couple weeks, but I cut that out." Reed answered. Tears welled in the corners of his eyes. Shame, regret, pain swirling together.

Reed turned away. He could feel it pressing at the back of his throat. That knot, that guilt, that unbearable grief. He clenched his jaw. It didn't help.

"That's good. That's really good. I hope…" Claire tried to respond.

"Claire, I'm so sorry," Reed interrupted her as he turned around quickly and let himself go. Crying now. "I'm so sorry for everything. You deserved so much better. I could've been a better dad. A better husband. Been a real partner rather than an angry, depressed drunk. I'm so sorry. I never wanted to hurt you. I regret everything I did to you. You never deserved that. Emily… I just miss her so much, you know?"

"It's all I thought about in that hospital bed. How much I had to make up for and never did." He couldn't talk anymore. It had become too much. He sank suddenly into the chair, bowing his head, fighting the tears and failing as they broke through despite him.

Claire set her coffee down and walked slowly over to him. She stopped in front of him. Stared for a long beat, weighing the choice, deciding whether this was something she could give him or not. Finally, she leaned down and wrapped her arms around him. "I know, Reed," she said softly, her voice carrying a fragile comfort.

It was the kind of hug that bent time sideways. He closed his eyes and let himself disappear into it. Just for a second. Just long enough to remember he used to be a man with a family. A daughter whose laugh still echoed somewhere behind the drywall of his memory.

They finally let go of each other and backed up slightly. Claire was crying now too. Both sniffing to gain composure.

Claire went first. "You thought about all that in the hospital?" she asked.

"It was probably just the fentanyl," Reed joked.

They laughed and sniffed.

"Fentanyl for an alcoholic. Great idea," Claire said, chuckling.

Reed grinned. "Yeah, right?"

Claire reached for the Kleenex box on the table and handed him a few. They both wiped their noses, then looked at each other and smiled.

They finished their coffee and caught up, letting the talk wander through the safe, ordinary places.

Reed asked about her work, and Claire about his parents, both of them curious in a way that felt almost tentative.

They laughed a little over old friends and where they'd ended up, reminisced about their respective families.

For a while, it almost felt like they were back in another life, one where the only things that mattered were family stories and the small turns of time.

When it was time to go, Claire walked him to the door. They hugged briefly, a quiet press of shared history, and said goodbye.

"Try not to disappear this time," she said.

Reed smiled and nodded. He turned and walked down the front steps.

Claire lingered in the doorway, watching him for a beat longer than she meant to. The bittersweetness hung in the air between them.

Reed felt it, each step away pulling at something tender he hadn't realized was still there.

Once upon a time, they had known each other better than anyone; each secret, each flaw, every small joy. Neither would ever say it now, not out loud, but they both carried the same quiet hope: that they would see each other again soon.

Not to reignite a flame, they didn't want that. But because they missed the best friend who had once lived at the heart of it all.

He slid into the car beside Maria and sighed. "Nice plan," he said, trying to cut through his emotions.

"We'll see," Maria said as she drove away.

They didn't speak for several blocks.

Reed watched the city blur past. The sun hung low just past 5:00 p.m., caught in a tangle of telephone wires and rusted fire escapes.

Mid-fall clung to the streets. The trees along the boulevard half-bare, leaves curling in gutters, the air sharp with the promise of winter. Shop windows glowed early with their lights, and steam rose in thin ghosts from the grates.

Reed sensed an oddness in the car, a silence that felt heavier than it should. But he brushed it off, still caught in the aftertaste of seeing Claire again. Still turning over the small relief of knowing it wasn't all bitterness between them.

It had felt good, better than he expected, to begin making amends.

Maria turned right, then right again, then suddenly left into a narrowing alley.

"Where are you going?" Reed said, confused and slightly alarmed.

No answer. Only the hum of the engine and the alley narrowing. Brick walls so close the side mirrors nearly scraped them. The car slowed to a crawl.

"Voss?" Reed asked, his voice uncertain. Maria didn't respond, her eyes fixed forward, ignoring him completely.

The car stopped. Maria put it into park.

"Voss?" he repeated, louder this time, the edge of fear cutting into his tone.

Before he could say more, his door yawned open with a frightening suddenness, the rush of cold air hitting him.

Something cracked behind his ear. White-hot pain. His head snapped sideways and then the world went black. The sting of cold air. Hands, gloved, rough, grabbing, pulling. His body folded, dragged. A sliding door. Metal clanking. A voice, flat and professional:

"Get him in the van. Let's go."

Reed's body was dragged into the back of a nondescript gray vehicle. No plates. No markings. The door slammed shut.

Three men climbed in after him with clipped precision, their movements efficient, almost military. No wasted motion, no words exchanged, just the cold choreography of men who had done this before.

Outside, Maria Voss stood next to her idling car, watching the van as it backed out of the alley and disappeared down the street.

She stood for a long moment, statuesque.

Then, slowly, she raised one hand and gave a graceful, deliberate wave. Palm cupped. Fingers fluid. A queen waving from a balcony.

Her grin widened: slow, unnatural.

It didn't belong to her.

It didn't belong to anyone human.

She turned with efficient calm, sliding back into the driver's seat.

From the console, she pulled a wipe and carefully went over the passenger side, erasing every trace with practiced precision.

When she finished, she flicked open a lighter, touched the flame to the cloth, and watched as fire consumed it, crawling fast toward her fingers. Just before it reached her skin, she tossed it out the window, the burning scrap spinning into the night.

She adjusted the driver's side mirror, her face settling into a calm expression that didn't quite belong to Maria. For a long moment she studied herself.

Then she blinked.

When her eyes opened again, the reflection staring back at her was wrong.

The eyes were nothing but black.

Acknowledgments

Thanks to Kent Priore and A.C. Hessenauer for reading early drafts and offering insight when the book was still finding its shape. Your time, honesty, and encouragement mattered more than you know.

To Mario Nevado — an extraordinary artist and an even better human being. Your vision, brilliance, and generosity were nothing short of transformative. Thank you for taking a chance on a writer like me and bringing this story to life visually in a way no one else on earth could have. I'll be forever grateful to have worked with someone of your caliber, your passion, and your heart.

My wife, Lyndsey, the love of my life. I couldn't have done this, or anything worth doing, without your love and constant belief in me.

To my parents, the kind of parents everyone wishes they had. My mom, whose love and unwavering support followed me down every crazy road I took. My dad, who was there for me no matter what happened. As he always told me, "You're just like me." To two people I never had the opportunity to meet — my Great-Grandpa C. and my Grandpa Dick. I grew up hearing stories about you both and wish I could have sat down with you, face-to-face, just once.

To my boys: Greyson, the smartest and most clever little man I've ever known. The real-life Eli. Asher, the most charming and chaotic force of nature to ever walk this earth. I have no idea what I did before I had you. Rhett, the real-life Tommy and the funniest guy I know. I couldn't imagine life without your energy in it. Max, you changed me as a man, a father, and a human being in ways no one else ever could. I love the crap out of all of you.

For my best friend and brother from another mother, Dave, years of experiences together have inspired me more than you'll ever know. And for the family that accepted me as one of their own: Stacy, Diane, and Gary. I couldn't have done this without you.

You've all made me the person I am. The person who could create this.

Lastly, for someone I didn't know personally but who inspired me artistically like no one else — David Lynch. Your passing left a hole in the world that will never be filled, one that will always be felt by anyone who cherishes true creativity and artistic expression. *See you in the trees.*

SUGGESTED LISTENING

Reflections in the Dark — Official Soundtrack

Music inspires everything I write. Every chapter in this novel has a specific song that helped shape its atmosphere, mood, and emotional tone. I built a complete soundtrack: 51 songs for 51 chapters, in order. I listened to this constantly while creating the world of this book.

If you're the kind of reader who enjoys music amplifying a story, feel free to explore it as you read. If that sounds overwhelming or takes you out of the experience, skip it entirely. There's no wrong way to engage with this world.

This soundtrack is simply a part of my own creative process, something I love deeply, and I wanted to extend an invitation to readers in case anyone loves combining music and reading the way I do.

Note on Music Selections

All suggested tracks are the property of their respective artists and copyright holders. No ownership or affiliation is implied. These selections are offered solely as recommended listening to enhance the reader's experience of *Reflections in the Dark*.

About the Cover Artist

The cover for *Reflections in the Dark* was created by **Mario Nevado**, a digital artist and designer known for his surreal, conceptual imagery and striking visual storytelling. His work spans book covers, album artwork, film posters, and creative collaborations across multiple industries.

Nevado's work often explores themes of identity, perception, and fractured realities. His style made him a natural fit for the psychological and cosmic horror themes of *Reflections in the Dark*.

Working with Mario on this project was a fantastic experience, and his ability to translate the atmosphere of the story into a single image exceeded every expectation.

More of his work can be found at:

About the Author

Jason Garman lives in central Illinois with his wife, three sons, and three dogs, spending most days trying to corral their family circus. A lifelong Midwesterner, he grew up surrounded by the quiet simplicity of small-town life, an ordinary backdrop that sparked an enduring fascination with the dark things that go bump in the night. He has been an avid lover of horror movies and literature since childhood, drawn to the paranormal, the unexplained, and the shadowy corners of the human psyche. Reflections in the Dark is his debut novel, equal parts hard-boiled detective story and surreal nightmare.

You can connect with me on:
- https://jasongarman.carrd.co
- https://x.com/JasonGWrites
- https://www.facebook.com/profile.php?id=61585954523384
- https://www.instagram.com/jasongarman.author
- https://www.tiktok.com/@jason.garman.auth

Subscribe to my newsletter:

✉ https://jasongarman.substack.com